DARK HARBOR

BOOKS BY STUART WOODS

FICTION

TRAVEL

A Romantic's Guide to the Country Inns of Britain and Ireland (1978)

MEMOIR

Blue Water, Green Skipper (1977)

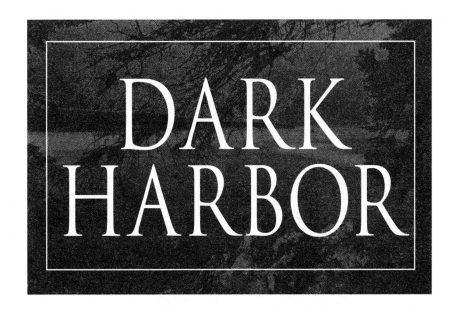

STUART WOODS

DOUBLEDAY LARGE PRINT HOME LIBRARY EDITION

G. P. PUTNAM'S SONS · NEW YORK

This Large Print Edition, prepared especially for Doubleday Large Print Home Library, contains the complete, unabridged text of the original Publisher's Edition.

G. P. PUTNAM'S SONS
Publishers Since 1838
Published by the Penguin Group
Penguin Group (USA) Inc., 375 Hudson Street, New York, New York 10014, USA • Penguin Group (Canada), 90 Eglinton Avenue East, Suite 700, Toronto, Ontario M4P 2Y3, Canada (a division of Pearson Penguin Canada Inc.) • Penguin Books Ltd, 80 Strand, London WC2R 0RL, England • Penguin Ireland, 25 St Stephen's Green, Dublin 2, Ireland (a division of Penguin Books Ltd) • Penguin Group (Australia), 250 Camberwell Road, Camberwell, Victoria 3124, Australia (a division of Pearson Australia Group Pty Ltd) • Penguin Books India Pvt Ltd, 11 Community Centre, Panchsheel Park, New Delhi–110 017, India • Penguin Group (NZ), Cnr Airborne and Rosedale Roads, Albany, Auckland 1310, New Zealand (a division of Pearson New Zealand Ltd) • Penguin Books (South Africa) (Pty) Ltd, 24 Sturdee Avenue, Rosebank, Johannesburg 2196, South Africa

Penguin Books Ltd, Registered Offices:
80 Strand, London WC2R 0RL, England

Purchase only authorized editions.
Published simultaneously in Canada

ISBN 13: 978-0-7394-6747-3
ISBN 10: 0-7394-6747-6

PRINTED IN THE UNITED STATES OF AMERICA

Photograph by Amanda Dewey

This Large Print Book carries the
Seal of Approval of N.A.V.H.

This book is for Kristin Larkin.

DARK
HARBOR

1

ELAINE'S, LATE.

Stone Barrington had already had a drink and had almost given up on Dino Bacchetti. It was unlike his former NYPD partner, now the lieutenant in charge of the detective squad at the 19th Precinct, to be late for eating or drinking. Stone was signaling a waiter for another drink and a menu when Dino trudged in.

"Why are you trudging?" Stone asked.

"I'm trudging because I'm depressed," Dino said, waving at a waiter and making drinking motions.

"And why, pray tell, are you depressed?"

"Mary Ann and I have just split."

"Yeah, sure," Stone said. "Just sleep on

the sofa tonight, and everything will be fine in the morning."

"Not this time," Dino replied, drinking greedily from the glass set before him. "Words were spoken that can't be taken back."

"Take it from a lawyer," Stone said, "the only words spoken that can't be taken back are 'Guilty, Your Honor.'"

"Those were pretty much the words," Dino said.

"And who spoke them?"

"Who the fuck do you think?" Dino asked. "You think *she* would ever cop to *anything*?"

"What did you plead guilty to?"

"To the new desk sergeant at the precinct."

Stone's eyebrows went up. "Dino, are you switch-hitting these days?"

"A *girl* desk sergeant."

"Oh."

"Yeah."

"So the sofa is not an option?"

"Nah. I guess I'm moving in with you."

Stone blinked loudly.

"Relax. It's only 'til I can find a place."

"Stay as long as you like, Dino," Stone said, patting his arm and hoping to God it wouldn't be more than a day or two before Mary Ann relented and let him back in the house.

"Thanks, pal, I appreciate it." Dino nodded toward the door. "Look who's coming."

Stone looked toward the door to find Lance Cabot and Holly Barker approaching.

"May we join you?" Lance asked.

"Sure." Stone waved them to chairs. Lance was in charge of some sort of New York CIA unit that Stone didn't really understand, and Holly had left her job as a chief of police in a small Florida town to work for him. Both Stone and Dino were contract "consultants," and Stone didn't really understand that, either, except that Lance sometimes asked him to do legal stuff. Stone and Holly were, occasionally, an item.

Lance ordered drinks.

"Why do I perceive that this isn't a social visit?" Stone asked.

"Because your perceptions are very keen," Lance replied.

"What's up?"

"Tell me everything you know about Richard Stone."

Stone blinked. It was the second time that

day that Dick Stone's name had come up. "He's my first cousin," Stone replied.

"I said everything you know," Lance pointed out.

"Okay, he's the son of my mother's older brother, now deceased; he grew up in Boston, went to Harvard and Harvard Law. I think he's something at the State Department."

"How long since you've seen him?"

Stone thought about it. "We had dinner eight, nine years ago, when I was still a cop. Last time before that was a little more than twenty years ago."

"Did you know him as a boy?"

"Okay, let me tell you about it. The summer after I graduated from high school my parents sat me down and told me I was going to spend the summer in Maine with some relatives of hers. This came as a surprise, because my mother's relatives had stopped speaking to her years before I was born, because she had married my father, who had been disowned by his family, because he was a Communist. He didn't seem too happy about my spending the summer with a bunch of Stones."

• • •

MALON BARRINGTON WAS, indeed, un-happy. "Why would you want your son to spend ten minutes with those plutocratic sons of bitches, let alone a whole summer?" he asked his wife.

"Because Richard was my brother, and Caleb and Dick Jr. are Stone's cousins, and he ought to take advantage of the opportunity to get to know them," Matilda Stone replied. "They have that very nice place on Islesboro, in Penobscot Bay, and it's a wonderful place to spend a summer."

"Stone was going to work for me in the shop," Malon said. Malon was a maker of fine furniture and cabinets.

"You're going to have to hire somebody when Stone goes to NYU in the fall anyway," Matilda said, "so it might as well be now as then."

Malon made a disgruntled noise.

Matilda got down an atlas and found Maine. "Here," she said, tapping her finger on a large body of water. "This is Penobscot Bay, the largest bay in Maine, and this long, skinny island is Islesboro. The Stones live here, in the village of Dark Harbor. I spent a couple of summers there in their big, drafty old house, which isn't insulated. It's one of those rambling summer 'cottages' that's unusable before June or after Labor Day."

"Sounds swell," Stone said drily.

"AND THAT WAS IT," Stone said to Lance. "I took a train to Bangor, where I was met by a retainer in a 1938 Ford station wagon. We drove to Lincolnville, then took a twenty-minute ferry ride to Islesboro."

"Dick had a brother named Caleb?"

"Yes. He was two years older than Dick, who was my age, and Caleb was a pain in the ass; he was a bully and a general all-round shit. Dick was a nice guy: smart, good in school, good athlete. All Caleb ever did in school was wrestle, and he liked nothing better than to grab Dick or me and get us in some sort of stranglehold. This went on until the day I kicked him in the balls and broke his nose with an uppercut. His mother almost sent me back to New York. When I left after Labor Day, she made it pretty clear that I wouldn't be invited back, and I wasn't."

"What did you do that summer?" Lance asked.

"We sailed and played golf and tennis. The Stones lived near the yacht club, and there was a nine-hole golf course and a tennis club. We didn't lack for activity."

"Did you and Dick keep in touch?"

"We exchanged a few letters over the next year or two, but that petered out. I didn't hear from him again until he turned up in New York and called me at the precinct and invited me to dinner. We went to the Harvard Club, I remember, and I was impressed."

"What did you talk about that evening?"

"About our work: He was stationed in Rome, as I recall—he was the agricultural attaché, or something—and I was working homicides with Dino. I remember he asked me if I was interested in government service, and I said I was already in government service. I asked him what he had in mind, but he was vague. I didn't hear from him again until this morning."

Lance nearly choked on his drink. "This *morning*?"

"Yes, I had a letter from Dick—a package, really—by FedEx. There was a letter saying that he wanted me to put the package, which was sealed, in my safe and not to open it, except in event of his death. There was a check for a thousand dollars, too, as a retainer. He wanted to formally hire me as his attorney. Why do you find it so odd that I heard from him this morning?"

Lance put a hand on Stone's arm. "Because, my friend, yesterday your cousin, Dick Stone, shot his wife and only daughter, then put a bullet in his own brain. At his house in Dark Harbor."

2

STONE UNLOCKED THE front door of his house and let everybody in. "Dino, put your stuff on the elevator, take it up to the third floor and put it in the big guest room. We'll be in my office." Dino complied.

Stone led the way downstairs to the basement and switched on the lights in his office. "Have a seat," he said to Lance and Holly. They did so. Stone went to his safe, punched the combination into the electronic keypad, removed a package and set it on his desk.

Lance bent over and looked at the package, then smiled. "Smart boy, Dick."

"Why?"

"Look at how he's done this: The package

is one large sheet of heavy paper, cut so that four corners come together and are sealed with wax and Dick's signet ring."

"Why?" Stone asked.

"Because it's impossible to open and reseal the package without his ring and without being detected. I think you should draw up a document saying that Holly, Dino and I witnessed your opening the package."

"Okay by me," Dino said, joining them.

Stone switched on his computer, typed out a brief statement, and the three of them witnessed his breaking the seals and opening the package. Then Stone put the package back into his safe and locked it.

"What are you doing?" Lance asked.

"It's your turn to answer some questions," Stone said. "What is your interest in my cousin Dick?"

"I don't have to answer your questions, Stone," Lance said.

"And I don't have to show you what's in Dick's package," Stone replied.

"All right, I guess we're all family here," Lance said. "Dick Stone wasn't with the State Department. Until recently, he was Assistant Deputy Director for European Operations for the CIA. Two weeks ago, he arrived with his family in Washington to re-place Hugh English as Deputy Director for Operations—that's the top job on the oper-ations side, reporting to the Director of Cen-tral Intelligence. After thirty years on the job, Hugh is retiring at the end of the summer. You remember when you and I met in Lon-don a couple of years ago?"

"Of course."

"I was working for Dick at the time. I've been assigned to investigate the deaths of him and his family."

"All right," Stone said, "now everybody go sit in my waiting room while I read what's in the package."

"Why?" Lance asked.

"Because I'm representing Dick as his at-torney and what passes between us is con-fidential, unless I determine that it doesn't need to be."

Lance stared at him for a moment, then got up and left the room, followed by Holly.

"You, too, Dino," Stone said. Dino got up and left the room.

Stone opened the safe, took out the package and spread its four flaps. On top there was a letter from Dick Stone and be-neath was a will. Stone read the letter:

My Dear Stone,

First of all, I wish to hire you as my attorney, and I enclose a check for $1,000.00 as a retainer. Of course, I know that your fees will surpass that amount, should I require services, but that will be taken care of in due course.

Barbara and I have written a will, which is enclosed, and I have had it properly witnessed by four people, whose names and addresses are noted. I have appointed you as our sole executor and, should it be necessary, guardian for our minor daughter, Esme, who is now eighteen, until she reaches her majority. She is entering Oxford this fall. I have also appointed you as her trustee, as she stands to inherit a lot of money if Barbara and I should both walk in front of the same oncoming bus.

You will note that, apart from a few bequests to distant relatives on Barbara's side of the family, there are none to members of my family. My only close relatives are Caleb, his wife and their twin sons, now twenty-one years old and seniors at Yale this fall. I have specifically excluded them from inherit-

ing any of my property. I have provided for our caretaker in Dark Harbor, Seth Hotchkiss (you'll remember him), and his family.

You will also note that, in the highly unlikely event of Barbara, Esme and I dying simultaneously, as in a plane crash, you would become a beneficiary, along with the foundation mentioned in the will. I say highly unlikely because we always travel on different airplanes.

Next time we meet, I will explain why I have made the decisions I have regarding our estate. In the meantime, I ask you to follow my wishes as you understand them.

It is not inconceivable that, should I die anytime soon, my employers may express an interest in my affairs, and I authorize you to cooperate with them to the extent you deem advisable.

Finally, I have attached a joint financial statement, giving account numbers, phone numbers of brokers, etc., which you would find useful in the event of our deaths. I should explain that most of our combined assets come from Barbara, inherited from her father.

I thank you for your kind attention to this matter, and the next time I find myself in New York, I'll take you to dinner again—it's been too long—or, alternatively, perhaps you might find some time to spend with us in June in Islesboro. I built my own house there four years ago, and you'll find it more comfortable than the old family barn, now occupied by Caleb and his ménage.

Warm regards,
Dick

Stone put the letter aside and read the will and the financial statement, then he called the group back into his office.

"All right. I have Dick's permission to talk with you about the package. Let me summarize: It contains a letter to me, his and his wife's will and a financial statement."

"What . . ." Lance began.

Stone held up a hand. "It's all very simple," he said. "If Dick dies first, Barbara gets everything; if she dies first, he gets everything; if they both die, their daughter, Esme, gets everything in trust. I am appointed their executor and their daughter's guardian and trustee."

"What happens if they all die?" Lance asked.

"Apart from a few bequests to Barbara's relatives and to a family retainer, the bulk of the estate would go to the Samuel Bernard Foundation. I would inherit the use of the Islesboro house for the life of myself and my heirs, along with the proceeds of a trust, set up to pay the expenses of maintaining and running the house. If I don't want the place, it would be sold, and the proceeds would go to the same foundation. Dick has specifically excluded his brother and his family as heirs, and if I sell the house, I am instructed to entail the deed in such a way that Caleb could never buy it."

"Sounds like some hard feeling between the two of them."

"Given my experience of them in their youth, I'm not surprised," Stone said. "I know Sam Bernard, of course, but what is the foundation?" Samuel Bernard had been a law-school professor of Stone's and had remained a mentor who had historic connections to the CIA.

"It's set up to provide for the families of

Agency officers killed or disabled in the line of duty," Lance said. "How much did Dick leave the foundation?"

"A million dollars," Stone said, "in the event of his own death. As I said, in the event of the whole family dying simultaneously, most of the estate goes to the foundation."

"And how much is that?"

"Thirty million dollars, give or take. Dick's wife was a very wealthy woman."

Lance drew in a quick breath. "That is astonishingly generous," he said.

"Lance," Stone said, "what reason do you have for thinking that Dick murdered his family and killed himself?"

"That is the opinion of the sheriff and the state police in Maine," Lance said. "My superiors would like for you and me to determine if he's right."

"Do you think Dick was mentally ill? You've seen him more recently than I."

"I have no reason to think so, and certainly the contents of his letter to you and his will are lucid and make him seem sound of mind."

"So the sheriff wants us to believe that a man who has spent his career handling intricate intelligence matters and who has just received the promotion of a lifetime is so nuts and despondent as to murder his family and commit suicide?"

"At this date, I suppose the sheriff's conclusions are preliminary and based only on the physical evidence."

"And what is the physical evidence?"

"I have no idea."

"Then I guess we'd better go to Maine," Stone said.

"I could take some time," Dino said. "Mind if I come along? It would keep me out of Mary Ann's way."

"We could always use another experienced homicide investigator," Lance said.

"Then I'll fly us up tomorrow morning," Stone said.

3

STONE CAME DOWN to breakfast to find Dino dressed and drinking orange juice in the kitchen. "Sleep well?"

"Not as well as I thought I would," Dino said. "I'm not used to sleeping alone."

Stone scrambled them some eggs and fried bacon in the microwave. "Was divorce mentioned?"

"No, but death was. Mine."

"You think she wants out?"

"She was madder than I've ever seen her, and that's saying a lot."

"You should leave a message about where we'll be."

"Where will we be?"

Stone picked up the phone and buzzed his office.

"Good morning," Joan Robertson, his secretary, said.

"Good morning. I have a couple of things for you to do."

"Shoot."

"There's an inn on the island of Islesboro, in Maine; I think it's called the Dark Harbor Inn. If it isn't, find it on the Internet and book four rooms for me, starting tonight. Make it for three nights, but tell them we might need to stay longer."

"Got it."

"There's a will on my desk, witnessed by four people. Please call them all and ask them to confirm that they witnessed the will of Richard Stone."

"Right."

"One of the witnesses is a man called Seth Hotchkiss, a family retainer. When you speak to him, ask him about a taxi service on the island and arrange for a cab to meet us at the airstrip on Islesboro at noon today."

"Got it."

"Also, find out what county Islesboro is in, call the sheriff, tell him I'm Richard Stone's executor, and I'd be grateful if the lead investigator on Stone's death would meet me at his house in Islesboro around one o'clock today."

"Done."

"I suppose they have cell-phone service up there, but in any event, I'll check in with you after we arrive."

"Okay. I'll hold the fort."

Stone hung up and finished his eggs.

"How's the flying weather?" Dino asked.

"Looks good on TV and the Internet. I'll get an aviation forecast in a few minutes and file a flight plan."

THE FOUR OF THEM arrived at Teterboro Airport in New Jersey a little before 10:00 A.M. in Lance's car. Stone did a preflight inspection of the airplane and got everybody aboard.

Their route took them north to Carmel, then northeast through Connecticut and Massachusetts to Kennebunk, Maine, then direct. Ceiling and visibility were unlimited.

"What kind of airport they got up there?" Dino asked.

"I looked it up in the directory," Stone

replied. "It's a paved strip of 2,450 feet, with a paved tiedown area. No fuel, no services."

"Isn't that kind of short?"

"The airplane can handle it."

"Can the pilot handle it?"

"Pray that he can."

Stone pointed out Rockland, as they flew over it during their descent. "That's a bigger airport that can take jets, for future reference. Islesboro is over there." He pointed at the long, narrow island ahead of them. "You can just make out the airstrip at the north end."

Stone began thinking ahead about making a short-field landing. The strip was long enough, but not if he touched halfway down the runway. He continued his descent and lined up for a straight-in approach. His traffic screen showed nothing in the immediate area, and he could see no movement near the strip, but he announced his intentions on the published radio frequency. He put down the landing gear and ten degrees of flaps, then performed his prelanding check: three green lights showing the gear down and locked, fuel selector on the fullest tank.

He wanted to touch down on the numbers, and as soon as he had cleared the trees at the end of the runway, he cut power and descended more steeply. He touched down a few yards past the numbers and applied the brakes. The airplane slowed in plenty of time, and he taxied off the runway onto the tiedown area. There was only one other airplane, a small Cessna, parked there.

Stone shut down the engine, and they deplaned. There was no taxi in sight, but after a couple of minutes, a 1938 Ford station wagon appeared, pulled up next to the airplane, and a man of about sixty got out. He was tall, skinny and weathered. Stone felt a wave of déjà vu. It was the same car and the same man who had met him at the Bangor Airport when he was eighteen.

"It's Stone, isn't it?" the man asked.

"It is, and it's Seth Hotchkiss, isn't it?"

"You've a good memory, Stone. Been a long time." His accent was distinctly Mainer.

"It certainly has," Stone replied, shaking the man's hand.

"We don't have taxi service around here until next week, when the summer folk start arriving," Seth said, "so I just came out. I expect we can get you all in the wagon."

"It's beautiful, Seth," Stone said, admiring the old car.

"Dick had it restored over at Rockland last year; they did a fine job. She's like new." He loaded their luggage, and Stone got into the front seat with Seth while the other three crowded into the rear seat.

"We're booked into the Dark Harbor Inn," Stone said.

"Nah, I told your secretary to forget about that. They don't open until next week. You'll be staying at Dick's house. There's plenty of room. We'll put two of you in the guest house and two in the main house. You've never seen the place, have you?"

"No, I stayed in the old family place."

"That barn," Seth said. "I'm glad I don't have nothing to do with it no more. It was a chore, just keeping it standing. Caleb's got three men doing what I used to do over there. Dick brought over me and my wife, Mabel—she's new since you were here—when he built his house, and we live in a nice apartment over the garage. We're comfortable there, but I don't know what'll happen to us now."

"Rest easy about that, Seth," Stone said.

"You'll be kept on as always. Dick provided for that."

"How do you know about that?" Seth asked.

"I'm Dick's executor, and I'll see that his wishes are carried out. He left me the use of the place for my lifetime and that of my heirs."

Seth nodded. "You married? You got any heirs?"

"Not married, but I've got one heir, a boy. I hope you'll get to meet him."

"We can still give a boy a good summer up here," Seth said.

They were quiet for a while. "Do you know what happened, Seth?" Stone asked finally.

"I know what I saw, and I don't put the same light on it that the sheriff does," Seth replied. "I'll tell you about it after we get everybody settled."

They drove through downtown Dark Harbor, which consisted of a few scattered houses and one business, a general store/real estate office/newsstand/ice cream parlor. It was astonishingly the same as it had been twenty years before.

They continued on past the Dark Harbor Inn, took a right and shortly drove through the gates of Dick Stone's house.

4

THE HOUSE WAS a perfect shingled New England dwelling with two front facades— one facing the front gate, the other facing the little harbor—with a garage wing big enough for four cars and a staff apartment and a guest house to one side of the main house.

Seth drove over to the guest house and unloaded Lance's and Dino's luggage. "We'll put the fellers here," he said, "and the lady over in the main house. That okay?"

Holly nodded. "Fine with me, Seth." She glanced at Stone, who pretended not to notice.

Seth showed Lance and Dino to neat little rooms, divided by a sitting room with a TV and a fireplace. "Mabel will have some lunch for you in half an hour," he said.

They got back into the wagon and drove the few yards to the main house. Seth carried the luggage upstairs and put Stone in what was, obviously, the master and Holly into an adjoining room, which seemed meant for guests. "Lunch is in half an hour in the kitchen," Seth said. "I'll leave you to get settled."

"I'll come down with you, Seth," Stone said.

"You want to see where it happened?" Seth asked.

"Didn't it happen in the master bedroom?"

Seth shook his head and beckoned. He led Stone down the hall to a large, pretty bedroom, full of stuffed animals and the detritus of childhood and the teen years. Everything was very neat. "For some reason, Barbara was in bed with Esme. They were both sleeping on their right sides, with their backs to the door. Somebody put two bullets in each of 'em's head. It was like they never woke up, never moved." He turned and led the way downstairs. They walked through a large living room with broad views of the harbor and into a smaller study.

Seth walked over to the desk. "Dick was sitting here, and he had this tiny, little gun in his left hand, and it had what looked like a silencer on it, like you see on TV. There was a hole in his left temple, and it was all black around it. The bullet went all the way through and ended up here." He tapped a hole in the leather desktop. "There was a lot of blood and brains."

"Who found them?"

"Mabel did, when she came down to fix breakfast. It was about six-thirty in the morning. She screamed real loud, and I was down quick."

"Did either of you touch anything?"

"No, *sir.* I've seen me enough *Law & Orders* not to do that."

"Why is there no crime-scene tape around the house, and why was Mabel allowed to clean up?"

"The trooper told us we could do that after they took the bodies away," Seth said. "By the way, he's coming over, getting the two o'clock ferry, so he'll be here by two-thirty."

"Did they take any photographs?"

"I'm not sure, but I did." Seth reached into a pocket and handed Stone a small electronic camera. "It was Dick's, just a point-and-shoot thing, then you put the pictures in the computer. I didn't know how to do that."

Stone put the camera into his pocket. "I'm sorry you and Mabel had to see that," he said.

"So'm I," Seth replied.

"Seth, Dick left you and Mabel some money, half a million dollars, and he left another half a million in a trust for your kids' education. How old are they now?"

"They're eighteen and nineteen; boy's younger. They're at Bowdoin, freshman and sophomore. Dick had been paying for their college. I'm relieved to hear that's going to keep on."

"That will continue, and they can go to graduate school, if they want to. When the older one is twenty-five, what's left in the trust will be divided between them."

"Nice little nest egg for them, then." Seth began to cry.

Stone patted him on the back, but didn't say anything.

"Lunch in half an hour, in the kitchen,"

Seth said. He handed Stone a bunch of keys. "These were Dick's." Then he hurried out of the room.

Stone walked around the study, looked at the view of the harbor, looked at the book titles. A remarkable number of them were in his own library. There were silver-framed photographs of Barbara and Esme on his desk. He suddenly felt closer to Dick, remembered his good cheer, his sense of humor, his innate kindness.

"Who are you?" a voice said.

Stone turned to find Caleb Stone standing behind him. He had put on some weight but was still recognizably the twenty-year-old Stone had known, with the same broken nose. "Hello, Caleb. I'm Stone Barrington."

Caleb stood stock-still for a moment and looked him up and down, then, remembering some vestige of manners, walked over and offered his hand. "Hello, Stone," he said. "What the hell are you doing here?" The question was made up of equal parts of amazement and hostility.

"I'm here at Dick's invitation."

"You mean, he invited you up here to stay?"

"Yes, he did. Along with some friends."

"You mean there are other people in the house?"

"Three, here and in the guest house."

"Christ, we planned to move in here tomorrow."

"I'm afraid you'll have to change your plans."

Caleb ignored this statement. "The boys are home from school to help, and their mother is packing right now."

"I'm afraid that won't be possible," Stone said.

"Now, you listen to me. I want you and your friends to get out of this house, and I want you on the next ferry."

Stone walked over to the sofa and chairs by the window. "Caleb, come and sit down for a minute; I need to tell you some things."

"Jesus, you haven't been up here in decades, and you're acting like you own the place."

Stone sat down and pointed at a chair. "I think you're going to want to hear this sitting down."

Caleb sank heavily into a chair facing him. "What have you got to say?"

"The day before yesterday, I received a Federal Express package from Dick, which contained a letter, hiring me as his attorney, and the original of a will he had written and had properly witnessed."

"What will? I've got Dick's will at home. He made it out eleven years ago, and I'm his executor."

"I'm afraid the new will supercedes that," Stone said. "Dick appointed me executor. It's a simple document: He provided for Seth Hotchkiss and his family, for a few of Barbara's relatives, and left the rest to a foundation that helps the families of dead CIA officers."

"Why the hell would he do that? Dick didn't have anything to do with the CIA. He was a diplomat."

Stone was surprised that Caleb knew nothing of Dick's work. "On the contrary, Dick was a career CIA officer, and he had recently been promoted to a high position in the Agency."

Caleb stared at him, speechless.

"There's something else," Stone said. "Dick and Barbara were each other's beneficiaries, and Esme was to inherit, if they both died. In the event that they all three died, as in an accident, Dick left this house to me for my lifetime and that of my heirs. If I choose to sell it, the proceeds will go to the foundation, and he instructed me to entail the deed so that you can't buy it."

"I want to see this will," Caleb said.

Stone reached into an inside pocket, produced a copy of the will and handed it to Caleb.

Caleb read it. "This will is invalid," he said, "because one of the witnesses is a named beneficiary. I'm a lawyer, and my specialty is estate planning."

"Three unnamed witnesses are enough to validate the will in any state in the union," Stone said. "You can sue, if you like, but I'm sure you've already realized that this is a proper and legal will, and there's nothing you can do about it."

"So you plan to take possession of this house?" Caleb demanded.

"I have already done so," Stone replied. "Would you like to stay to lunch and meet my friends?"

Caleb got up and walked out without a word, the will clutched tightly in his hand.

Stone got up and went in to lunch.

5

THE OTHERS WERE already gathered at the table in the large kitchen. Stone went over to Mabel Hotchkiss, who was stirring something on the stove. "Hello, Mabel. I'm Stone Barrington."

She shook his hand. "Hello, Mr. Stone."

"Just Stone will do."

"It'll be on the table in a minute," she said. Stone sat down. "Anybody hungry?"

"Was that Caleb Stone I saw leaving?" Lance asked.

"Yes, and I'm afraid Caleb isn't having a very good day. He had planned to move into this house tomorrow."

"I take it you disabused him of that notion."

"I did, and I gave him a copy of Dick's will. The poor guy has also learned that he's not inheriting any money from his brother."

"Does he know how much he's not inheriting?"

"He probably has some idea."

"Is he going to sue?"

"If he can think of grounds. Turns out, he's an estate attorney, with a Boston firm, I suppose."

"You'd better file that will for probate as soon as possible."

"I intend to. I have to get a death certificate, though. There's a state trooper coming this afternoon; maybe he can help me with that. How much do you know about Dick's affairs, Lance? Did he have a residence in Washington?"

"Not yet. I learned from the DDO's office that they were house shopping in Georgetown, but they hadn't found anything yet."

"How long had they been back in Washington?"

"Less than a week. They sold the house in London, apparently."

"I guess that means this house was Dick's only residence, so I can go to the local probate court. Mabel, what's the name of this county?"

"Waldo."

"And what's the county seat?"

"Belfast, up the coast."

"How long a drive?"

"From Lincolnville, half an hour, forty-five minutes."

"Thanks. I guess I'll go up there first thing tomorrow."

A lunch of shrimp and rice was served, and everyone ate quietly until Mabel left the room.

"What did you learn from Seth this morning?" Lance asked.

"The two women were sleeping in Esme's room and took two shots in the head, each. Dick was sitting at his desk downstairs and suffered a contact wound to the left temple."

"Dick was right-handed," Lance said.

"You're sure?"

"I worked for him for four years."

"Seth said that he had a very small pistol with a silencer in his hand when he was found."

"Sounds like a Keltec .380; it's one of a

number of handguns issued by Agency technical services."

"Do you have any insight into Dick's state of mind the past few weeks?"

"I spoke to his deputy, who's replacing him in London. He said Dick was his usual cheerful self, and he was excited about the new job. He said that he'd had a farewell dinner with Dick and Barbara the night before they left London, and they were in great form."

Dino spoke up. "Is anybody ready to say this wasn't a murder-suicide yet?"

"Let's talk to the trooper first," Stone said.

AFTER LUNCH THEY went into the study. Lance pointed at a door near Dick's desk, which sported a dead-bolt lock. "I think I know what that is," he said. "Let's find a key."

Stone fished Dick's keys out of his pocket and found one that fit the lock. He opened the door to find what appeared to be a small office, containing a computer, a large fax machine and an odd-looking telephone, along with a filing cabinet. "This is strange," Stone said.

"No, it isn't. Dick spent a month or so here every year, and this is Agency equipment. The computer is linked to the Agency mainframe, and the phone and fax are scrambled."

"I take it you know how to use such a computer?"

"I do."

"Do you think you could get me some background on Caleb Stone?"

Lance sat down at the computer. "Sure."

"I'd particularly like a credit report and any other financial information you can dig up. Also, any criminal record."

"Give me a couple of minutes," Lance said, switching on the machine. He picked up the scrambled phone and dialed a number. "Give me your supervisor," he said. "This is Lance Cabot. I'm authorized by the DDO to conduct an investigation into the death of Richard Stone; that office will confirm. I'm at Stone's Maine residence now, using his scrambled phone and his computer. I want to use my own access card in the computer. Thank you." Lance hung up. "It'll be a few minutes while the necessary checks and setup are done."

"Let's lock up this room, then; the trooper

will be here soon, and I doubt if you want him looking in here." He locked the room, and they sat down to wait.

"This is a beautiful house, Stone," Holly said. "You're lucky to have it."

"I haven't gotten used to the idea yet," Stone replied. "It's all very strange. Most of my mother's and father's families haven't spoken to them since long before I was born, and yet I've inherited two houses from my mother's side of the family. The Turtle Bay town house came from my great aunt, who took an interest in me. She also gave my father his first large commission: the cabinet work and much of the furniture for the house. And now there's this place. The strange thing is, if I'd built it myself it would be exactly as it is. The whole thing is spooky."

The doorbell rang, and Mabel answered it. A moment later, she showed a uniformed sergeant of the Maine State Police into the study. Stone introduced himself and the others.

"What can I do for you, Mr. Barrington?"

"I am Richard Stone's first cousin, his attorney, and the executor of his will. I'd like to know as much as possible about the circumstances of his death."

"The local constable called my office in Belfast two days ago and said that the caretaker here had found the owner and his wife and daughter dead in the house, apparently shot. I and a crime-scene investigator choppered over here, and when we got to the house we found the wife and daughter in the same bed upstairs with two bullets in each of their heads. We found Mr. Stone's body at the desk with a wound to the head and a small pistol in his hand.

"We fingerprinted the corpses and had them removed to the Belfast morgue for postmortem examination. We dusted the study and the upstairs bedroom and found only the fingerprints of the occupants and the housekeeper. There were no fingerprints of any other person in the house. The place was locked, and there was no sign of an intruder.

"In the absence of any evidence to the contrary, I judged the circumstances to be murder-suicide, possibly while the mind of the perpetrator was disturbed. I removed the weapon to our offices for ballistic comparison with the bullets removed from the bodies."

"I notice that the bullet that killed Mr. Stone passed through his head and lodged in the desk."

"Yes, we were able to extricate that. It will be of less use than the ones removed from the two women, but I think that my preliminary conclusion will be confirmed: that the weapon in Mr. Stone's hand was both the murder and suicide weapon."

"Did you investigate Mr. Stone's state of mind?"

"I interviewed the caretaker and his wife, and they maintained that he seemed normal at dinner the night before."

"Did you determine the time of death?"

"The medical examiner has put it somewhere between midnight and four A.M. By the way, an inquest will be held tomorrow at eleven A.M. in the Belfast courthouse. You're welcome to attend, if you like."

"Thank you. What will be your recommendation at the inquest?"

"Death by murder and suicide."

"I should tell you that our investigations"—Stone indicated the other people in the room—"have determined that Richard

Stone was of sound mind and cheerful disposition and that he was excited and happy about his appointment to a new, high position by his employers."

"And you consider yourselves investigators?" the sergeant asked.

"A reasonable question. I am a retired officer of the New York Police Department, where I spent eleven years as a detective, specializing in homicides. Lieutenant Bacchetti, here, commands the detective squad at the Nineteenth Precinct of the NYPD, and Ms. Barker is a retired military police officer and chief of police in the state of Florida." He didn't mention Lance.

"Well, that's all very impressive," the sergeant said. "I'm interested to know what you've learned about Mr. Stone's state of mind, but do you have any other evidence that this was anything but a murder-suicide?"

"Take a look at this," Stone said, beckoning the trooper to the desk. He took a pencil from a coffee mug on the desk and placed it in the hole left by the bullet. "Note that the angle of the bullet's trajectory was only about twenty degrees off the vertical. I think that might indicate someone standing over Mr. Stone and firing a bullet into his head. Also, in your scenario, he would have fired with his left hand, and he was right-handed."

"My crime-scene investigator, an experienced man, concluded that Mr. Stone laid his head on the desk before firing the fatal shot. That would account for the angle. I didn't know he was right-handed, but there was nothing to prevent him using his left hand."

"Our consensus, based on Mr. Cabot's investigation into Mr. Stone's state of mind in the days and weeks before his death, is that an unknown person shot him in the head with a silenced pistol, then went upstairs and shot his wife and daughter."

"You're entitled to your theory, Mr. Barrington, but my investigation has not found any reason to believe that any person on this island had a motive to kill this family. I should point out that they resided in London for many years and they came into contact with the locals only for a few weeks a year and that no one knows of any local who had any animosity toward the family. Indeed, they were very popular summer residents. Also, my investigation revealed that no summer residents had yet arrived on the island at the time of the deaths. Mr. Stone's brother and his family arrived only yesterday—we have the ferry operator's testimony for that—and only one aircraft was parked at the airstrip, that belonging to a local. The people who live nearest the strip tell us that no aircraft landed or took off on the day or the day before the deaths. It's a small island; people pay attention to who comes and goes."

"Did you take any photographs of the crime scene?" Stone asked.

"Yes, but I didn't bring them with me. If you come to the inquest, I'd be glad to show them to you, and the gun, as well."

"Thank you, Sergeant. I appreciate your taking the time to come to the island to brief us. I'll see you tomorrow."

The trooper handed Stone an envelope. "Here's the original of the death certificate," he said. "You'll need it to file the will for probate."

They shook hands, and the trooper left.

Stone turned to the group with a questioning look.

"The sergeant has some good points," Dino said. "He did his job."

"He didn't spend much time on state of mind," Stone said.

"I wouldn't have spent much more time on that, in the circumstances," Dino said.

Holly spoke up. "You didn't mention to the trooper that Caleb Stone had been disinherited by Dick. That's motive."

"Not really. It would be motive if Caleb had known that he was *about* to be disinherited, but there is no indication of that. Caleb was *very* surprised to learn that Dick had made a new will. I'd be surprised to learn that they'd even communicated in recent months."

"I can check Caleb's home and office phone records, as well as Dick's," Lance said.

"Yes," Stone said, "I would like you to do that. Maybe you'd better get started."

6

LANCE WENT TO WORK on Dick Stone's Agency computer while Stone called his office.

"The Barrington Practice," Joan said.

"Hi, it's me. What's up?"

"I trust you were met at the airport?"

"Yes, and we're comfortably ensconced in the house. There are three phone lines, one for the fax." He gave her all of them.

"How long will you be there?"

"I'm not sure; there's a lot to do. There's the inquest tomorrow morning, and I have to file the will for probate."

"I take it you're now the proud owner of a Maine house?"

"In a manner of speaking. I can't seem to get used to the idea."

"Oh, by the way, for your information, the three witnesses who signed the will, besides Seth Hotchkiss, were the pilot, copilot and flight attendant on the private jet that delivered the Stone family to Rockport the day before they died. Apparently, they were considering buying into some sort of fractional jet program, and the trip from D.C. to Rockport was a sort of test run."

"Good to know."

"There's no interesting mail. Can I reach you at this number?"

"For all of today; tomorrow morning, try the cell. I'll talk to you sometime tomorrow.

"Bye-bye."

Stone hung up and turned to Lance in the little office. The printer was spitting out sheets of paper. "What are you learning?" he asked.

Lance picked up the papers and consulted them. "Our boy, Caleb, is married to the former Vivian Smith; two sons, Eben and Enos, who share a birthday. Caleb graduated Yale and Yale Law in the bottom half of both classes; he is employed by the Boston law firm of Marsh, Andrews, Fields and Schwartz. Note his name is not on the letterhead. He's been with the firm since law school but took twelve years to make partner. He heads their estate planning division, and given the number of the firm's employees, I'm inclined to think he *is* the firm's estate planning division.

"He belongs to a couple of good clubs, lives in a respectable suburb of Boston, summers here, and from his tax returns and credit report, it appears that he lives at the very limit of his income while still managing to pay his bills on time. I think he will be very relieved when his boys finish Yale next year."

"Any criminal record?"

"None. He appears to have trod the straight and narrow his whole life long."

"If he's as financially strapped as you say he is, he must have been very disappointed, indeed, when he read Dick's will."

"No doubt. I expect he's reassessing his retirement plans as we speak. One good thing: Since he now has no hope of ever seeing Dick's and Barbara's money, he has no motive to kill you."

"Yes, well . . ."

"Caleb has led the most boring of all lives,

I expect," Lance said. "One of quiet desperation, as the saying goes. I hope his family loves him, because it seems to me that's about his only comfort."

"My experience of him is that he's not an easy fellow to love," Stone said.

Seth Hotchkiss came into the room. "Anything I can do for anybody?"

"Seth," Stone said, "let's you and I have a talk." Stone led the caretaker outside, and they took seats on teak furniture on the stone patio. The sun was pleasantly warm, though Stone knew that by nightfall there would be a chill in the air. After all, it was only June in Maine.

"What can I do for you, Stone?"

"Tell me what Dick's and Caleb's relationship was like."

"Well, you remember what it was like when they were boys?"

"Yes."

"It was pretty much like that, except that Dick seemed to do better in life than Caleb, had a better job and a nicer wife. Dick was able to build this house, while Caleb had to be content with propping up the old family place. Funny, I would have stayed on there out of loyalty, but Caleb fired me a week after his parents died in that car crash. Dick hired me the same day, and I've been very happy ever since."

"Caleb inherited the house?"

"They both did, but Dick signed his half over to Caleb, said to me he didn't want any part of it; the place was filled with unhappy memories for him."

"Why did he stay on the island?"

"Oh, he loved the island, he just didn't love the old house. I think he took some pleasure in sticking Caleb with it."

"Have you ever heard Caleb express any animosity toward Dick?"

"Caleb's whole attitude toward most everybody is animosity, I guess. He was nice to those folks he had to get along with, which were most of the summer people. After all, he wanted the yacht club and the golf club, so he was nice to the members. The year-rounders hated him pretty good; he had trouble keeping help and all that. When he wanted a new roof, he had to go to somebody on the mainland, which cost him more money. He puts away the booze pretty good, and so does his wife."

"How did the locals feel about Dick and his family?"

"Oh, Dick was a sweetheart, and everybody knew it. Barbara and Esme, too. If Mabel and I weren't doing this job, folks would be lined up to get it."

"I expect there's a pretty good grapevine on the island among the locals?"

"There is."

"I'd like to know what you hear on it."

"Folks are real interested in you, Stone."

"Well, I don't have any secrets, so feel free to talk. In particular, you might let it be known that I'm not very happy with the murder/suicide theory held by your state trooper."

"Me, neither," Seth said, "and nobody who knew Dick is going to put much stock in it. Folks start arriving tomorrow, and they'll have seen about it in the Boston papers, so there'll be a lot of curiosity."

"Well, let's not starve them for information, but don't give anybody the impression that I think Caleb is in any way responsible. He and his family hadn't even arrived on the island at the time, so let's not hang it around his neck." Then they got up and went back into the house.

•   •   •

THAT NIGHT, after dinner, the group enjoyed coffee and brandy before a crackling fire in the living room.

"Lance," Stone said, "there's a possibility we haven't talked about."

"What's that?"

"Could these murders have been work related? Dick's work, I mean."

"Don't worry, I've thought a lot about it. I've reviewed the threats Dick received in London over the years. There were more of them than you might think, but most from nuts or the ineffectual. Generally speaking, terrorist groups don't tell you they're going to kill you; they just kill you. Anyway, there was nothing in the file less than a year old. The other thing is that it just doesn't happen that foreigners murder Agency personnel in the U.S. I can't think of a single case when that's happened. Add to that fact that Dick and his family were in, if not an inaccessible place, then one very difficult to access without being noticed."

Dino spoke up. "We haven't talked about the possibility of someone arriving in a small boat to do the job. A team, or even an individual, could have pulled a rubber dinghy out of the water less than thirty yards from this house."

"I grant you that," Lance said. "A commando-style raid, in the middle of the night, would have been the way to do it, if you wanted to do it, but nobody's claimed responsibility, and these groups usually do. Nobody at the Agency has been able to detect the slightest sign that a group had or was about to conduct an operation of this sort. I've checked the weather that night, and there was thick fog all night and into the morning, and believe me, the fog gets really thick up here.

"Frankly, in my own mind, I've ruled out the possibility of an incursion from outside, and my report will so state. I'm more inclined to think that somebody local had it in for Dick."

"Seth tells me that Dick and his family were very popular locally," Stone said.

"And Caleb is accounted for," Dino said. "We're getting no-where fast."

"Well," Holly said, "I'm going to turn in, I think." She got up. "Good night all." She headed for the stairs.

After a few more minutes of chat, the others headed for their rooms, too.

• • •

STONE WAS PLEASED to find Holly in his bed, and when he slid in beside her, even more pleased to find her naked. He snuggled up to her back and nestled between her cheeks. Holly reached back between her hands and fondled him, bringing him erect. "I thought you'd never come upstairs," she said, guiding him into her. She rolled over on her stomach, pulling him with her, and they kept that position until they had both come. Finally, she turned over, slung a wet leg over his and snuggled into his shoulder.

Stone reflected that it was nice to have her sleeping beside him. He didn't fall asleep for a long time, though, because he was running every possible permutation of the events in the house through his head and getting nowhere. He resolved to get to the bottom of Dick's and his family's death. It was the last thing he could do for them.

7

AT BREAKFAST the following morning Stone asked Mabel if he should make a ferry reservation for his trip to Belfast.

"Well," Mabel said, "you won't need a reservation going over to the mainland, and you won't get one coming back. Too many folks are arriving today for the summer, and the ferry's been booked up for weeks."

"Is there an airport in Belfast?" Stone asked.

"Yup. Bigger than ours, too."

"Okay, I'll fly," he said.

"I'll come with you," Dino chipped in. "I don't have anything else to do."

Lance spoke up. "Now that I've got Dick's computer up and running, I'm going to check out some things. Holly, I'd like you here with me to see what I'm doing. You'll find the knowledge useful, eventually."

"Okay by me," Holly said, rubbing Stone's leg with her toe under the table.

Stone looked at his watch. "I'd better get a weather forecast," he said, getting up from the table.

STONE AND DINO LANDED at the Belfast airport at 9:30 and took a cab to the Waldo County Courthouse. Stone found the probate office, filed Dick's will and was sworn in as his executor. By 10:30, he had all the necessary documents for disbursing Dick's estate. He and Dino walked outside and found a bench in the sunshine where they could wait for the inquest to begin.

Shortly, Sergeant Young appeared with an envelope and handed it to Stone. "Morning," he said to Stone. "Here are the photographs of the scene, the autopsy report, the ballistics report and a copy of my report. Will you have anything to say at the inquest?"

"I'll take a look at your material and then decide," Stone said.

"I'll tell the coroner who you are," the trooper said. "See you in the small courtroom downstairs." He walked back into the courthouse.

Stone opened the envelope, and he and Dino began poring over its contents. The ballistics report confirmed that the gun in Dick's hand had killed all three, and the photographs were competently taken and in color.

Stone picked up an autopsy photograph, a closeup of Dick's head. He pointed at Dick's forehead. "Look at that," he said.

THE CORONER CALLED the inquest to order at five minutes past eleven. There were no more than half a dozen attendees, one of whom, a young woman with a notebook, appeared to be a reporter from the local press. They had passed a television crew in the hallway outside the courtroom.

Sergeant Young was called as the first witness and gave twenty minutes of testimony, using a large television set to display the photographs of the scene. When he was done, the medical examiner gave the autopsy results and agreed with the trooper's assessment of the events.

"Is there anyone else who has relevant testimony?" the coroner asked.

Stone stood up. "Your Honor, my name is Stone Barrington. I am the attorney for Richard Stone and executor of his estate. I have some questions for the medical examiner, if I may."

The coroner instructed the M.E. to take the stand again.

"Doctor, I refer to your photograph number four taken at the autopsy. May we have that on the screen, Your Honor?"

A technician brought up the photograph.

"Doctor, as part of your autopsy, did you place a rod or other object in the head wound to determine the trajectory of the gunshot?"

"I did," the doctor replied. "I inserted a twelve-inch rod into the wound."

"And what angle did the rod indicate?"

"It indicated that the gunshot came from the left side of the head and from an elevated angle of fifteen degrees."

"Was the wound a contact wound? That is, was the barrel of the gun held against the head before firing?"

"Yes, it was a contact wound."

Stone held his left hand, finger pointing, to his head and elevated his elbow. "So, in order to create that trajectory, the gun would have to have been held in this fashion?"

"Yes, I suppose so."

"Doctor, have you ever conducted another autopsy on a person who killed himself with a self-inflicted gunshot wound to the head?"

"Yes, at least a dozen times. It's a very common way of committing suicide."

"In any of those cases, was there a gunshot trajectory similar or identical to the one in this case?"

The doctor thought for a moment. "No, I don't believe there was."

"Doctor are you aware that Mr. Stone was right-handed?"

"Yes. It was in the trooper's preliminary report."

"But, if Mr. Stone indeed shot himself, he would have done so with his left hand?"

"Yes, that is so."

"In any of the other cases you mentioned, did the victim use other than his dominant hand to fire the shot?"

The doctor thought again. "I can't be positive from memory, but I don't recall such a case."

"Doctor, the trooper has testified that it is his belief that Mr. Stone laid his head on the desk, then fired the fatal shot. On reflection, do you believe that the trajectory of the gunshot is consistent with his theory?"

"Perhaps not," the doctor said.

"Your Honor, may I use the blackboard?" Stone pointed to the board at one side of the courtroom.

"Go ahead," the coroner said.

Stone walked to the blackboard and quickly sketched a man's head lying on a desktop, then he drew a line through the head and into the desktop.

"Doctor, is this approximately the path that the trooper described in his report, with the bullet lodging in the desktop?"

"Yes," the doctor replied.

Stone drew another line through the head, approximating the trajectory of the bullet described by the doctor. "Doctor, is this the approximate path of the bullet, given the trajectory in your report?"

"Yes, I suppose it is."

"Do you see that the bullet would have

lodged in an entirely different place in the desk, if fired in this manner?"

"Yes, I do."

"It would then appear that the only way to reconcile the trajectory of the bullet with the place where it struck the desk would be with Mr. Stone sitting in an upright position?"

"It would seem so."

"With the gun held so?" Stone again assumed the awkward position he had demonstrated earlier.

"Yes."

"Would this trajectory also be consistent with the gun being fired by a person unknown standing next to and above Mr. Stone's position?"

The doctor took a deep breath. "Yes, it would be."

"Thank you, Doctor. Your Honor, I suggest that the preponderance of the evidence suggests that this was murder, not suicide, that it was likely that the shooter first shot Mr. Stone, then went upstairs and shot his wife and daughter."

"What about the noise of the gunshot?" the coroner asked.

Stone went to the evidence table and

picked up the Keltec .380 in its plastic bag. "The pistol was silenced, Your Honor."

The coroner turned to Trooper Young. "Sergeant, do you have anything further to add?"

"No, sir," the trooper said.

The coroner faced his small audience again. "The verdict of this court is declared to be open, that the victims could have been killed by either Mr. Stone or by an unknown party, and that the police investigation should continue. This court is adjourned until such time that there is further evidence to hear in this case. The bodies of the victims are released for burial."

The coroner rapped once with his gavel, then gathered his papers, got up and left the room.

Outside the courtroom Stone was met by the television crew and the young woman from the press, but he declined to speak further, referring them to the testimony in the courtroom.

As they were standing on the street, looking for a cab, Sergeant Young approached them. "You'd have to phone for a taxi," he said. "Can I give you a lift somewhere?"

"I need to go to a funeral parlor, then to the airport," Stone said.

"I'll drive you."

They got into the state police car and drove away.

"Looks like you've made some more work for me," Young said.

"Sorry about that," Stone said.

"Don't be. You made a valid point. I'll come over there tomorrow and go over the whole thing again."

"Thank you," Stone said.

AT THE FUNERAL PARLOR, Stone made arrangements for the cremation of Dick, Barbara and Esme Stone and instructed that their ashes should be mingled and shipped to him in Dark Harbor. He and Dino were back on Islesboro by two o'clock.

8

WHEN STONE AND DINO left the Islesboro airport to drive back to the house, they were amazed at the number of cars on the road and parked outside the Dark Harbor ice cream parlor. Apparently, summer residents were pouring off the ferry.

Back at the house he found Lance and Holly working in Dick's secret office.

"How'd everything go?" Lance asked.

Stone told him about the autopsy photographs. "At least I managed to get an open verdict, pending further investigation," he said. He began looking for a secure place to lock up the crime scene, autopsy and ballistic reports, and to his surprise, he opened a cabinet and found a safe inside.

There had been nothing about a safe in Dick's will or in the accompanying letter. Below the safe's dial was a keyhole, and Stone went through Dick's keys until he found one that fit, but it didn't open the safe.

"Maybe I can help," Holly said from behind him.

"You a safecracker?" Stone asked.

"I had some training at the Farm," she said. The Farm was the CIA's training facility for agents.

"You go right ahead," Stone said, stepping out of her way.

Three minutes later, Holly stepped back from the safe.

"Now try your key," she said.

Stone inserted Dick's key in the lock and opened the door. "That was spectacular," Stone said.

"Piece of cake," Holly replied.

Stone removed the contents of the safe—a couple of bundles of documents and envelopes—and placed them on the desk. Holly wrote down the combination to the safe and handed it to Stone. Stone went through the papers and found a deed to the house, a cancelled mortgage, the household insurance policies and some correspondence with the house's architect. He also found two insurance policies with a face value of a million dollars each: the beneficiary of one was Dick's parents, and the other, Caleb Stone. They had both been taken out on the same day, some twelve years before, with an agent in Camden. He opened the safe, put all the papers back inside and locked it.

Lance came out of the little office reading a sheet of paper. "Uh, oh," he said. "Holly and I have business back in New York; Langley is sending an airplane to Rockland for us."

Stone picked up the phone and paged Seth Hotchkiss, who came into the room a moment later. "What's up?" he asked.

"Seth, Mr. Cabot and Ms. Barker have to get to Rockland, where an airplane is meeting them this afternoon. Should I fly them over there, or is there another way, given the packed ferries today?"

"Easiest thing is for them to take the ferry, and I'll call a taxi from Camden to meet them on the other side," Seth said. "What time's the plane at Rockland?"

"It's landing at four o'clock," Lance said.

"Then we'd better get started. You can

make the three-thirty ferry, and you'll be a few minutes late getting to Rockland."

"They'll wait for us," Lance said. He turned to Holly. "Let's get packed."

Dino came into the room. "What's going on?"

"Holly and I have to go back to New York."

"Can you take me with you?"

"Sure. Get packed."

Dino turned to Stone. "I just talked to Mary Ann. She's hired a lawyer, and he wants a meeting, so I'd better get back down there."

"I guess you'd better," Stone agreed. "You've got your key to my house and the alarm codes. I'll tell Joan you're coming, and the housekeeper will lay in some food for you. You're going to need a lawyer, and I'm going to be tied up with this, so call Bill Eggers at Woodman & Weld and ask him to recommend somebody. Do *not* meet with them without your own lawyer present."

"Gotcha."

A few minutes later they were standing beside the old Ford station wagon in front of the house.

"So much for a Maine vacation," Holly said.

"You can come back later in the summer," Stone said.

"Are you staying all summer?"

"I'm not planning to, but who knows? I've got a triple homicide on my hands and no suspects."

"Good luck," Holly said. "Call me on my cell if you want to bounce anything off me."

"Will do." Stone hugged Holly and shook Lance's hand.

"I'm still on this," Lance said, "and I'll be in touch if I come up with anything. Please keep Dick's little office locked until I can get somebody up here to remove the equipment." He handed Stone the key.

"Sure." Stone shook Dino's hand. "Let me know what's happening, and give Elaine a kiss for me."

A moment later, they were driving away, and Stone went back into the house. It seemed suddenly very empty.

Mabel came into the room. "Stone, what should I do about all the clothes upstairs?"

Stone thought about it for a moment. "Take anything that you and Seth want, then pack it all up and give it to some local charity."

"The church has a clothing drive every summer," she said.

"That's perfect." Stone called Joan and told her to expect Dino. As he was hanging up, the doorbell rang. He opened it to find Caleb Stone standing on the doorstep.

"Come in, Caleb," Stone said, offering his hand.

"Can I talk with you for a minute?" Caleb asked.

"Sure, come on into Dick's study. You want a drink?"

"I wouldn't mind a Scotch."

Stone poured the drink, and they sat down in the big wing chairs before the fireplace. Stone waited for Caleb to speak.

"I owe you an apology," Caleb said.

"What for?"

"First of all, for the way I behaved that summer when you were up here."

"That was a long time ago." It may have been a long time ago, he reflected, but every time he saw Caleb he felt a flash of anxiety and anger at the way Caleb had treated Dick and him that summer.

"It's been on my mind. Also, for the way I

behaved when you told me about Dick's will."

"I know it came from out of the blue," Stone said. "You had a right to be upset. Caleb, I wish I had some leeway in disbursing the estate, but I just don't. As I'm sure you've noted, Dick's will was so explicit as not to allow any interpretation."

"I understand that," Caleb said, "and I'll just have to learn to live with it. How did the inquest go? I couldn't bring myself to be there."

"You've another shock in store, I'm afraid. There's little doubt in my mind that Dick, Barbara and Esme were all murdered by some unknown person. Dick didn't kill his family or himself."

Caleb looked stunned. He took a deep swig from his drink. "Well, that's both a shock and a relief. I couldn't imagine that Dick had done that, but I can't imagine that there's anyone who'd want them dead, either."

Stone opened the safe, took out the inquest papers and took Caleb through the procedure, showing him the photographs.

"I see your point," Caleb said.

"I intend to pursue this," Stone said.

"You're probably not aware that I spent fourteen years in the New York Police Department, eleven of them as a detective investigating homicides. Dino Bacchetti, who just left, was my partner. He and I agree that this wasn't a murder/ suicide, and the coroner has issued an open verdict."

"I knew you were a cop, but that was all I knew. I'm glad you've got the experience to look into this. I want Dick's killer caught and punished."

"I'm going to need your help," Stone said. "Can you think of anyone, on the island or off, who had any sort of grudge against Dick?"

Caleb looked thoughtful but shook his head. "I can't. Dick wasn't the sort of fellow that people had grudges against."

"That's my memory of him, too. I'd like you to think about this, and if you come up with anything at all, please call me. I'll be here for a while, and this is my number in New York, when I go back." Stone handed him a card.

"I'll certainly do that," Caleb said.

"There's something else, Caleb, and I'm glad to say this is good news." Stone took the insurance policies from the safe and handed them to him. "Dick took out these policies twelve years ago, leaving a million dollars each to his parents and to you."

Caleb's mouth dropped open. "Good God," he finally managed to say.

"Your parents are dead, aren't they?"

Caleb nodded. "Both of them."

"Were you and Dick their heirs?"

"Yes, their only heirs."

"Then half of their policy will go to you, the other half to the foundation."

"A million and a half dollars," Caleb said tonelessly.

Stone took the policies back. "I'll get in touch with the insurance agent and make the claim, and I'll have the insurance company send you both checks. You're well equipped to handle the estate and tax consequences."

"Yes, I can do that." Caleb stood up. "Thank you, Stone, for telling me about this."

"I would have told you sooner, but I found the policies only a few minutes ago." Stone walked him to the front door. "One more thing: As you're aware, Dick specified that his ashes be scattered in the harbor here; do you want me to take care of that?"

"I'd like to do it myself," Caleb said. "It's the last thing I can do for him."

"I've made arrangements with a funeral parlor in Belfast. I'll call you when I receive the ashes."

"Thank you." Caleb dug into a pocket. "Oh, I expect you'll want my key to this house. Dick gave it to me when he built it, in case of an emergency, but you've got Seth and Mabel Hotchkiss here to deal with any problems."

Stone took the key. "Thank you, Caleb." They shook hands, and Stone went back into the house. He looked at the key. There was a tag attached to it, and written on the tag was "Dick's House, all doors."

9

STONE HAD DINNER alone that evening, watched a movie on satellite television and got to bed late. It was after nine when he woke up the following morning.

He was having breakfast when Seth came into the kitchen. "I thought I might take a drive around the island this morning," Stone said. "You need the station wagon?"

"I've got to go over to Camden to pick up some parts for the washing machine," Seth said, "but Dick's other car is in the garage, ready to go. The key is in the bunch I gave you."

"Thanks," Stone said, pushing back from the table. He got his sunglasses, walked out of the house and opened the garage door.

"Wow," he said, walking up to the little car. A moment's inspection revealed it to be an MG TF 1500, the last of the classic series, built in 1954. It was silver, with a red leather interior, beautifully restored. Apparently, Dick Stone had not liked newer cars.

Stone got into the car, switched on the ignition, pressed the starter button, and the engine caught. He let it warm up for a moment, then found reverse and backed out of the garage. A moment later he was wending his way down the road toward Dark Harbor, the wind in his hair and a song in his heart.

He stopped in front of the Dark Harbor Shop, went inside and bought a *New York Times.* The owner, who also was a real estate agent, was working at his desk in the back of the shop and gave him a wave. The young girl working behind the old-fashioned soda fountain smiled at him as he left.

Stone took the little car north until he ran out of road, then turned around and went back by a different route, passing the ferry terminal and the golf course. Soon he was back in the village and on the way home. You could see all of Islesboro in under an hour.

As he approached the house he saw another dirt road forking to the left and, just for the hell of it, turned down it. It immediately began to narrow, but there was no place to turn around, so he continued. After a hundred yards he drove through an open gate, then another fifty yards down the road came to an abrupt halt. A large tree trunk, trimmed of its branches, was stretched across the road.

Stone looked around. He was going to have to reverse for a hundred and fifty yards. He had begun to do so, when the gate behind him swung shut. Now he was trapped on the narrow road between the gate and the fallen tree trunk.

He got out of the car and looked around. He was surrounded by thick woods and underbrush, with nobody and no house in sight. He was about to walk to the gate and try to open it when he saw a tiny red flash, and then he looked down at his chest to find a pinpoint of red light dancing around it. Laser gunsight. He hit the ground and crawled behind the car.

"Stand up and keep your hands where I can see you!" a deep voice shouted.

"Are you going to shoot me?" Stone called back.

"Maybe. We'll see. Now get up."

Stone sat up and looked over the car. On the other side stood a large, bearlike man somewhere in his sixties, Stone reckoned, with a thick head of salt-and-pepper hair, a large moustache and round, steel-rimmed glasses. He was holding a Sigarms P220 pistol, and the laser sight was still on him.

"I said, 'Stand up,'" the man said.

Stone stood up.

"Now walk to the front of the car and put your hands on the grille."

Stone did so, and the man walked over and frisked him from his neck to his ankles in a thoroughly professional manner.

The man backed away. "Now stand up straight, turn around and stand still."

Stone did so.

"Why are you driving Dick Stone's car?" the man demanded.

"Can I show you some I.D.?"

"Do it carefully."

Stone produced a wallet with his badge and I.D.

The man snatched it away from him and read it carefully, keeping his aim with the gun. "Your first name is Stone?"

"Dick was my first cousin."

"And you're a retired cop?"

"Yes, and you seem to be, too."

"Not exactly."

"I'm Dick's executor. I'm up here to settle his estate."

The man lowered the gun but didn't put it away. "Okay," he said. "You ought to be more careful whose driveway you drive down."

"I'm sorry about that. I didn't know it was a driveway; there was no sign or mailbox. I was just exploring."

The man put the gun in his belt and held out a hand. "I'm Ed Rawls," he said. He took a remote control from his pocket and pressed a button. The log ahead of Stone swung slowly out of his way. "Explore your way down to the end of the drive, and I'll buy you a cup of coffee," he said, then he turned and disappeared into the trees.

The gate behind him was still closed, so Stone got into the car and drove another fifty yards before the drive ended at a sharp turn into a clearing. Stone noticed a large convex mirror mounted on a tree at the turn. Ed Rawls was a very careful man.

He got out of the car and approached a small, handsome, shingled cottage. As he stepped onto the porch, Ed Rawls opened the front door.

"Come on in," Rawls said. "The coffee is already on."

Stone stepped into a large room paneled in old pine, with a fieldstone fireplace to his right. Two walls were covered in pictures, oils and watercolors of Maine and European scenes and landscapes. Rawls disappeared and came back with a coffee pot and two mugs on a tray.

"Have a seat," he said. "You take cream or milk?"

"Black is fine." Stone sat down in a leather chair.

"Good. I don't have any cream or milk." He poured them both a mug of coffee, handed one to Stone and sat down himself. "So you're a retired cop? I wouldn't have thought there was a cop in Dick's family."

"I'm from the black sheep branch," Stone said. "Since I retired I practice law in New York."

"You look pretty young to be retired."

"A bullet in the knee retired me."

Rawls nodded. "So you're Dick's executor? Why, is Caleb dead, too?"

"No."

Rawls stared at him for a moment, then

decided not to pursue that line of questioning. "You gonna be on Islesboro long?"

"As long as it takes."

"As long as it takes to what?"

"To find out who murdered Dick and his family."

Rawls looked at him carefully. "And why do you think he was murdered?"

Stone shrugged. "I've seen a lot of homicides and quite a few suicides, and I know the difference." Stone sipped his coffee. "And what are you retired from, Mr. Rawls?"

"You call me Ed and I'll call you Stone, all right?"

"All right."

"I'm retired from the State Department," Rawls said. "Dick and I used to work together."

"Ed," Stone said, "I know who Dick worked for, and it wasn't the State Department."

"Oh, yeah?"

"Oh, yeah. And why do you have all this security and why are you walking around in this lovely place with a Sig P220 in your hand?"

"Well," Rawls said, "I reckon the folks who got Dick Stone might be coming for me, too."

10

STONE THOUGHT FOR a minute about what Ed Rawls had just said. "So you think Dick's death was work related?"

Rawls nodded gravely. "Certainly."

"Why?"

Rawls held up a finger. "One: This island has a population of fifty or sixty in the winter and maybe six hundred in the summer. All of them, local and summer folk, have known each other for years—generations, some of them—and the atmosphere on Islesboro is not the sort to engender grudges that end in multiple homicides. Two: Dick Stone was not the kind of guy that anybody could hold a grudge against. And three: I'm just guessing, of course, but

I'd be willing to bet that there wasn't a trace of any kind of evidence in the house. Am I right?"

"On all three points," Stone said.

"And the weapon was silenced, right? This was a pro hit," Rawls said, sitting back in his chair. "No doubt about it."

"The weapon was Dick's own," Stone said.

"Well," Rawls said, sitting back again, "if you were a pro staging a murder-suicide, you'd use the victim's own gun, wouldn't you? Lends plausibility."

"That brings us to who sent the pro," Stone said. "Any ideas, Ed?"

Rawls sipped his coffee contemplatively. "You make enemies in that line of work."

"Which ones did Dick make?"

"Irish? Russian mafia? Islamics? Take your pick."

"So you have no idea?"

"Not specifically."

"Who would want to kill *you,* then?"

"Ah," Rawls chuckled. "The field broadens. With me, you have to consider domestic sources."

"Domestic? The Agency deals only in foreign matters, doesn't it?"

"Well, not any more . . . not since 9/11, anyway. It did in my day, though, at least mostly."

"You fear your own countrymen, then?"

"More than anybody else."

"Why?"

"Let's just say that my countrymen were not always happy with the way I did my work."

"I've heard your name before, haven't I?" He knew he had, but he couldn't place it.

Rawls shrugged. "Possibly."

"Why would I have heard it, Ed?"

Rawls shrugged again but said nothing.

"Come on, Ed. I can run a check on you half a dozen ways. Hell, I can probably get most of it by Googling you."

"I suppose you could," Rawls said. "I was running the Scandinavian station out of Stockholm some years back, looking forward to retirement. I got involved with a lovely Swedish creature who turned out to be a lovely Russian creature. This was before the fuckers all became democrats. They blackmailed me, and I gave them some fairly useless information, but a meet went south, and a couple of my people bought it. I was blamed, and they hung me out to dry."

"I remember now," Stone said. "You're supposed to be in prison, aren't you?"

"I was, until a few months ago, but a couple of nice things happened. One: The former KGB station chief in Stockholm told the Brits that I had nothing to do with the two deaths, that it was an accident not related to me, and the Brits told our people. Two: Even in the Atlanta pen I was able to do my country a valuable service, and a combination of the two things got me a presidential pardon. And a very nice cash reward, I might add."

"I didn't hear about the pardon."

"Almost nobody did. I think they announced it in the middle of the night. It probably won't be out until Will Lee isn't president anymore."

"And how'd you end up on Islesboro?"

"Oh, I'm a fourth-generation islander; my great-grandfather built this house, and I've owned it for more than twenty years."

"How did the islanders react to your, ah, problems?"

"Pretty well. I actually got some encouraging mail in prison, and when I came back, it was like I'd never left. During the whole business I was never asked to resign from the yacht club or the golf club. You play golf?"

"In a manner of speaking."

"Let's do that soon. I'll introduce you to some islanders."

"Ed, are you convinced that nobody who lives here had anything to do with the murders of Dick and his family?"

Rawls nodded. "I am. Nobody knows this place and these people better than I do, and, believe me, it's just not in the cards."

"But you can't suggest exactly who might have been involved?"

"Not yet, but I've got some feelers out. You'll have to be patient; these things aren't on the clock."

"You're making me feel helpless," Stone said. "I'm out of my depth with the kind of people you're talking about."

"Yeah, but you know people who can help, Stone."

"Do I?"

"Well, until yesterday, you were up here with Lance Cabot, weren't you?"

"There is a local grapevine, isn't there?"

"Sure, there is."

"You know Lance?"

"I helped train him," Rawls said. "He worked for me later. So did Kate Rule." Katharine Rule Lee was the president's wife and the Director of Central Intelligence.

"You are well connected, aren't you, Ed?"

"I know quite a few folks; not all of 'em want to know me."

"Because of your indiscretions?"

Rawls nodded. "Stone, I can see you're here with the idea of tracking down Dick's killer and putting him in jail, but that's not how it works in this particular game."

"How does it work?"

"We find out who gave the order, and after a while, we make something happen to him in such a way that doesn't seem connected to the Stone murders."

Stone noted the "we." "And how do *we* make that happen?"

"Oh, somebody has an auto accident on an icy road, or maybe he has a few sips of a dioxin cocktail. Satisfaction comes slow in this game."

Stone looked at his watch. "I'd better be going; I have to make some calls, and I still have quite a lot of work to do on Dick's estate."

"Tell you what, let's play golf tomorrow morning—nine holes at, say, ten and then I'll take you to lunch at the yacht club. Pick you up at Dick's at nine-forty-five?"

"Sounds good," Stone said. He shook hands with Rawls and went to his car. As he drove back up Ed Rawls's drive, the gate was open again. Then, in his rearview mirror, he saw it close behind him.

11

STONE DROVE BACK TO the house and called Lance's cell phone.

"Yes?"

"It's Stone."

"Everything all right?"

"So far. Tell me about Ed Rawls."

There was silence for a moment, while Lance thought about it. "Oh, God," he said. "Ed lives up there, doesn't he? I'd forgotten."

"Tell me about him."

"What do you want to know?"

"Everything you've got time for."

"All right. Ed was a second-generation guy; his father worked for Bill Donovan in the OSS during World War Two and was with Dulles when the Agency was created. Ed became a star in Operations; he initially made his name as a new agent in Viet Nam. He had a talent for recruiting, even people whose language he didn't speak, but it didn't take him long to learn the language. He ran teams of South Vietnamese into Laos and the North to gather intelligence, take and interrogate prisoners and destroy weapons stockpiles; he jumped out of airplanes into the jungle, got what he was after and walked home if a chopper couldn't get to him without attracting too much attention.

"By the time the war was over, he was a near-legend, and by the time I met him, when I was in training, he was the actual thing. He was a great mentor, and everybody loved him, except the colleagues who had to compete with him.

"After the Farm, he was posted to Berlin and made a whole new name for himself then. He preceded Dick in running the London station, then he got caught in bed with somebody's wife and got sent to Stockholm, which was a demotion. Ed never could keep his cock in his pants, and the cold winters didn't slow him down.

"Unfortunately, one of his girls was a setup of the Soviets, and they took the usual embarrassing photographs. He was up against it, due to retire in a couple of years, and exposure would have gotten him fired, after his debacle in London. He began feeding them information, probably harmless stuff. Two of our people were designated to follow him to a possible meet with the Soviets, and they were both shot. Kate Rule, herself, found him out and got him sent to prison. He spent four or five years in the Atlanta Federal Prison, until the Agency got some backdoor information from a former source that seemed to clear him.

"He was also the source of a tip that put somebody we were looking for in a cottage on North Islesboro. That, apparently, tipped the balance, and the top echelon at Langley, including Kate Rule, recommended a presidential pardon. He also got a million-dollar reward and repaired to his ancestral home in Dark Harbor to amuse himself as best he could and await death. That's about it."

"Is he somebody I can trust?"

"Trust to what?"

"Tell me the truth."

"Probably, especially if it's in his interest to do so. Why do you ask?"

"Rawls told me he thinks Dick's death was work related."

A brief silence. "Did he give you any details?"

"He said he had some feelers out, and I'd have to be patient. He's also afraid whoever killed Dick and his family may have a go at him as well, and he's taken security precautions at his house. I wandered down his drive, exploring, and he trapped my car and drew down on me."

"Well, assuming prison didn't send Ed around the bend, there may be something to it. We all have a certain amount of paranoia trained into us, and Ed would be no exception. Did he seem to make sense to you?"

"Yes, he did."

"Then I'd take him seriously and find out what, if anything, he has to offer. How could it hurt?"

"Well, it's not like I have anything else to go on."

"You'll find Ed an entertaining character, full of stories, and he's very smart. You could do worse than to have him on your side."

"I didn't see any evidence of a wife."

"She bailed out when Ed was arrested, took half of everything and bought a house in Florida. Last I heard, she'd remarried."

"Tell me, Lance, in what sort of repute is Rawls held by his former colleagues?"

"Some are sympathetic; some hate his guts. Hugh English, whom Dick was succeeding as Deputy Director for Operations, was one of the haters, but he signed off on the pardon recommendation. Incidentally, I don't know if Ed mentioned it to you, but there are a few other retired spooks living out their years on that island. I understand they do some drinking together and call themselves the Old Farts."

Stone laughed. "Thanks for the information, Lance."

"Call me when I can help." Lance hung up.

It suddenly occurred to Stone that he had a golf date the following morning, and he didn't have any golf clubs. He saw Seth Hotchkiss working in the back garden, and he walked outside.

"Hey, Stone," Seth said.

"Hey, yourself. Tell me, Seth, did Dick have any golf clubs?"

Seth nodded. "There's a big cupboard in the garage, next to the MG."

"I noticed, but I didn't look inside."

"There's a lot of sports stuff in that cupboard." Then Seth nodded toward a sailboat resting at the end of Dick's dock. "There's that, too, got delivered from the yard this morning, and there's a picnic boat, ought to be delivered from the yard this afternoon. You'll get a big bill for the maintenance and storage."

"What's the sailing boat?"

"It's a one-off. Dick designed it himself maybe ten years ago and had it built over at Hinckley's, in Southwest Harbor. They built the picnic boat, too, but Dick got that last year."

"Thanks, Seth." Stone went back into the house and then to the garage, where he opened the large cupboard. It was a veritable sporting goods store: There was a set of titanium Callaway clubs, tennis racquets, a croquet set, fishing equipment and more. Dick was nothing if not well equipped; he had spent his wife's money well.

Stone went back into the house, opened

the safe and read Dick's will again. The bequest of the use of the house to Stone included outright ownership of all its "appurtenances." Stone read that to include the cars and boats and whatever else he hadn't discovered yet.

"Holy shit," he muttered to himself.

12

STONE WAS STANDING in front of the house with his golf clubs when Ed Rawls pulled into the driveway in a shiny, new Range Rover. Stone put his clubs in the back and got into the passenger seat. "Morning."

"Good morning," Rawls said. "Looks like we've got a good day for it."

"Yep."

"I had a call from Lance Cabot last night. We had a nice chat, and he offered me any support I might need in helping you with the Stone murders."

"That's good. Take him up on it."

"He gave me a name at Langley as a liaison. I talked with her this morning, and she's running down some things for me."

"You want to tell me about the things?"

"Nah, it would take too long, and it wouldn't help you. The information she gets might help, though, and I'll tell you about that when I get it."

"Okay."

They drove through Dark Harbor and out to the golf course, where they unloaded their clubs. There was a wait while a foursome teed off before them.

"Let's give them a good head start," Rawls said. He looked down at Stone's loafers. "What kind of golf shoes are those?"

"Oh, Dick's were too small, and I didn't have any of my own. I'll have to send for some, I guess."

Stone looked around; there were no carts. "We going to walk?" he asked.

"Oh, sure; it's how I get my exercise."

They teed off, and Rawls set a rapid pace down the fairway. Stone followed as best he could, but his loafers were not built for this.

TWO HOURS LATER they sat at a table at the Tarrantine Yacht Club, which was a modest building with a big dock and a lot of moorings, waiting for cheeseburgers. Stone took off his ruined loafers, which were soaking wet after a few tramps through the rough, and rubbed his feet.

"You gotta get some better shoes," Rawls said, sipping his Coke.

"Tell me about it." He had to replace the loafers, too. It had been an expensive round of golf.

"What did you shoot, finally?" Rawls asked.

"Don't ask."

"How'm I going to play you for money, if you won't tell me your score?"

"All right, I shot a fifty-two. How about you?"

"Forty, a little off my handicap."

"Which is . . . ?"

"Six."

"Jesus, Ed, how the hell are you playing to that kind of handicap at your age?"

"I practice a lot. There's fuck-all else to do around here, if you don't sail or play tennis. What's your handicap?"

"I don't know, probably around twenty-five."

"You need to practice more."

"Well, if I spend enough time up here, I might do that. Golf is tough when you live in the city. I have a place in Connecticut, and I belong to a club there, but I don't get up there often enough."

"You going to be spending any time around here?"

"Maybe. Dick left me his house."

"No kidding? That's a very tidy inheritance. You know what that place is worth?"

"I get to use it, and so do my heirs, but if it's sold, the proceeds go to the Samuel Bernard Foundation."

"You know what that is?"

"Yes. Bernard was a mentor of mine in law school."

"I'm surprised he didn't recruit you."

"He tried to, but I didn't know it at the time. It was many years later he told me he thought I might not have been suited for the life. Lance signed me as a consultant, though."

"That speaks well of you; Lance is a good judge of talent."

Stone shrugged.

"Well, if you're going to be spending some time here, we'd better get you in the yacht club and the golf club. I'll work with you, and we'll bring your handicap down." Rawls raised a hand and waved over two men who were standing in line for hamburgers. He introduced both men.

"I hear you're Dick Stone's cousin," one of them said.

"That's right."

"How does that work? I thought I knew all of Dick's family."

"His father and my mother were brother and sister. I grew up in New York."

"This your first time in Islesboro?" the other asked.

"No, I spent a summer up here with Dick's family when I was eighteen."

"Hey, I remember you," the man said, laughing. "You're the kid who knocked Caleb Stone on his ass."

"I remember that, too," the other man said. "It was the talk of the club for a week. Why did you never come back?"

"Caleb's mother didn't take the news as well as everybody else did. After that, I was persona non grata."

"Welcome back," the man said, then they excused themselves and went to get their food.

"Well done," Rawls said.

"Well done what?"

"The tall guy was the commodore, and

the other was the chairman of the membership committee. The commodore is on the golf club board, too. I'll get forms and propose you today."

"You think the business with Caleb will hurt?"

"Are you kidding? Everybody hated that kid; judging from their reaction, you were a hero."

Stone glanced toward the door and nearly dropped his Coke. A ghost from his past had just walked in the door. He had a rush of déjà vu in which he and Dick were sitting in this club at this table when Dick's brother, Caleb, entered the room. His gut tightened, just as it always had when Caleb was around, teasing and bullying the two younger boys. Now Caleb, aged twenty or so, was back, young again.

"What's wrong?" Rawls asked.

Stone had trouble speaking. "Who is that?" And as he asked the question, he began to see double.

"Oh, those are the Stone twins, Caleb's boys, Eben and Enos. I can never tell which is which."

Stone breathed a little easier. "God, I thought I was going crazy for a moment;

they're both the image of Caleb at that age."

"I guess they are, at that," Rawls said.

The twins were loud, too, just like their father. They approached a table of teenagers, and the noise level went up with their arrival.

"I haven't seen those boys since they were about twelve," Rawls said. "I didn't like them then; they were bullies, always picking on some younger kids. They'd double-team them."

"Thank God there was only one of their father," Stone muttered. He could not imagine what his summer in Islesboro would have been like if there had been two of Caleb. But now there were, and he didn't like the idea much. He decided not to go over and introduce himself as Cousin Stone.

13

DINO BACCHETTI'S UNMARKED CAR
pulled up in front of the Palatine mansion in
the outer reaches of Brooklyn, the home of
his father-in-law, Eduardo Bianchi. "Wait
here," Dino said to his driver. "My guess is,
this won't take long."

Dino got out of the car and trudged
toward the front door, dreading every step.
He had never had lunch alone with Eduardo, and he wasn't looking forward to it.
The meeting with Mary Ann and her lawyer
yesterday had been a disaster that had
ended in shouting and harsh words, and
Dino thought he had probably been sum-
moned here to be disciplined. He was well
aware that Eduardo had only to lift an eye-

brow and some obedient servant would slip a stiletto between his ribs.

Dino rang the bell, and the front door was opened by just such a servant, Pietro, a cadaverous sixty-year-old who had once had a fearsome reputation as an assassin. But that was back in the days when Eduardo was still taking an active part in the ruling of his Cosa Nostra family, which ran large parts of Brooklyn and Manhattan.

Eduardo had since, over the past thirty years, made himself into an elder statesman of everything: the Metropolitan Museum of Art, the New York Public Library and nearly every important charity in the city. His Mafia connections had been mostly forgotten by the very few surviving people who knew anything about them. But Dino knew Eduardo still had the power to deal with people in any way he saw fit.

Pietro led Dino through the elegantly appointed house into the rear garden, where Eduardo sat at a table set for two. Eduardo rose and offered his hand, a good sign, Dino thought.

"Dino, welcome," the old man said. He carried his eighty-odd years lightly, looking trim, even athletic, and there was only a little gray in his hair. "Please sit down and have some lunch."

Dino sat. "Beautiful day," he said, because he couldn't think of anything else to say.

"Yes, one appreciates good weather as one grows older," Eduardo replied.

A waiter came and opened a bottle of Frascati, while another man set before them plates of bruschetta, little slices of bread fried in olive oil, then topped with chopped plum tomatoes, garlic and basil. Dino tried not to eat too greedily, but Eduardo's younger sister was the best cook he had ever known, and he loved bruschetta.

"I understand things didn't go well yesterday," Eduardo said.

"That's understating the case," Dino replied.

"You know that I disapproved of your marriage to Anna Maria," the old man said. He refused to refer to her as Mary Ann, as she preferred to be called.

"Yes, I knew that."

"I was, of course, upset that Anna Maria was pregnant, but my principal objection was that you were a policeman."

"I'll take that as a compliment," Dino said.

"However, as the years have passed I

have come to respect your personal integrity. You would never allow me to use my influence to improve your position in the police department, though I could easily have done so, and you would never accept any gift from me, insisting that everything be in Anna Maria's name. I realize now that you are being divorced, that works to your disadvantage."

Dino shrugged. "All I want is shared custody of Benito," he said.

"You will have that," Eduardo said. "I do not approve of divorce, being a good Catholic, but I understand that people can come to a place in their lives where they can no longer live together, and I see little reason to deny them remarriage at some point. I once put that directly to the Pope, who was unhappy with me for a while, as a result."

Dino thought that the Pope would have been at a disadvantage, arguing with Eduardo.

"You are aware, are you not, that Anna Maria has worked very hard at investing the money that came to her when she was twenty-one?"

"We never discussed that," Dino said. "I told her I didn't want to know."

"I understand your position, but I assure you that the funds she started with came from entirely legitimate sources, and that that can be documented to the satisfaction of the New York Police Department or even the Internal Revenue Service."

"I'm glad to hear it," Dino said.

"You have lived a long time in an unhappy marriage," Eduardo said, "and the law entitles you to an equitable division of property."

"I don't want her property," Dino said, though the thought of existing on a lieutenant's salary and benefits did not thrill him.

"Anna Maria was able to do so well with her investments because you insisted on supporting her. That way, she could devote all her capital to making more."

Dino shrugged.

"You are morally entitled to leave this marriage with more than you earn as a policeman," Eduardo said, "so I have made certain arrangements."

Dino said nothing but started in on the veal that had been placed before him.

"Anna Maria's holdings now amount to about eleven million dollars, including the value of the apartment you shared, which was bought with earnings from her money. Tomorrow, a million dollars of her holdings will be placed in the trust that you set up at Benito's birth and to which you would never allow me to contribute. This will be used as you have specified, for his education, and anything left over can be used to buy a home after he is twenty-five, though surely by that time he will have come into a considerable inheritance from me."

"That's very generous of her," Dino said. This was Eduardo's move, of course, not Mary Ann's, but it lifted a load from his mind.

"Further, five million dollars of her funds go to you, as a complete and total settlement. I know you do not want any part of the apartment or any other wealth deriving from me."

"Thank you for understanding that, Eduardo," Dino said. "And I don't want her money."

"Five million of it is your money, Dino," Eduardo said, "and it was placed in your checking account this morning."

Dino put down his fork and stared at Eduardo.

"I can hear the gears turning in your mind,

Dino," the old man said. "You are trying to figure out how this money is ill-gotten gains, but I assure you none of it is. It is a reasonable and proper settlement of your divorce; it will stand up to any possible scrutiny by the department, the district attorney or the state and federal tax authorities, and I will not tolerate its return."

Dino had never heard Eduardo use the words "I will not tolerate," and they stopped him in his tracks. "I am uncomfortable with this," he said, when he had found his voice.

"I know, but you will grow more comfortable with it as your life grows more comfortable, particularly when you are as old as I. You can now purchase a home of your own, where Benito can visit you regularly and have his own room. If you wish to invest the rest, I will be pleased to recommend someone who I can guarantee will not steal from you or charge unreasonable fees."

Dino stared at his father-in-law again.

Eduardo held up a hand. "Please," he said. "I ask this of you as a favor. Make an old man happy."

Dino sighed. "All right. And thank you, Eduardo."

Eduardo snapped his fingers and a man

with a briefcase whom Dino had not noticed approached, appeared at his elbow. He opened the case and produced a sheaf of papers. "This," Eduardo said, accepting them, "will be the settlement agreement between you and Anna Maria. It includes the financial settlement I have just outlined and a guarantee of joint custody. You will have Benito two weekends each month, two days each week and six weeks each summer, all to be mutually agreed on by you and Anna Maria. Anna Maria's signature is already affixed and notarized. If you should ever feel that Anna Maria is not living up to the agreement's provisions, you need not go to a lawyer or judge, simply telephone me. Please read it."

Dino took a pen from his pocket and signed both copies of the document without reading it. The man in the suit notarized both, handed one to Dino and put the other into his briefcase, then disappeared as quickly as he had appeared.

The two men finished their lunch at their leisure and spoke of whatever came into their minds. It was the only time in the years Dino had known Eduardo that he had ever felt comfortable in his presence.

14

STONE SPENT THE NEXT DAY working on
his cousin's estate, distributing funds to
those named in the will, paying the bills that
had come in and dealing with the life insurance company on the two policies that Dick
had taken out.

Around noon, the doorbell rang, and two
packages were delivered. One bore the return address of the funeral directors who
had handled the cremation and obviously
contained the family's ashes; the other was
from Sergeant Young. Stone opened that
package.

Inside were a pair of khaki trousers and a
plastic bag containing a number of items. A
letter from the sergeant said that these were

Dick's clothes and the contents of his pockets, and that Dick's pistol and silencer were being retained as evidence, pending resolution of his case.

Stone examined the trousers. They were ordinary, from L.L. Bean, and a belt was among the effects. He went through the other effects and found a steel Rolex Submariner wristwatch and bracelet, a wallet, ninety-four dollars in cash held by a money clip, a clump of keys on a ring, a handkerchief, a pocket comb, a silver Mont Blanc pen, a mint Chapstick and a pocket-sized packet of Kleenex.

Stone's first interest lay in the fact that Dick's clothes did not include shoes, shirt or underwear, just the trousers. He imagined Dick being wakened by a noise, slipping on the trousers and coming downstairs, where his killer greeted him with his own gun. He could not think of any other reason why his cousin would be wandering around the house in the middle of the night wearing only trousers. It was still cool at night, and the furnace in the house was programmed not to come on after midnight.

The wallet was small, since Dick had carried his cash in a money clip. He emptied it of its contents, one compartment at a time, and replaced the items in the same order after he had inspected them. There were a Maine driver's license, American Express and Visa cards, a bank ATM card on Dick's Camden bank, a membership card from a London club, a pilot's license for single-engine land and multi-engine land with instrument ratings for both and a third-class FAA medical certificate with the date of Dick's last examination, two days before his death, from a doctor in Camden. Stone had not known that Dick was a pilot. The wallet also contained business cards, identifying Dick as the agricultural attaché at London's American embassy, obviously a cover job. The last item was a Maine license to carry concealed firearms.

Stone returned the items to their bag and put them in a cupboard in the study, then he looked up Caleb Stone's number in the local phone book and called him. Caleb answered.

"It's Stone," he said.

"Hi."

"I've received the ashes from the funeral directors, and you said you wanted to scatter them in the harbor."

"Yes, thank you."

"The three were intermingled, according to Dick's instructions. Would you like me to bring them over?"

"I'll pick them up," Caleb said. "Is now a good time?"

"Yes, come ahead." The two men hung up.

Five minutes later, the doorbell rang, and Stone ushered Caleb inside and handed him the box.

"I haven't opened them," he said. "I don't know what sort of container they're in."

"I don't suppose it matters," Caleb said, tucking the box under his arm.

Stone struggled for something else to say. "I saw your boys over at the yacht club yesterday," he said finally. "They're the image of you at that age."

"Yes, they are," Caleb said. "I'm very proud of them. They're doing well at Yale, and they're the stars of the wrestling team, as I was."

Stone nodded.

Caleb looked uncomfortable. "Would you mind if we borrowed the picnic boat to scatter the ashes? All we've got is a Boston

Whaler, and it doesn't seem appropriate to the occasion."

"Please do," Stone replied. "I suppose the keys are in it, since the yard delivered it yesterday."

"Thank you," Caleb said. "I'll have the boys bring it back when we're done." He stood still for another moment, then said, "Well, I suppose I'd better go. Thank you for taking care of the funeral directors. Will you send me a bill?"

"The estate paid for it," Stone said. "I've already sent them a check. I've dealt with the insurance company, and you should have a check from them within a week."

"Thank you for that, too," Caleb said and headed for the door.

Stone walked him to the door, shook his hand and closed it after him. Stone had still not become accustomed to Caleb's new-found civility and quiet nature.

The phone rang, and Stone answered it in the study, at Dick's desk.

"It's Dino."

"How are you? How did the meeting with Mary Ann and the lawyers go?"

"Lousy, but the one with Eduardo went better."

"Why with Eduardo?"

"It was at his invitation." Dino told him what had happened.

"That's very good news, Dino."

"Yeah, now I'm not stuck with just a salary and a pension."

"What are you going to do with it?"

"I'm going to buy an apartment and invest the rest with a guy Eduardo recommended. So I'll be out of your house as soon as I can find the right place."

"Take your time."

"How's it going up there?"

"It's all very pleasant. I played golf yesterday with an old cohort of Dick's and had lunch at the yacht club, but I have no leads on the murders."

"Am I going to have to come back up there and solve this for you?"

"Any help would be appreciated."

"I'm going to be tied up here for a few days, then maybe I'll do that."

"You'd be welcome. How's Elaine?"

"As ever. What did you expect?"

"As ever."

"I gotta run; I've got an appointment with a real estate agent."

"Take care." Stone hung up. It was past

his lunchtime, and he went into the kitchen and found Mabel fixing him a shrimp salad.

"Oh," she said, "I thought of something. About that night."

"What did you think of?" Stone asked.

"It was the vacuum cleaner."

"What about the vacuum cleaner?"

"It was in Mr. Dick's study, over by the door to the terrace."

"Where would it ordinarily be?" he asked.

She pointed to a door across the kitchen. "In there, in the broom closet."

"Do you think Dick used it?"

She shook her head. "Mr. Dick never lifted a finger to clean anything; I don't think he would know how to operate a vacuum cleaner."

"Did you mention this to the police?"

"Yes, and they put some powder on the handle, but they didn't seem to find any fingerprints. When they were through with it, I cleaned the powder off and put it back in the broom closet." She set his plate on the kitchen table.

Stone sat down to eat. So whoever had killed Dick and his family had vacuumed as he left the house through the terrace door. Very neat fellow. Very smart, too. "Mabel, have you changed the bag in the vacuum since that night?"

"There was no bag in it," she said. "I put a new one in."

Very smart fellow, indeed, Stone thought.

15

THE NEXT DAY STONE was sitting at Dick's desk, trying to clean up the last details of the estate before sending a check to the foundation, when the phone rang. His hand was on the receiver before he realized that none of the buttons was lit and that the sound of the phone was very muffled. He put his ear to the door of Dick's secret office, and the bell became louder.

Stone got out his keys, opened the door and picked up the phone. "Yes?" he said.

There was a silence on the other end, then a man's voice: "Stone?"

"Yes, speaking."

"This is warning," the man said. His voice was heavily accented.

"Yes?"

"Kirov."

"What?"

"You understand me?"

"I understood Kirov."

"Then you know."

"Know what?"

The man was silent for another long moment. "Is Stone?" he asked.

"Yes."

"Then you know." He hung up.

Then it dawned on Stone that the man had thought he was talking to Dick. "I'm a little slow on the uptake," he said aloud, then hung up the phone. He locked up the office, went back to the desk and called Lance's cell phone.

"Yes?"

"It's Stone."

"Hello."

"Dick just got a call in his other office."

"You mean the phone rang?"

"Yes."

"For how long?"

"Until I answered it."

"You answered Dick's hotline?"

"Is that what it is?"

"Yes, did you answer it?"

"Yes." Stone told him about the conversation, such as it was.

"He said Kirov?"

"Yes."

"Like the ballet company in St. Petersburg?"

"Yes."

"You're sure he said Kirov?"

"Positive. And he had a heavy accent, maybe Russian, maybe Eastern European."

"Kirov is a code word," Lance said.

"You think?"

"It means that something has happened."

"What?"

"Or that something is going to happen."

"What has happened or is going to happen?"

"I don't know; I'll have to do some checking with London."

"Okay. If something is going to happen, I'd like to know about it."

"I'll call you back."

"Okay."

"Wait a minute."

"I'm still here."

"Call me when you get back Dick's personal effects, the things that the police took from his body."

"They arrived yesterday."

"There should be a small coinlike object, larger than a penny, smaller than a nickel."

"There were no coins, just ninety-four dollars in a money clip."

"Look through them again. I'll hold."

Stone put the phone down, went to the cupboard, retrieved the bag and shook the contents out on the desk.

"No coins," he said.

"Tell me what's there."

"Small wallet, ninety-four dollars, money clip, handkerchief, comb, Chapstick, keys, Kleenex."

"It's got to be there. Take a minute and go through everything again, especially the wallet."

Stone removed everything from the wallet and inspected it carefully. Nothing. He went through the money. Nothing. Nothing anywhere. He sneezed.

"Bless you," he heard Lance say.

"Just a minute." He picked up the Kleenex pack, got one out and blew his nose. "Hang on," he said. He took all the Kleenex out of the pack, and left inside the plastic was a small disc. "Got it," he said. "It was in the pack of Kleenex."

"Okay, are you in the little office?"

"No."

"Get in there, and take the disc with you."

Stone unlocked the door and went inside again, taking the phone with him. "Okay, I'm in."

"Look at the bottom of the computer; there's a little panel."

Stone looked at the black computer tower. "Yes, I see it."

"Push on the panel."

Stone did so, and out slid a little tray that had an indentation the size of the disc. "Okay, do I put the disc in the tray?"

"Yes, smooth side down."

There were four little bumps on one side, so Stone put the disk, bumps up, into the tray and closed it. "Done."

"Now turn on the computer and the monitor. There's a button at the top of the tower, next to the floppy-disk drive, and another on the monitor."

Stone turned them both on. "Booting up."

"Wait a minute, and you'll get a prompt at the top of the screen."

Stone waited, and the prompt appeared. "It's there."

"Type in, all caps, TELOG."

Stone typed it in, and instantly a list of names and phone numbers appeared. "I have a telephone log."

"Tell me what the top line says."

"It says, 'Cell' and gives a number." He read the number to Lance.

"Thank you," Lance said. "Now switch off the monitor and the computer, remove the disk and put it in Dick's safe. It will be collected."

"Okay. Now what?"

"Now I'll run down the phone number and find out what the hell is going on. I'll get back to you, maybe today, maybe not. Bye-bye." Lance hung up.

"Spooky," Stone said.

16

THE PHONE RANG, and Stone picked it up. "Hello?"

"It's Rawls," a gruff voice drawled.

"Good morning."

"You free for lunch? I'd like you to meet some people."

"Yes."

"Noon at the yacht club?"

"Good."

"See you then." Rawls hung up.

The phone rang again. "Hello?"

"It's Lance."

"That was fast."

"I checked with the London station; *Kirov* means trouble is coming, watch your ass."

"A little late," Stone replied.

"Obviously, Dick's contact hadn't heard about his death."

"Is that it, trouble is coming?"

"*Kirov* is used as a specific warning, based on solid information. It was just too late."

"What was the solid information?"

"The man who called was a paid source of Dick's; you'd call him a snitch. He was at a card game last week in East Germany when he overheard two players, Russians, discussing a revenge hit on a highly placed American. The snitch is Hungarian, but he speaks Russian."

"Then why the hell didn't he call Dick last week, when it might have done some good?"

"He was in jail; got into an accident while driving home from the card game, drunk."

"What was the revenge for?"

"Apparently the Agency was responsible for the breakup of a large drug ring in which the two Russians had a stake. The hit was meant to be a warning to the London station."

"This doesn't make any sense," Stone said. "They would send a hit man from Eastern Europe to a small island in Penobscot Bay just to send a message to London?"

"I know it's a stretch, but crime is worldwide these days; the whole thing could have been arranged with a single phone call or e-mail. Anyway, we know the result."

"I'm having lunch with Ed Rawls and some friends of his," Stone said. "Is there any reason to think these same people would have an interest in Rawls?"

"None that I know of. You can tell him about this; it might set his mind at ease. By the way, are you armed?"

"No."

"Does Dick have any guns in the house?"

"Well, he had the Keltec, but the state police have still got that. Why do I need to be armed?"

"I'm not certain that you do, but I have some concerns."

"Please tell me about your concerns."

"When the man called and you answered, he said, 'Is this Stone?,' and you replied, 'Yes,' because that's your name, too. So he thought he was talking to Dick, right?"

"I suppose so."

"This source is classed as unreliable, so he may be working both sides of the street. He may have called to make sure Dick was dead."

"Come on, Lance. Whoever killed Dick knows that he's dead."

"Try and follow me: The shooter would have reported back to whoever sent him that Dick was dead, and it may very well be that the person who sent the shooter also killed him, for security reasons. The phone call could have simply been a check to see if the shooter was lying."

"I suppose that makes a perverted kind of sense," Stone said.

"These people would not casually kill a senior officer of the CIA; it would have been carefully planned, with cutouts at every level, to protect those who ordered the killing. Shooting the shooter is a very good cutout. If caught, he might give up the people who hired him to save his own neck."

"Well, yes, I've had some experience with that."

"Anyway, when you spoke to the guy this morning, that may have indicated to these people that the shooter lied about having completed the hit and that Dick is still alive and well. And you, of course, are also named Stone, and you are living in Dick's house."

Stone sighed. "Are you doing anything about this?"

"People from the London station are looking for Dick's snitch as we speak. When they find him, they'll work their way up the food chain until they find the people who gave the order for the hit."

"And what, do you estimate, are the chances of their reaching the top of the food chain?"

"I think good; the Agency does not take lightly the murder of their officers and especially the murder of an officer's family in the United States. I'll keep you posted on developments. In the meantime, buy a shotgun and watch your ass." Lance hung up.

Stone called his secretary, Joan. "Hi."

"Good morning."

"I'd like you to send me some things, overnight."

"Shoot."

"Go up to my dressing room, find my golf shoes—they're the ones with the plastic spikes . . ."

"No kidding?"

". . . and also a pair of brown alligator moccasins and a pair of boat shoes."

"They're the ones with the nonslip soles, I guess."

"Don't be a smart-ass. Also, go into the safe in my dressing room—you have the combination—and send me that little .45 that Terry Tussey made for me, the one with the pearl handle. Send the holster next to it—make sure it fits, that it's the right one—and the heavy gun belt that's hanging on my belt rack. Also, send three magazines and the double-magazine holder that's with the holster, and send me a box of .45 caliber ammo, the Federal Hydrashock. Got all that?"

"Is it the shoulder holster you want or the belt holster?"

"The belt holster. . . . Oh, what the hell, send both."

Joan read back the list to him. "Anything else?"

"Oh, send me a couple of thousand in cash, too, just put it in an envelope and stick it in a shoe."

"The usual denominations?"

"Plenty of smaller bills."

"Will do. I'll send along some mail, too."

"Goodbye." Stone hung up. Now, if he could just survive until tomorrow.

17

ED RAWLS WAS ALREADY SEATED at a corner table when Stone arrived at the little yacht club. They shook hands, and Stone sat down.

Rawls pushed a slip of paper across the table. "Send checks in those amounts to those addresses for the yacht and golf club memberships," he said. "You're in."

"Already?" Stone asked, astonished. It usually took a while to get into any club.

"You had good backers, and like I told you, your cousin, Dick, was highly regarded around here," Rawls replied. "You met the three requisite members at lunch here yesterday. The committee met last night, and it got done."

"Thank you, Ed. I'm sure I'll enjoy using both. Who am I meeting today?"

"See the two guys standing on the dock?"

Stone turned and saw two elderly men standing outside, one sweeping the horizon, the other looking toward shore. "What are they doing?"

"Just checking. They would never go into any building without checking, especially in light of recent events."

The screen door to the club was bumped open by an electric invalid scooter, and its rider moved it quickly toward their table.

"Stone, this is Don Brown," Rawls said. The other two men came in and sat down. "And this is Harley Davis and Mack Morris."

Stone shook hands all around. "Gentlemen, glad to meet you."

"We're a kind of club of old boys," Rawls said. "We call ourselves the Old Farts."

"Your reputation precedes you," Stone said.

The three men looked wary and exchanged glances. "How's that?" Mack Morris asked.

"I told you, he knows Lance Cabot," Rawls said. "In fact, Stone is one of Lance's contract people. And he's Dick Stone's first cousin."

Everybody nodded, seemingly satisfied with Stone's credentials. They all ordered sandwiches and iced tea and chatted desultorily about golf and boats for a while, then Rawls called the meeting to order, after a fashion.

"My sources are telling me somebody ordered a hit on Dick," he said, without preamble. Everybody became very still.

"We know why?" Davis asked.

"Haven't gotten that far yet," Rawls replied.

Stone spoke up. "My information is a revenge killing, in return for the Agency's busting up a drug ring in East Germany."

"*Your* information?" Don Brown asked, with laconic incredulity.

Stone shrugged.

"Details?" Brown asked.

"I answered Dick's office phone, and somebody used a code word, *Kirov,* which turned out to be a warning."

"Okay," Brown said.

"Problem is, the caller may have thought I was Dick."

"So," Harley Davis said, "if they think Dick

is still alive, somebody may make another house call."

Stone nodded. "So I'm told."

"Are you armed, Stone?" Rawls asked.

"I will be tomorrow."

"That may not be soon enough. I've got a shotgun in the car you can borrow until you're equipped."

"Thanks."

Their sandwiches arrived, and everybody ate in silence for a while.

"For what it's worth, Ed," Stone said, "Lance didn't think any of this had spilled over on you."

"It's nice that Lance thinks that," Rawls said, "but he don't know everything."

"Who knows everything?" Mack Morris observed.

There were affirmative grunts around the table. Then Rawls's three cohorts began to grill Stone.

"How come you're Dick's first cousin and we never heard of you?" Harley Davis asked.

"There was a rift in the family," Stone said. "I spent a summer up here when I was eighteen, and that was about the only contact we had with the Boston branch. I had a great aunt who lived in New York. She was the only one who was friendly."

"What was the cause of the rift?" Don Brown asked.

"My father left Yale to become a carpenter in New York. He was also a member of the Communist Party for a little while." He watched the four men exchange glances.

"How little a while?" Harley asked.

"A couple of years. His family disowned him, and my mother's family disowned her for marrying him."

"She was a Stone?"

"Yes, Matilda."

Don looked up from his sandwich. "She a painter?"

"Yes."

"My wife was a painter; she thought your mother was the greatest artist since Rembrandt."

"My father thought so, too."

"Where'd you go to school?"

"New York public schools, then NYU, both undergraduate and law."

"You ever run into Sam Bernard there?"

"He taught me constitutional law."

Harley looked at Rawls. "I'm surprised Sam didn't recruit him."

"He tried, but Stone preferred the NYPD," Rawls replied.

"That was dumb," Harley said.

Stone couldn't help laughing. "It was pretty good, actually, until I took a bullet in the knee." That wasn't all of it, but it was as much as he told people.

"I heard that wasn't all of it," Mack said.

Stone suppressed another laugh.

"We're careful people," Rawls said, "by nature and by training. We do our homework."

"What did you hear?" Stone asked.

"I heard you were a pain in the ass to your superiors, particularly on that last homicide you worked, and they took advantage of your injury to bounce you."

"That's a fair description," Stone said. "Did you also hear I was right about the homicide?"

"I heard you were a *little* right," Mack replied, "but that your partner had to save your ass before it was over."

"That's fair, too, I guess," Stone admitted.

Mack turned to Rawls. "I guess he'll do," he said.

Stone felt lucky: the approval of the yacht

club, the golf club and the Old Farts, all in one day.

THAT NIGHT, he slept with Rawls's shotgun on the floor next to his bed.

18

STONE WAS WORKING on Dick's estate when the phone rang.

"Hello?"

"This is the Dark Harbor Shop. We have a package for you. Can you come pick it up?"

So much for overnight delivery, Stone thought. "Sure. Be right over." What the hell, he had to pick up a newspaper anyway. He drove into the village and to the shop.

"Heavy," the girl commented, handing the package to him. "You got guns in there?"

Stone smiled. "Just shoes with shoe trees in them."

"Feels like guns," she said, returning to her work at the soda fountain.

Stone bought a paper and went back to

the house. He unwrapped the package, put his golf shoes with his clubs in the garage and the new loafers in his dressing room upstairs. He took a few hundred in cash from the money Joan had sent and put the rest in the safe. She had also sent a light, Italian cotton windbreaker, which would be useful for covering the gun as well as for the cool Maine days. Trust Joan to think of that.

He loaded the three magazines she had sent, put two in the little magazine pouch, then slapped one into the beautiful little custom-made Terry Tussey .45, with its Damascus steel slide, black anodized light-weight frame and mother-of-pearl handle. Small guns were a specialty of Terry's, and this one weighed only twenty-one ounces, tiny for a .45.

He took off his belt and threaded the two by 1/4–inch gun belt through his trouser loops, adding the magazine pouch and the gun holster at the appropriate points. With the belt tightened and the gun in its Mitch Rosen holster, everything felt secure, with the gun lying flat against his side and at an angle. When he slipped on the light wind-breaker or a sweater, or left his shirttail out, everything would be concealed. He drew the .45, worked the slide, put on the safety and added another round to the magazine. With the pistol loaded, cocked and locked, ready for use, he felt better.

Stone called Ed Rawls. "My equipment has arrived. May I return your shotgun without getting blown away?"

"Come ahead. Blow the horn three times as you reach the gate, and I probably won't kill you."

Stone followed Rawls's instructions to the letter and pulled into the clearing before the little house without incident. Rawls came out to meet him, and Stone handed him the shotgun. "There's still one in the chamber, and the safety's on," he said.

"Come on in," Rawls said. "Coffee?"

"Sure."

Rawls poured him a cup from a Thermos and handed it to him. "So what are you packing?"

Stone removed the .45 from its holster, popped out the magazine, ejected the cartridge in the chamber, locked back the slide and handed it to Rawls.

Rawls thumbed the slide catch, aimed it out the window and squeezed off an imaginary round. "Sweet trigger," he said. "Who's Tussey?"

"A guy out in Carson City, Nevada. I saw something of his in a magazine, and we talked on the phone a couple of times. I've got a couple more of his guns, too."

"I never had any need for a gunsmith," Rawls said. "Tech Services supplied what we needed. It didn't have pearl grips, but it always worked good." He handed back Stone's gun.

Stone picked up the ejected round, reloaded the pistol, cocked and locked it and returned it to its holster.

"I had a call from Lance a minute ago," Rawls said. "He tried you first, but I guess you'd already left the house."

"What news?"

"Bad news: The two Russians Dick's source overheard at the poker game are *very* bad actors named Gorky and Rastropov, former KGB. Like a lot of their colleagues they discovered that there was money to be made when the Soviet Union crumbled, and their training and experience, combined with their sociopathic tendencies, make them very dangerous. The Berlin station is looking for them now, but they've gone to ground, and it won't be easy to find them. The word's out, though, and you never know. If they buy a pack of cigarettes in the wrong shop, they're toast."

"So what do we do?"

"Use the burglar alarm and sleep lightly," Rawls replied.

"Will do."

"You've got a very secure house, you know. Did you ever take a close look at the front door?"

"No. I've noticed it's heavy."

"Take a look at mine," Rawls said, beckoning him to the front door. He opened the door and showed Stone the edge. "It's two one-inch-thick sheets of mahogany with a half-inch of steel plate sandwiched between. The door frame is steel, too, and it's bolted to eight-by-eight posts set in concrete. It's hanging on eight hinges." He turned the thumb bolt on the inside, and three extra-large bolts slid out of the door, one each at the top and bottom of the door and the third in the traditional spot.

"That's very impressive," Stone said. "What about the rest of the house? The windows, for instance?"

"They're all steel-framed, and the glass is

armored and an inch thick. Dick's house has the same."

"None of it seemed to work for Dick."

"He made a mistake; everybody does it sooner or later. If he'd had the Kirov call promptly, nobody would ever have gotten into the house alive. I'm surprised you didn't find any weapons in the house."

"I looked in all the cupboards," Stone said. "I couldn't find anything. I figure Dick kept the Keltec at his bedside. He heard something in the night, put on his pants and went downstairs. Somebody disarmed him, sat him down at the desk and shot him with his own gun, then went upstairs and shot his wife and daughter. He was wearing only trousers when they found him."

"Sounds right," Rawls said. "I don't think anybody rang the doorbell; that would have woken the girls. I think what happened was, Dick didn't lock up right and didn't set the alarm system. By the way, the system isn't monitored locally. If somebody set off a motion detector or something, an alarm at Langley would go off."

"Are there motion detectors?" Stone asked. "I hadn't noticed."

"It's why Dick didn't have a dog. If you

have a dog, it has to be highly trained, so you can forego the motion detectors. Otherwise, they have to be set high enough so that a dog won't set them off, and intruders can duck under them."

"Dick sounds too careful to have made a mistake."

"Everybody does, eventually."

"Either that or he knew the person who killed him and let him into the house."

"That's a disturbing thought, given where we are," Rawls said. "It's a tightly contained population."

"All it takes is one," Stone said. He finished his coffee and went home.

As he walked into the house, the phone was ringing. "Hello?"

"It's Dino. Can you meet me at the airport?"

"What airport?"

"The one on the fucking island, dummy. Half an hour." Dino hung up.

19

STONE STOOD BESIDE the Islesboro airport landing strip and watched an airplane
materialize in the sky to the south. It got
larger fast, and a moment later a Pilatus
PC12 set down just past the numbers, re-
versed its prop and taxied to the ramp. The
lettering on the side said NEW YORK STATE PO-
LICE. The airstair door swung down, and
Dino stepped onto the tarmac carrying two
bags. Somebody tossed him a briefcase,
then the door closed, and the airplane taxied to the other end of the runway and took
off again.

"Jesus, why don't you get an airplane like
that?" Dino said.

"Because it costs three million dollars,"

Stone replied. "I'm thinking about having my Malibu Mirage converted to a turboprop, though, and upgrading the avionics. I can do that for half a million."

Dino put his bags into the rear of the station wagon and got into the passenger seat.

Stone started the wagon. "So, why didn't you tell me you were coming?"

"This state cop was at the precinct and said he was flying up to Bar Harbor, so I asked if he could drop me here, and he did. What with the panic packing, I didn't have time to call you. What's happening?"

As they drove into Dark Harbor, Stone brought Dino up to date on the threat against Dick as well as Ed Rawls and the Old Farts.

"So now it's an investigation by committee? Swell."

"They have sources of information I don't," Stone said. "By the way, did you come armed?"

"Nope. I didn't realize I'd be in danger."

"I guess I'll have to borrow Rawls's shotgun again."

"Whatever."

They stopped at the Dark Harbor Shop. "I

have to get a *Times*," he said. "It gets here later than in the city."

Dino got out and came in with him, had a look around the shop. A slender man with blond hair and beard was having a cup of coffee, and Dino glanced at him.

When they were back in the car, Dino said, "You saw the guy at the soda fountain, right?"

"Sort of. You know him?"

"Yeah, and so do you. We busted him for more than a hundred burglaries about seven, eight years ago, back when you were earning an honest living."

"Harold Rhinehart? That was him?"

"Yeah. He has a beard now, and his hair is shorter, but that's the guy."

"How much time did he get?"

"He plead out for five to seven, which means he could have been out two and a half years ago, if he kept his nose clean in the joint and really impressed the parole board. You had any burglaries up here?"

"Not that I've heard about, but I'll ask Rawls; he seems to know everything that's going on. Maybe Rhinehart took his ill-gotten gains and retired up here."

"I doubt it," Dino said. "The guy was a

pro, but he was obsessive about stealing. I don't think there are any New York State parole officers on this island, either. If he got out in half his sentence, he should be reporting to a P.O. every week."

"Dino, you're a wonder; you've been here fifteen minutes, and already you've spotted a perp."

"They're everywhere," Dino said. "Maybe I'll just clean up this burg while I'm here."

"How long can you stay?"

"I got a lot of vacation time built up; we'll see."

"How's it going with Mary Ann?"

"Everything's squared. We're just waiting for a judge to sign off on the agreement and give us a decree, then I'll be a free man."

"How do you feel about that?"

"Relieved."

"No regrets?"

"Can't think of any. It wasn't like it was a marriage made in heaven, y'know. If the kid hadn't been in the picture, we'd have screwed each other for a few months and called it a day the first time she complained about something. She knew it, I knew it."

"Any luck on the apartment hunt?"

"Yeah, I found a nice six on Park in the sixties."

"Sounds expensive."

"By the time it's done up I'll have a couple mil in it."

"Sounds nice."

"Had to be; the court has to approve it for Benito's visits."

"When do you close?"

"Yesterday," Dino said. "Things move fast when it's an all-cash deal. I've already got a designer working on the renovations and buying me some furniture."

"You're going to let a designer furnish the place?"

"Jesus, Stone, you think I give a shit about furniture? I told her, make it nice for the kid so the court will sign off on it. She's going to get it painted, put in some new stuff in the kitchen and get the floors refinished. I'll be in it in a month."

"Dino, it's New York; nothing happens in a month."

"This designer lady is a real hard-ass; she'll get it done. She's already got her people lined up, and she gets paid more if it's ready on time."

"And you're letting her pick out *every-thing*?"

"I picked out the TVs and the stereo and my chair for the den. The rest is up to her."

"Good luck."

"Listen, I'm a better judge of people than I am of furniture. Anyway, it'll piss off Mary Ann if I'm in a really nice place, and I'll enjoy that."

They drove in silence until they got to the house and started unloading Dino's bags.

"I just thought of something," Dino said.

"What?"

"Hal Rhinehart."

"What about him?"

"I heard a pretty good rumor one time from a guy on the organized crime task force that Rhinehart was doing some contract hit work, but they could never nail him."

That stopped Stone in his tracks. "Why don't you get on the phone and find out whether Rhinehart has jumped parole?"

20

DINO PUT THE PHONE DOWN. "Rhinehart must have a very smart lawyer; he did a deal that allows him to live up here and report in by phone every week."

"Ankle bracelet?"

"I didn't ask," Dino said, "but he could be out of range up here."

"Put your stuff in the guest house, then let's go see Rhinehart."

"You know where he lives?"

"No, but I know how to find out."

THEY WENT BACK to the Dark Harbor Shop, and Stone led Dino to the rear office, where he rapped on the door. The man at the desk looked up.

"Hi," Stone said, "I'm Stone Barrington, and this is Dino Bacchetti."

The man stood up. "Jimmy Hotchkiss."

"You're Seth's cousin, right?"

"Right, and you're Dick's cousin."

"Right."

"Take a seat." Jimmy waved them to a pair of rickety chairs next to the desk.

"We were in here earlier and saw somebody we used to know," Stone said.

"And who would that be?"

"His name is Harold Rhinehart."

"Sure, I know Hal."

"You know where he lives?"

"Yep. It's about three miles north on the main road. You'll see a sign: RHINEHART CABINETS."

"He's a cabinet maker?"

"And his father before him. Hal took over the business when his old man died a few years back."

"He grew up on the island?"

"Yeah, then he went away to some tech college in New York State, and we didn't see much of him after that, until he came back and took over the business. His dad was sick then, lived a few more months. Hal grew up in that shop, though, so he didn't have any problem taking over."

"Is there a police officer on the island?"

"Constable," Jimmy said. "You're looking at him."

"Jimmy, have you had any reports of burglaries on the island?"

"Over what period of time?"

"After Hal Rhinehart came back."

Jimmy looked at them both carefully before replying. "What's your interest in this?"

"Dino is a police lieutenant in New York. He and I used to be partners in the NYPD, and we arrested Rhinehart for burglary a few years back."

"I heard about that," Jimmy said. "I also heard from his parole officer—indirectly, through the state police—when he came back."

"That's what we were wondering about," Dino said. "How Rhinehart could be here, when he's supposed to be on parole." As if he didn't know.

"Apparently, he arranged things with his parole officer when his dad got sick," Jimmy said. "He reports by phone, I'm told."

"You never answered my question, Jimmy," Stone said.

"Which question was that?"

"Have there been any burglaries on the island since Rhinehart came home?"

"No." Jimmy took a long beat. "But Camden and Rockland have had a rash of them. You think it's Hal?"

"What kind of burglaries?"

"What do you mean?"

"Big, small? Jewelry, lawnmowers, what?"

"Jewelry and cash, it said in the paper."

Stone and Dino exchanged a glance.

"We had some burglaries here, too," Jimmy said.

"When and how many?"

"When Hal was a teenager; a dozen or more. Come to think of it, they stopped when he went to college. I never made the connection." Jimmy sighed. "I hope to hell this new rash is not Hal's doing. We need a cabinet maker around here; you go to the mainland for something like that, and it's a lot more money, and Hal's gotten to be as good as his dad."

"I expect the folks in Camden and Rockland wouldn't feel the same regrets you would, if he turned out to be the guy," Stone said.

"You want me to talk to him?" Jimmy asked.

Dino spoke up. "Let me do that," he said.

"Okay, you're the pro; I'm just here to call the state boys if something happens. You want me to call them about this?"

"Not yet," Dino said.

21

THE CABINET SHOP was in a low building behind a neat, shingled house close to the road, and the smell of sawdust rolled over Stone in a wave of memory. All woodworking shops smelled like this, and his father's shop had been no exception. It was a clean, fresh smell, sometimes tinged with burning when a saw cut hardwood.

There was a lot of machinery, some of it not new. A huge bandsaw appeared to be at least fifty years old, but it was clean, rust-free and well oiled. Three men were working on different machines, each with hearing protection and goggles. Half a dozen newly completed kitchen cabinets hung on a wall, awaiting painting and hardware.

Stone let Dino take the lead into the shop. He could do most of the talking, too, and it was just as well, given the size of the lump in Stone's throat brought on by the scent of sawed wood.

A tall man near the front of the shop switched off his machine when he saw them enter. He pulled off his earmuffs and let the goggles fall to his neck as he walked slowly toward them. "This way," he said, beckoning. He led the way into a spacious office containing an old rolltop desk and a large drawing table. Rolls of plans protruded from pigeonholes next to the desk. He pointed to a pair of nicely built chairs, and they sat down.

"Remember us?" Dino asked.

Rhinehart nodded but didn't speak.

"Wonder why we're here?"

"Yes, I do," he said slowly. His voice was deep. "I didn't think we had any further business."

"Looks like we do," Dino said. "There've been a bunch of burglaries."

"In Camden and Rockland? I knew the state cops would get around to me sooner or later, but why is the NYPD interested?"

"Your parole officer wants to know if you're involved, Hal," Stone said.

Rhinehart shook his head. "I haven't been off the island since I got back here. I'm confined to it, according to my agreement with my parole officer. I can't get on the ferry, unless I have his permission, and I've made a point of not leaving."

"Do you own a boat?" Dino asked.

"Yes, my father's, but it's been laid up in a shed since he died."

"Do you own a gun?"

"My father had a deer rifle. It's locked in a case over at the house, and it hasn't been fired since he got sick."

"You know Dick Stone's house?" Stone asked.

"Sure, I do; my dad and I built the study, the kitchen and the dressing rooms. Why?"

"I recall that you once did some other work, besides burglary," Dino said. "Something more specialized."

"I don't know what you're talking about," Rhinehart said.

"Vito Thomasini, shot in his bed," Dino said. "Edgar Bromfield, shot on his front doorstep from a roof across the street."

"I've heard of Thomasini. Who hasn't?

Never heard of Bromfield, and I was no-where near either of them when they were killed."

"If you've never heard of Bromfield, why do you know you were nowhere near him when he was shot?" Stone asked.

"I mean, I heard of him, when I saw it in the papers, but I never laid eyes on the guy."

"Not even through a scope?" Dino asked.

"Listen, if there'd been the slightest evi-dence against me for those killings, you guys would have been all over me at the time. Why are you asking about Dick Stone? You think I killed him, too?"

"Did you?" Stone asked.

"Of course not. I liked the guy, and he paid us well for our work. I had no motive to kill him."

"Sometimes, all the motive you need is a phone call and some cash," Dino pointed out. "It's not as though you have a con-science about these things."

"Look, I stole a lot of jewelry, cash and other stuff, but I've never killed anybody."

"Funny how you have this reputation, then," Dino said.

"I don't believe I do. Anyway, the only

people who know I'm even on this island are those who live here, the state cops and my parole officer. Nobody I ever knew in that old life has ever even heard of Islesboro."

"You're in the phone book," Stone said.

"The cabinet shop is; I'm not. I'm dug in here. I've got a wife and a kid and a fine business; I don't need to steal from people or kill them for money. Go talk to my banker."

"I believe you," Stone said.

Dino looked at him as if he were crazy.

"I don't think anybody who built that study for Dick Stone, who knew him, could kill him."

"Thank you," Rhinehart said.

"Let's go, Dino," Stone said, standing up.

"You really think we're done here?" Dino asked. They were all on their feet now.

"What's your interest in Dick Stone?" Rhinehart asked, as they moved back into the shop and toward the front door.

"He was my first cousin."

"I see."

Stone looked around the shop. "My father was a cabinet and furniture maker in New York."

Rhinehart looked thoughtful. "Not Malon Barrington?"

"Yes."

"I've seen some of his work. He was as good as they come."

Stone wondered if he'd seen that work in people's homes, after breaking in. "You said you liked Dick?"

"I did. He was easy to work with, and he paid on time. He understood what we were doing for him and how good the work was."

"Would you like to do something for Dick?" Stone asked.

"What could I do for him now?" Rhinehart asked, as they reached the front door.

"You could break into his house," Stone said.

"What?"

"I want to know how hard it is. You know the place."

"I know he has an elaborate security system," Rhinehart said. "A bunch of guys from out of the state were just beginning to install it when we were finishing the study."

"Will you come and take a look?" Stone said. "I'd really like your opinion; it might help me learn who killed Dick."

"Since you put it that way," Rhinehart said.

Stone shook his hand. "After work?"

"Around six."

"See you then." Stone led Dino out of the place.

22

DINO WAS FUMING as they drove away from the cabinet shop.

"Jesus, I'm glad you're not a cop anymore. You've gone all squishy soft. We might have gotten something out of him."

"No, we wouldn't," Stone said. "He was trying to be cooperative, against his better instincts, and I didn't want to piss him off."

"Why the hell should you care if you piss him off?"

"Because it's a small island, and I might need some cabinet work done someday. And because we need him."

"What, that business about breaking into Dick's house?"

"You know anybody more qualified?"

"Now that you mentioned it, no," Dino replied, settling down a little. "Of course, it's a perfect opportunity for him to case the place in preparation for a later visit, maybe in the winter, when you're not here."

"No, Rhinehart has too much to lose. He's got a new life now and, apparently, a good one. He's not going to piss in his own well."

"Oh, all right," Dino said. "I never could talk to you when you get this way."

RHINEHART SHOWED UP at six, when Stone and Dino were having a drink in the study.

"Would you like a drink, Hal?"

"Thanks, no. I'd better get started. I'm going to go outside, and I want you to go through the house and make sure that every window and door is closed and locked, then turn on the alarm system." He turned and left.

"You take the upstairs," Stone said to Dino, then headed for the kitchen. He went around the ground floor, checking and locking windows and doors, then went to the front door, tapped in the alarm code, then back to the study and his drink. Dino was already there. He had barely sat down when he looked up to see Hal Rhinehart standing in the doorway.

"How the hell did you get in?" Dino asked.

"Upstairs bathroom window on the south side," Rhinehart said.

"What are you, a human fly?"

"No, the climbing part was easy; there was a ladder leaning against the house."

Stone looked at Dino. "I believe that was one of your windows," he said. "You want to go close it and double-check the others?"

Dino got up and stalked from the room.

Rhinehart crooked a finger. "Come here, I want to show you something." He led Stone to the keypad by the front door, then opened the door. "Tap in the code," he said, looking away.

Stone tapped in the code.

"Now look at the little screen on the keypad. What does it say?"

Stone peered at the screen. "Front door open," he said.

"Before, it would have said 'Upstairs bathroom window open.' And the alarm won't arm if there's something open. The house has to be sealed tight."

Dino came back downstairs. "All right, everything's closed."

"I'm going outside again," Rhinehart said. "Arm the alarm."

Stone did so, then returned to the study with Dino. They had finished their drinks when the front doorbell rang. He went and let Rhinehart in. "Will you have a drink now?"

"Yes, thanks. Scotch, if you have it."

Stone poured them all another one, and they sat down in front of the fireplace.

"I couldn't get in," Rhinehart said. "Not without taking a chainsaw to a wall, anyway. This is the most secure family home I've ever been in, and I've been in a lot of them. The front door is steel, sheathed in mahogany; the windows are steel and the glass armored; and there are no gaps in the installation—every door and window is alarmed."

"I'm glad to hear it," Stone said.

"What the hell was Dick expecting?" Rhinehart asked. "He must have spent fifty thousand dollars on security."

"Dick worked for the State Department," Stone said. "I think they had the work done."

"State Department? More like the CIA or NSA," Rhinehart said. "I doubt if the Secretary of State has this much hard-wired security."

Stone shrugged.

"The problem, though, is the same as with any two-thousand-dollar installation: You leave a window cracked or just forget to arm the system, and all this security is useless."

Stone nodded. "You have a point."

"Is that what happened? Did Dick screw up and not arm the system?"

"Either that, or he let somebody in," Stone said.

"The locks are something special, too. They're Swedish, and they use a key that has magnetic points built into it as well as tumblers. I couldn't pick one of them, and I'm pretty good."

"I'll bet you are," Dino said.

"Hal," Stone said, "do you have any theories about how or why Dick died?"

"Was anything taken from the house?"

"No."

"You mean, nothing that you *knew* about was gone, but then, had you ever set foot in the place before Dick was killed?"

"No, and I wouldn't have known what he had here. The caretaker and his wife would have known, though, especially the wife, since she cleans the place every day. The only thing she noticed amiss was that a vacuum cleaner was left by that door over there." He pointed at the door to the terrace.

"So the killer cleaned up after himself."

"It appears so, and he took the vacuum bag with him."

"Did the alarm go off?"

"No."

"Then it wasn't armed, unless the killer had the code. What time of night did it happen?"

"Some time after midnight, according to the state police."

"Anybody see anybody come or go?"

"No."

"Nobody moves on this island after ten o'clock. It would be noticed if somebody was driving around. Maybe the guy came by boat."

"That's a good guess," Stone said.

"You don't think it was a local?"

"Do you?"

"Nah; everybody liked Dick. I mean, there

are some folks on this island I wouldn't trust with a gun after a few drinks, but nobody had anything against Dick; word would have gotten around. From what I read in the papers about the inquest, it sure sounds like a pro hit, doesn't it?"

"More and more," Stone said. "But I'd appreciate it if you'd keep that notion to yourself. I wouldn't want the folks to start worrying about hitmen stalking their island."

Rhinehart tossed off the rest of his drink and stood up. "I've got to get home for supper."

Stone walked him to the door and thanked him for coming, then returned to the study.

"This case sure is a pisser, ain't it?" Dino asked.

"It sure is."

23

ARRINGTON WAS wonderfully naked, seated atop Stone, and he was sitting up, so that he could feel her breasts against his chest. They were moving rhythmically, and she was making little noises and contracting her vagina each time she moved. They were both nearly there, just on the brink, when a noise intruded.

"Stop that noise!" Arrington panted. "I'm going to come!"

Stone woke up in a sitting position, sweating, tumescent and angry about losing the orgasm. He could hear a noise from downstairs. What the hell was going on? He heard the noise again; it seemed louder. He struggled out of bed and into his trousers, picked up the .45 from the bedside table and left the bedroom, pausing on the landing to listen. He heard it again, and it seemed to be coming from the study. He started down the stairs, then stopped. This was what Dick had done, going downstairs in only his trousers, armed, and still he had died.

Stone thought for a moment, then went back into his bedroom, unlocked a window and opened it. Nothing happened; no alarm. Somebody had defeated it, in spite of Hal Rhinehart's assurances. He picked up the phone to buzz the guest house and wake up Dino, then put it down again. Dino was unarmed, and Stone couldn't let him walk into this without a gun.

Stone went back to the landing and listened again. Nothing for a moment, then the noise came, but more softly. He flicked off the gun's safety and began to creep slowly down the stairs, staying close to the wall to avoid squeaks from the steps. He stopped on the landing midway down the stairs to listen again. Nothing.

His heart pounding, Stone continued down the stairs, stopping every step or two to listen. At the bottom, he pressed his back against the wall and listened again. The noise came, as if someone were grinding something. Then, as from a great distance, a phone began to ring. It was faint, so it had to be coming from Dick's secret office.

Stone took a deep breath, held the gun out in front of him in a combat stance and whipped around the corner, looking for any sign of movement, listening for any noise. The downstairs hallway was empty, but he heard the noise again, coming from the study.

Walking on tiptoe, even though he was barefoot, he went to the open study door and listened again. Nothing. He charged into the room yelling "Freeze, police!" the way he had done hundreds of times before, when he still was the police. Nothing. No one. He walked around the study, checking every corner, until he came to the alarm keypad glowing in the dark, near the door to the terrace. He checked the little screen: "Open window in master BR," it said. The phone continued to ring. Stone tapped in the alarm code. The phone still rang.

Stone did a quick tour of the downstairs, checking every room, but found nothing. He got out his keys, went to Dick's secret office door and opened it. The phone stopped ringing. Stone switched on the light in the little office and looked around, half expecting to find somebody there. Then he saw something he hadn't noticed before. The wall opposite Dick's desk was lined with cabinets, and one of them, with double doors, had a substantial lock on it.

He went through his keys until he found one that fit, then opened the cabinet. Inside, hanging on pegs, was an array of weapons: a stainless-steel riot gun with an extra-long magazine; a Beretta 9 mm semi-automatic, model 92, which was used by the armed services; a model 1911 Colt .45 officer's model, with a beautiful mirror-blue finish and ivory grips; and a pair of Colt Government .380s finished identically to the larger pistol. So Dick had been well armed, after all.

The phone in the study started to ring. Stone rushed to answer it, lest it wake someone, then realized he was alone in the house. He picked it up. "Hello?"

"Stone? It's Lance. What's wrong?"

"I don't know," Stone said. "I was sound asleep, and I was wakened by a noise. I got my pants on and started downstairs, then I thought better of it, remembering that's what Dick did. So I opened a window in my bedroom to set off the alarm, but it didn't go off."

"Yes, it did go off," Lance said. "It's silent, unless you program it not to be. The signal was transmitted to Operations, at Langley, and they called the house, but you didn't answer, so they called me. Are you all right? Is someone in the house?"

"I'm all right," Stone said, "and it appears I'm alone. I heard the phone ringing in Dick's little office, but by the time I was able to get the door unlocked, it stopped. Then you called."

"Are you alone up there?"

"Dino's here, but he's in the guest house."

"There's a manual for the alarm system somewhere in the house, probably in the little office, if you want to change the alarm from silent. It appears to be working properly."

"Yes, I had the house checked out by an expert, and he says it's pretty much impenetrable, unless you saw through a wall."

"What expert?"

"A burglar."

"What?"

"A guy Dino and I once busted for more than a hundred burglaries in New York. He's out of prison now and living here. He's a cabinetmaker."

"Well, I guess that's one kind of expert. If you're all right, I'm going back to bed."

"Sure, and thanks for calling." They both hung up.

Suddenly, the front doorbell rang, and there was a hammering on the front door. Stone ran to the door, switched on the front porch light and looked through the peephole. Dino was standing there in his pajamas and robe. Stone opened the door.

"What's going on?" Dino asked.

"I heard a noise in the house," Stone said. "What woke you up?"

"The phone. I had just gotten up to piss, and I heard it ring. I wasn't sleepy, anyway, so I came over."

Stone closed the door. "Come in the study. You want a drink?"

"Couldn't hurt," Dino said. "Keep out the cold night air."

"Oh, let me show you something." He led Dino into Dick's little office and showed him the array of weapons. Dino picked up the officer's .45. "I like this," he said. "I'll sleep with it under my pillow." He checked and found a full magazine in the gun.

Stone pointed to a shelf that held a lot of gun leather. "Find yourself a belt and holster." He went to the bar and got down a couple of glasses. As he was about to open the door to the ice machine, he heard the noise again.

Dino approached. "Is that the noise you heard?"

"Yes," Stone said sheepishly.

"The ice machine, making ice?"

Stone sighed. "Yes. I wonder why I've never heard it before."

"I think you're a little too tightly wound," Dino said. "Sit down and drink that bourbon."

Stone followed orders.

24

STONE WENT BACK to bed and tried to retrieve the dream with Arrington, but it wouldn't come back. He overslept, not waking until after ten, and he felt fuzzy around the edges. He wasn't accustomed to drinking in the middle of the night.

He sat up in bed and called Arrington's home in Virginia. A maid answered.

"She's not here, Mr. Barrington. She's in New York, she and Peter. You can reach her at the Carlyle."

"Thank you," Stone said. He called the Carlyle and asked for Mrs. Calder.

"Hello?" she said, sounding chipper and cheerful.

"It's Stone."

"Oh, hi. I was about to call you. I'm in New York."

"I know; I just called you."

"Oh, that's right. Sorry. You want to have dinner tonight?"

"I'd love to, but it's a plane ride."

"What?"

"I'm in Maine."

"Why? What are you doing in Maine?"

"I have a new house on an island called Islesboro. Why don't you summon up the Centurion jet, and you and Peter come up here for a few days?" As the widow of Centurion Studios' largest stockholder, she had access to their jet.

She was silent for a moment. "All right, but it will have to be tomorrow, maybe the next day. I have some shopping to do here."

"Tell the flight department at Centurion that you'll be landing at Rockland. I'll meet you there in my airplane. It's only another ten minutes of flying, but the strip on the island is too short for a jet."

"All right. What will I need in the way of clothes?"

"Nothing you couldn't find at L.L. Bean."

"I've got to run; I have a hair appointment, but I'll call you later and give you an ETA."

He gave her the number and hung up, feeling wonderful. He bounded out of bed, shaved, showered and began getting dressed when the phone rang. "Hello?"

"It's Ed Rawls. I need to see you at Don Brown's house right now."

"Okay. Where's the house?"

Rawls gave him directions.

"What's going on?"

"I'll tell you when you get here."

Stone finished dressing and went downstairs. Dino was having breakfast in the kitchen, and Stone grabbed a piece of his toast. "Come on. We have to be somewhere."

"Where?"

"Not far."

It was a beautiful day, and they took the little MG, top down.

"Arrington and Peter are coming up tomorrow or the next day," Stone said.

"You're horny, huh?"

"Oh, shut up."

They drove through some woods and stopped at the end of a short, paved driveway. There were other cars parked there.

The house was a shingled Cape Cod with a porch. The front door was opened by an obviously upset woman wearing an apron.

Rawls emerged from another room and waved them in. Harley Davis and Mack Morris were seated in the living room, while Jimmy Hotchkiss talked on the phone. Stone introduced Dino to everybody, then followed Rawls into a bedroom.

"Uh, oh," Dino said.

Don Brown, the Old Fart who used the electric scooter, was sitting up in bed, a bullet hole in his right temple and a much larger hole in his left. A Colt .45 lay on the bed, and brains and blood were scattered around the bedspread.

"We've got another one," Rawls said.

"How long have you been here?" Stone asked.

"Less than half an hour. I've mostly been on the phone calling people."

"Has somebody called the state police?"

"Jimmy's on the phone with them now."

"Let's get out of this room," Stone said. "Have you touched anything?"

Rawls shook his head. "I know better than that."

They went back into the living room and took seats, while the woman served them coffee.

"This is Hilda," Rawls said. "She found him when she came to clean the house."

"What time do you normally get here, Hilda?" Stone said.

"Usually, at nine," the woman replied. "But it was ten, today; I had to do Mr. Brown's grocery shopping. I always do that for him." She went back to the kitchen.

"Dino," Stone said, "you ask the questions."

Dino nodded. "Gentlemen, did any of you know Mr. Brown to be depressed?"

"This wasn't suicide," Harley Davis replied.

"Please, just answer the question."

"Don wasn't depressed," Mack Morris said. "He was pissed off."

"About what?" Dino asked.

"About being in that fucking wheelchair thing. He didn't like it at all; he was permanently pissed off about it."

"Did he ever talk about suicide?"

All three men shook their heads. "He wasn't the type," Rawls said.

"Is the gun his?" Dino asked.

"Probably; he had a .45," Rawls said. "If the cops don't find another one, then it's his."

Jimmy hung up the phone. "The state boys will be on the next ferry," he said, looking at his watch. "They should be here in an hour or so."

"Gentlemen," Dino said, "I'd appreciate it if you'd all go sit on the porch until the cops get here. Stone and I will take a look around the house."

The four men went outside, and Dino went into the kitchen, followed by Stone.

"Hilda," Dino said, "when you got here this morning, did you find anything unusual about the state of the house?"

"Well, Mr. Brown was dead in his bed," she said.

Dino nodded. "Yes, ma'am. Anything else?"

"Well, the vacuum cleaner is normally in the broom closet, but it was sitting in the kitchen, by the back door, there." She pointed. "And there wasn't no bag inside it."

25

STONE AND DINO WENT and stood in the bedroom door, so as not to disturb anything further by entering the room.

"He's sitting up in bed," Stone said, "so whoever shot him woke him up first."

"Unless he wasn't asleep when the guy arrived," Dino said.

"The TV isn't on, and there's no book present, so he wasn't sitting up in bed reading. Nobody just sits in bed, doing nothin'."

"Maybe you're right. But why would the guy wake him up?"

Stone shrugged. "Maybe he had something to say to him before he shot him."

"Like what?"

"Like, 'Here's one from your pal, Joe,' or whoever ordered the hit."

"You should write novels."

"Short stories, maybe. There's always a little story that goes with a murder. This wasn't the burglary story, was it?"

"Nothing seems disturbed."

"Let's take a look outside," Stone said.

They walked through the kitchen, where Hilda was sitting, disconsolately, drinking coffee, and out the back door. The sea was, perhaps, thirty paces away, and they avoided walking on the path, looking for footprints.

"Got a good one here," Dino said, pointing.

"Deck shoe," Stone said. "See the little ridges? That narrows the suspect list to everybody on the island and everybody on the coast of Maine."

"Big deck shoe," Dino said. "Size eleven or twelve. There are other partials here, going in both directions, but just this one good one."

"That's more than the cops found at Dick's house," Stone said. "I'd consider that a break." He walked down to the rocky beach and pointed. "Some scrapes on the stones here; our man arrived by boat and pulled it ashore, but only a foot or two."

"Must have been a sizable boat," Dino said. "Not just a what-chacallit . . . ?"

"Dinghy."

"Yeah."

They walked back up toward the porch, and Dino pointed: "Sand and dirt on the porch."

"That's about it," Stone said. "Let's take a look out front."

They walked around the house.

"Too many cars and people here to find any usable footprints," Dino said, "but I'm satisfied the killer came by boat."

Stone walked up to the porch, where the Old Farts and Jimmy Hotchkiss had sat down. "Where's the nearest house?"

Rawls pointed. "Over there, a couple of hundred yards."

"The cops will want to know if anybody heard the shot."

"Why? We know he was shot."

"Fix the time of death," Dino said.

"Oh, yeah."

"Anybody got any thoughts about this killing?" Stone asked the group.

"We've all got the same thought," Harley Davis said.

"Don and Dick were of different generations," Stone said. "Would they have ever worked together on something?"

"Not recently," Rawls said. "Don's been retired for, I think, six years."

"Where was his last posting?"

"Berlin."

"And where was Dick at the time?"

"I'm not sure."

"Could it have been Berlin?"

Rawls shrugged. "Everybody based in Europe got to Berlin sooner or later."

Stone and Dino sat down on the front steps, and everybody fell silent.

An hour later a state police car drove up, and four men got out. Sergeant Young was the driver. "Good morning," he said.

"No, it ain't," Rawls replied.

"What have we got here?"

Stone and Dino took him into the house and showed him the corpse in the bedroom, then told him what they had observed since arriving, including the footprint. "Nearest house is a couple of hundred yards over there," Stone said, pointing. "They should have heard the shot."

"It's a whole lot like the other killing, isn't it?" Young asked.

"Sure is," Stone replied.

"What did Dick Stone and Don Brown have in common?"

Stone spoke up. "They both lived on the same island, and they both worked for the same government agency. Brown retired six years ago."

Stone and Dino left the sergeant and the crime-scene people to their work and went back to the front porch.

"Ed, when did you last talk to Don?"

"Last night, after supper, about nine."

"What did you talk about?"

"Don called me, wanted to have lunch with the three of us tomorrow, that is, today. Said he had something to tell us."

"Any hints about what he wanted to tell you?"

"No. Don liked to think things over before he spoke."

"You think it had anything to do with Dick's murder?"

"My guess is yes. He asked me to call Harley and Mack, and I did."

The other two men nodded.

"He wouldn't have made a lunch date if he'd intended to shoot himself," Rawls said.

"That makes sense. Be sure and tell the sergeant about the call."

Rawls nodded. "This sort of stuff isn't supposed to happen," he said. "You do your work for thirty-five or forty years and you retire, and you're out of it. Nobody comes looking for you five or six years later."

"Don found out something," Harley said. "God knows what."

"Any of you know how Don spent his day yesterday?"

Jimmy Hotchkiss spoke up. "I know he was here at lunchtime, because I send the papers out to him every day." He looked around him. "And don't you other fellers get any ideas; I'm not running a paper-delivery service, except for a couple of people, like Don, who couldn't get in the store easy."

"So we need to know what he was doing between lunchtime and bedtime."

Sergeant Young had appeared in the front doorway. "Hilda says he got in his car and went out about one o'clock. He had this way of getting his scooter in and out of the trunk. We'll ask around, see if anybody saw him around the island."

"You need us anymore?" Stone asked.

The sergeant shook his head. "I'll call you if I think of anything."

Stone and Dino got into the MG and headed down the drive. "Dino," Stone said, "I think it would be good if you moved into the house, into Esme's bedroom. Arrington can bunk with me, and there's another bedroom for Peter."

"Why move? To cover your ass?"

"That and because there's no alarm system in the guest house."

"Oh."

26

TWO DAYS LATER, Stone stood on the tarmac and watched the Centurion Studios' Gulfstream IV land at Rockland Airport. Peter was the first down the airplane's stairs, at a run. He was six now and taller than when Stone had last seen him the year before. His mother followed, carrying her overnight case, and the two pilots then dealt with the luggage.

There were hugs, then Stone loaded their luggage into his airplane. "Peter, I think we'll let you be copilot today, and your mother can be the passenger."

The boy was delighted. Soon Stone had them buckled in and was running through his checklist, giving Peter a running commentary.

"I hope this isn't going to be like my last ride with you," the boy said.

Stone laughed. On their last ride Stone had been at the controls of a helicopter, a machine he hadn't known how to fly, had made a very rough landing, and they were both lucky to be alive. "I think you'll find this a smoother trip; shorter, too."

They lifted off and turned out over Penobscot Bay. "There's our island," Stone said, pointing. "Can you see it, Arrington?"

Arrington could hear and speak from the rear through her headset. "Yes, it's beautiful."

"There's our landing strip," Stone said to Peter.

"It looks a lot shorter than the one we just landed on," Peter said.

"It is, but my airplane is a lot smaller than the Centurion jet, so it can use shorter strips." Stone lined up for the runway, announced his intentions over the radio and looked for traffic. A moment later they were on the runway and braking. Dino sat in the station wagon, waiting for them.

They stopped at the Dark Harbor Shop for

the papers and an ice cream cone for Peter, then continued to the house.

"It's lovely, Stone," Arrington said. "How did you find it?"

"I'll tell you the story later," Stone said. He took them into the house and got them settled. Peter ran out to the dock to have a look at the boats, and Arrington relaxed in the study.

"So, tell me why you bought a house in Maine," she said.

Stone sat down beside her. "It belonged to my first cousin, Dick Stone, who died recently and left me the house. Well, the use of the house for my lifetime and that of my heirs."

"How old a man was Dick?"

"My age."

"Heart attack?"

"Not exactly."

"Stone, I'm beginning to get the feeling that I'm not going to like the rest of this story."

"Dick and his wife and daughter were murdered a couple of weeks ago."

"Not in this house, I hope."

"Dick was at his desk, over there; his wife and daughter were in Dino's room."

"Who murdered them, and why?"

"Dick was CIA; the murders seem to be related to his work."

"*Seem* to be related to his work?"

"There's evidence to suggest that and no evidence to suggest otherwise."

"Am I going to find his wife's clothes in my closet?"

"All their personal effects have been removed. It's my house now."

"Why is Dino sleeping upstairs instead of in the guest house?" Arrington didn't miss much.

"There's no security system in the guest house."

"And why do we need a security system on this tiny island?"

"It's only a precaution. Another man, this one a retired CIA officer, was killed in a fashion similar to the way Dick was killed a couple of days ago."

"Has anyone tried to kill you yet?"

"No, and there isn't the slightest reason to suppose that anyone might."

"Stone, every time I see you somebody is trying to kill you or trying to kill me."

"Those incidents were not my fault."

"No, it's never your fault; it just seems to happen to you."

"I have that history, but I believe we're all quite safe here."

"How good is the security system?"

"It was designed and installed by the CIA. By the way, don't go downstairs at night before I disable the system. There are motion detectors downstairs."

"I'm relieved to hear it."

Peter came running back into the house.

"Peter, don't run indoors," his mother said.

"I'm sorry. The boats are neat, Stone. Can we go out in one of them?"

"Sure, we can. Which one would you like to go out in?"

"The sailboat."

"All right, we'll go out after lunch." Stone glanced at Arrington. "I think there's a life jacket just your size on board, Peter."

Arrington nodded approvingly.

AFTER LUNCH IT TOOK an hour for Stone to get familiar enough with the yacht to be comfortable, and to get the engine started and check the chart for deep water and hazards to navigation, before they were skimming smoothly over small waves in a good breeze, with Peter steering the boat from Stone's lap. Dino stretched out in the cockpit and went to sleep, a beer still clutched in his hand, while Arrington sat quietly next to Stone and Peter, taking in the scenery.

Stone felt eighteen again, except that his son was along for the ride. He and Arrington had had an affair years before, when she had chosen to marry Vance Calder, the movie star, not knowing that she was already carrying Stone's child. It had taken a long time for her to admit to Stone, if not to herself, that Peter was his son.

Stone wondered if Peter would ever know. He saw a small island coming up and showed the boy how to tack the boat. He hoped to show him a lot more while they were here.

As Peter was turning the boat and Dino was hauling in on the jib sheet, a motorboat appeared from nowhere, dousing them with spray and making their ride bumpier.

Dino laughed. "I think you've just had sand kicked in your face, Stone."

Stone watched the boat disappear toward

the yacht club. The two occupants were Caleb Stone's twin sons.

THAT NIGHT, after Peter was sound asleep in his room, Stone lay in bed and watched Arrington undress. Her body had changed little with childbirth, and she obviously took very good care of herself. She switched off the bedside lamp and got into bed, snuggling close to him.

"This is why you wanted me here, isn't it?" she asked, flicking his ear with her tongue. "You were just randy."

"I'm always randy when you're around," Stone said, kissing her and cupping a breast in his hand. "But that's not the only reason I invited you."

"We can discuss the other reasons in the morning," she said, taking him in her hand and kneading gently.

Stone responded instantly. He rolled on top of her, and she guided him in.

"It's not the only reason for me, either," she said, her hips rising to meet him. "But I love it all the same."

27

THE FOLLOWING MORNING a fax came from Sergeant Young of the state police. Stone read the report, and as he did, the phone rang.

"It's Ed Rawls," the gruff voice said. "Did you get the report?"

"I've just read it," Stone said. "It's nice that Young didn't call it a suicide."

"I think you and Dino saw to that," Rawls said. "I'm glad you were there, because none of the rest of us has any credentials that would make Young take us seriously."

"I would have thought that your careers would have been enough."

"We don't talk about that to civilians," Rawls said.

"A state cop is a civilian?"

"Everybody who isn't Agency is a civilian."

"What about me?"

"You're kind of a semipro, because of your relationship with Lance Cabot."

"Thanks."

"The fellows and I put together Don's day, before he died," Rawls said.

"And?"

"He had lunch at the yacht club, picked up his mail and went home. He had dinner alone, called me, then got himself murdered."

"That's it?"

"That's it. If he'd been anywhere on the island, he'd have been seen."

"Did he talk to anybody anywhere, except at the yacht club?"

"Nothing more than to say hello."

"Who'd he have lunch with?"

"He had lunch alone, talked to anybody who dropped by, nothing important."

"And then he called you and said he'd found out something?"

"After thinking about it all day."

"Was he alone at home when he called?"

"Until he was joined by his murderer later in the evening."

"Did he make any phone calls?"

There was a brief silence.

"I'd like to see his phone records," Stone said.

"He had that caller ID thing," Rawls replied.

"Then there might be a log of the calls he received."

"Yeah, but not the calls he made."

"Can we get into the house?"

"I've got a key, and Harley and I are his executors. Fifteen minutes?"

"See you there." Stone hung up.

RAWLS WAS ALREADY at Don Brown's house when Stone arrived. He let them into the house, and they went into Brown's den.

"Here we go," Stone said. The phone was a Japanese-made combination of answering machine and cordless phone with other features. Stone looked at the buttons carefully, pressed a couple, then a number appeared on the little screen. "Looks like he received only one call." It was an 800 number.

"That's an Agency WATS line," Rawls said. "It's unpublished, of course, but it's one of the lines that Agency people can call in on from outside or, of course, receive calls from."

"Any way to tell who called?" Stone asked.

Rawls shook his head. "Nope. Anybody with an extension from the main switchboard can pick up a phone, dial a number and get a dial tone, then call anywhere in the world."

"There must be an internal record of which extension used the WATS line," Stone said.

"I expect there would be."

"Do you have any way of checking on it?"

"The best way would be through Lance; he's active, and most of my friends are retired."

"I'll call him," Stone said.

"You can use this phone."

Stone dialed Lance's cell number.

"Yes?"

"It's Stone. Bad news from up here."

"Don Brown? I heard. This is not a good development."

"Lance, Don received a call from Langley

in the late afternoon on the day of his death. Whoever called used an Agency WATS line. Can you find out who made the call?"

"Probably."

"I'm going to ask the state police to get Don's phone records, so we can find out who he might have called at Langley."

"I don't think that will work," Lance said.

"Why not?"

"Because he would have called in on the WATS line and asked for a name or an extension. All the Agency would have would be a record that he called in, not which extension he asked for. It's a deficiency, I know, and it's being corrected, but it hasn't been done yet."

"Whatever you say."

"That's not to say that Don might not have made local calls in Maine that might be significant, so I'd ask the cops for his local records."

"Thanks. When will you get back to me about the WATS line?"

"Later today, if I can." Lance hung up.

Stone called Sergeant Young and asked for Don Brown's phone records, and Young promised to fax them to him.

"I guess that's all we can do for the moment," Rawls said.

"A thought," Stone said. "Did Don have an ex-wife who hated him?"

"No, his wife died less than a year ago. They were married for more than fifty years, and I don't think she had learned to hate him yet. I've got a couple who hate me; so does Harley. Mack is a lifelong bachelor."

"What was the medical condition that required Don to use the wheelchair?"

"It was some complication of diabetes, I think," Rawls said. "He could get around a bit, not much more than a few steps. I mean, he could get to the bathroom at night, and he could get his scooter in and out of the trunk of his car."

"Do you know where he kept the .45 that was used to kill him?"

"Bedside table drawer," Rawls said.

"So it wouldn't have been hard to find. The murderer could have come in with another gun and found it easily."

"Yeah, especially if Don tried to go for it."

"Who knew this house well, besides his housekeeper?"

"Harley, Mack and me; we played poker

over here one night a week. Probably a few locals: repairmen, those sorts of folks."

"So we don't have any more to go on than we had with Dick's murder."

"Looks that way, don't it."

"Maybe Lance will be able to tell us something."

"You're grasping at straws," Rawls said, "but then, that's all we've got to grab at."

"I know."

"We're having a little ceremony to scatter Don's ashes at the yacht club tomorrow morning at ten, if you'd like to join us. I think Don would like that."

"I'll be there."

28

AFTER BREAKFAST the following morning Stone made a few phone calls and worked on Dick's estate. He was clearing the desk when Peter came into the room and flopped down on the rug. He opened a book and began to laboriously write on a pad.

Stone came over and looked over his shoulder. "What are you doing?"

"I'm practicing my calligraphy," Peter said. "I'm copying this book, see?"

Stone glanced at the book, which seemed handwritten in a beautiful copperplate. "Do you study calligraphy at school?"

"I don't take a class in it or anything, but I was having trouble with my handwriting, and my teacher said it would help if I copied from a book, just for practice."

"That's a great idea," Stone said. "I have to go out for a while; when your mother gets up, please tell her I'll be back in an hour or so."

"Okay." The boy went back to work.

Stone walked over to the yacht club and found a little group of people boarding a small motor yacht at the end of the pier. Rawls, Harley Davis and Mack Morris were there, along with a couple and their teenaged daughter, who was in tears. Rawls introduced them.

"This is Ralph and Martha Harris and their daughter, Janey," he said. "Martha is Don's sister."

The boat was Ralph's, apparently, and he got the engine started. They motored out a ways, then Rawls and Martha said a few words, and she emptied the ashes into the water. Janey seemed more upset than anybody, Stone thought.

They returned to the yacht club, and Stone excused himself and returned home.

Peter was still copying lines from the book, and Arrington was seated by the fireplace, drinking coffee with Dino. Stone poured himself a cup and was about to sit down when the phone rang, and he went to the desk to answer it.

"It's Lance. I've got the phone information."

"Great."

"On the day Don Brown died, he called the Agency WATS line a little after three P.M. and was connected to an Operations officer named Jake Burns. I tried to call Jake, but he's left on an assignment and is unreachable. An office assistant said that Jake did a criminal records search for Don, but she doesn't know the results or even who the subject was. That's all I could get."

"Well, that's very interesting, indeed, and very frustrating, too."

"I know. I left a message for Jake, but there's no way of knowing when he'll be able to respond to it. I wish there were something else I could do."

"Thanks, Lance. I appreciate that." Stone hung up, called Rawls and told him the results.

"Shit," Rawls said.

"That's pretty much how I feel about it, too."

"I guess we'll just have to wait for Jake Burns to get back."

"I guess so."

"Thanks for coming this morning. Martha appreciated it."

"I was glad to be there. Janey seemed particularly upset."

"Yeah, Don was her favorite uncle; they were close."

The fax machine rang and began to spit out pages.

"Hold on a minute," Stone said. He went to the machine and retrieved two pages, then returned to the phone. "Sergeant Young faxed me Don's phone records," he said, looking over the pages.

"What've we got?"

"Not much. He called you a few times and a couple of other numbers." Stone read them to Rawls.

"That's Harley and Mack."

"Then there's the call to the WATS line, and that's it for the past week."

"Shit again," Rawls said.

"Yeah. Do you have any idea at all whose criminal records Don could have been checking on?"

"Not a clue."

"Do Harley and Mack have security systems in their houses?"

"Harley does. Mack's having one installed today."

"Good. Make sure they both use them, will you?"

"Don't worry; they won't need any prodding."

"Talk to you later." Stone hung up and returned to his coffee. Arrington was on her knees on the floor next to Peter.

"What are you copying, honey?" she asked.

"A book," he said.

"Where did you get it?"

"I found it in a desk drawer in my room."

"Can I see it for a minute?"

"Sure."

Arrington picked up the book, which was bound in leather, and flipped through it slowly. "Peter, this is somebody's diary."

"It is?"

"Yes, and a diary is a very private thing. You shouldn't be reading it."

"I wasn't reading it. I was just copying."

"Well, I think you should find something else to copy."

"All right." Peter gathered up his papers and went upstairs.

Arrington handed the book to Stone. "It's the diary of somebody called Esme Stone," she said, handing it to him.

"That was Dick's daughter," he said.

"Perhaps you should put it away somewhere."

Stone looked at the book. Esme's name was stamped in gold on the cover. It had probably been a Christmas or birthday present from her parents. He flipped through it, marveling at the beautiful handwriting, then closed it. He shouldn't be reading it any more than Peter should.

Stone went to the cupboard where the safe was, opened it, put the diary inside and closed it again. Next time they built a fire, he would burn it, and Esme's secrets would be safe.

29

AFTER LUNCH Stone remembered that he had not gone for the *New York Times,* and he asked Peter if he'd like an ice cream cone.

"I think I can handle that," Peter replied.

Stone laughed. "I bet you can."

They got into the MG and started for the village.

"I like this car," Peter said. "What kind is it?"

"It's called an MG," Stone replied, "and it's old. It was built a long time before you were born."

"Where did you buy it?"

"I didn't buy it. It belonged to my cousin Dick, and when he died, he left it to me."

"My mom has a Mercedes SL 55," Peter said, "and it's very fast, but it's not as . . ." He seemed to search for a word. "Elegant as this."

"That's a good word for it," Stone said. "You have a very good vocabulary for a boy your age."

"That's what my teacher told me." He pointed out the window. "What's that pond?"

"It isn't a pond, really. It's a little cove, saltwater. A long time ago there was a resort hotel on the shore over there, and they built a kind of dam to keep water in the cove when the tide was out so the guests could swim. The hotel burned down, but the dam is still there."

"Why did it burn down?"

"I imagine it was a wooden structure, covered in shingles, like most of the houses on the island, and it's easy for them to catch fire."

They were approaching the Dark Harbor Shop, and Stone could see three state police cars parked in front of it. He wondered what could possibly have happened on the island that would require three state police cars.

Stone and Peter went into the shop, and Stone set Peter on a stool at the soda fountain and told him to order whatever he wanted, then went to the rear of the shop to get a paper. Jimmy Hotchkiss's office was crowded with state police officers, and Stone couldn't hear what they were saying. He went back to the soda fountain. "What's going on with the police?" he asked the girl behind the counter.

"A little girl has disappeared," the girl said, "and I think they're organizing a search party."

Stone started to ask the little girl's name, but it occurred to him that he wouldn't know her or her family, in any case. He paid for his paper and Peter's ice cream, and they got back into the car.

"Do you think they'll find the little girl?" Peter asked.

"I expect so," Stone said. "It's not all that big an island; she probably just got lost in the woods."

They drove on toward the house, and as they pulled into the driveway, Stone saw Ed Rawls getting out of his Range Rover.

"Hey, Ed," Stone said, "have you met my . . . friend, Peter?"

"How are you, Peter?" Rawls said.

"How do you do?" Peter replied, offering his hand like a gentleman.

"I've got some news," Rawls said to Stone, and he looked worried.

"Peter, you go on inside, all right? And don't spill ice cream on the rugs." The boy ran inside, and Stone turned to Rawls. "What is it?"

"You know the girl you met yesterday? Janey Harris?"

"Sure."

"She didn't come home from a friend's house last night."

"I was at the Dark Harbor Shop, and the soda jerk told me a little girl was missing. There were a lot of state cops in Jimmy's office, and she said they're organizing a search party."

"I'm worried about her," Rawls said. "You saw how upset she was yesterday?"

"Yes, I noticed that. Even more upset than her parents. You said she and Don were close."

"Right, but there was more going on, I think."

"What was going on?"

"I don't know, but I've been thinking about

this since I got the call about Janey a few minutes ago, and I think her disappearance has to be connected to Don's death."

"Why do you think that?"

"Remember where you are, boy. Things like this just don't happen on this island. There are no perverts kidnapping seventeen-year-old girls on Islesboro."

"Right, and no hitmen murdering ex-CIA officers and their families, either. Do you have any details of the girl's disappearance?"

"Her mother told me Janey went to a friend's house for dinner last night, and when she wasn't home by ten o'clock, Martha called the house, and they said Janey had been gone for over an hour. The houses are only a quarter of a mile apart, and Janey would have walked home along the road. She had a flashlight. The Harrises went looking for her, and they found her flashlight in the road. That was all they found."

"I don't suppose there are bears on the island?"

"Not since before World War Two, and I doubt if she was attacked by raccoons."

"What could possibly connect Janey's disappearance with Don's death?"

"All I can do is guess. Maybe they both knew something about somebody that they shouldn't have known."

"But what could they possibly know?"

"Maybe they found out who killed Dick and his family."

"That seems farfetched; if Don had known something about that, he'd have told you, wouldn't he?"

"He would have, if he'd lived through the night," Rawls said. "Remember, he wanted to meet the next day, said he had something to tell me."

"Why didn't he just tell you on the phone when he called?"

"People in our line of work have a nicely developed aversion to passing important information on the phone. It's not that he would have thought his line was tapped; it's just that he would have been uncomfortable discussing something like that, except face to face."

"But how does Janey come into it?"

"I don't know, but I'm going to find out," Rawls said. "I'm going to talk to everybody who clapped eyes on Don and Janey the

day Don died. I should have done it sooner."
He got into the Range Rover and drove
away.

Stone went back into the house. He
wasn't about to mention this to Arrington.

30

THEY HAD AN ESPECIALLY good dinner that evening: Seth had found some lobsters, and his wife had steamed them perfectly. There were clams, too, and corn on the cob, dripping with butter, and two bottles of a Beringer reserve chardonnay from Dick's cellar.

After dinner they moved into the study, where Arrington found a Scrabble board in a bookcase, and they played game after game until they were all sleepy. Arrington sent Peter to bed, and after a while, the adults drifted upstairs.

Stone and Arrington made wonderful love for nearly an hour, fueled by the good wine and good feeling from their evening, then they lay in each other's arms, getting their breath back.

Stone stroked her hair and kissed her on the forehead. "You know," he said, "we really ought to start thinking about making this a more permanent relationship."

Arrington sat up in bed and tucked her legs under her. "I've thought about that a lot," she said, "and it wouldn't work."

Stone said nothing, just waited for her to continue.

"First of all, I love you, Stone, and I always will, and I know you love me in the same way."

"That's perfectly true," Stone said, "but somehow I don't see that as an impediment to a relationship."

"Think about our lives," she said. "They're completely incompatible."

"I don't see why."

"Then I'll explain it to you. Peter and I live in Virginia, and we both love it there. You wouldn't last a month in Virginia. You need New York: You need Elaine's and you need to earn a living, and New York is the only place you can do that. Sure, you could hang out a shingle in Virginia, but you'd hate the work, and although I'm certainly rich enough to support you in the style to which you've become accustomed, you'd never let me do that, and I'd have a lot less respect for you if you did.

"Peter is in a wonderful school that will take him right through high school, and when he's ready for college he'll be able to choose between the Ivy League and the University of Virginia, which is right down the road, in Charlottesville. I know you can raise children in New York, but I would never subject him to the things we'd have to do to keep him safe: limos to school, organized play groups, security guards. In Virginia he'll be able to ride his horse every day, ride it to school in a couple of years. He has the fields and woods to roam and plenty of great, unspoiled kids his own age."

"You don't want to get married again, do you?" Stone asked.

"There's that, too. I've been married, I've had my child and I enjoy my freedom. There isn't a single thing that being married could do for me that I can't do anyway. Then there's you: You've been following your cock around since you were fifteen, and you're not going to stop now."

"You don't think I could be faithful?"

"I'd give you three months, tops," she said, laughing. "Then you'd meet some girl at Elaine's, and you'd be in the sack in the blink of an eye. Look, I don't mind that about you, at least not in our present relationship, but if we were married, it would piss me off royally, and we'd be divorced in no time."

"I think we could make it work," Stone said.

Arrington sighed. "There's something else," she said.

"What?"

"I wasn't going to bring this up, at least not on this trip, but it would have come up eventually, so we'd better face it."

"What are you talking about?"

"You're still not sure that I didn't kill Vance." Arrington's husband had been shot dead in their home; Arrington had been suspected, but Stone had gotten her cleared. Another woman had been tried for the crime, but acquitted. The murder was still unsolved.

Stone knew he had to choose his words carefully. "Arrington, is there something you want to tell me?"

"That's just the point, I don't want to tell

you anything, but maybe I should. It's just that you are a very moral person, and if you thought I had killed Vance you'd never look at me the same way again."

"You're starting to worry me, Arrington."

"I don't want you to worry. Let's just say that, if I had killed Vance, I would have done it for very good reasons and to protect myself and Peter. Could you believe that of me?"

"I believe that you would not murder your husband, but that if you did, there would have been some justifiable reason, yes."

"More than justifiable," she said. "Imperative. And if I had done that and the facts had been presented in court, I would very likely have been acquitted, but it would have destroyed Peter's life. So my decision would have been between that and keeping quiet and risking conviction. That would have been an impossible situation."

"What are you saying, Arrington?"

"I'm not saying anything, Stone. This is all hypothetical, don't you see?"

"All right."

"Then let's leave it at that," Arrington said. "It would not improve our relationship to go any further, and I don't want anything to change."

Stone thought about that. "As you wish," he said finally. "Let's leave it at that."

Arrington crawled under the covers, snuggled close to Stone and rested her head on his shoulder. "Then let's never speak of it again," she said, fondling him.

The phone rang.

"Shit," Stone said.

"Who could that be at this hour?"

Stone reached over her and picked up the phone. "Hello?"

"It's Ed Rawls. They found Janey."

"Is she all right?"

"She was floating face down in Dark Harbor."

"Oh, God," Stone breathed.

"She'd been beaten, raped and strangled."

"Are the state cops on top of this?"

"They're all over it. They've taken the body back to Augusta for autopsy."

"When did they find her?"

"At sundown. They kept it as quiet as they could until they told the parents and got the body off the island."

"And you think this is connected to Don?"

"I think Janey knew something about somebody, and she told Don, and that person killed them both. I just can't see it any other way. I think all this Kirov horseshit is just that, and we ought to forget about it."

"I'll let Lance know in the morning."

"I'm sorry I called you so late."

"It's all right. I'll talk to you tomorrow." Stone hung up.

Arrington was staring at him intently. "Who's dead?"

"A seventeen-year-old girl," Stone said. "Her name was Janey. She was kidnapped, raped and murdered."

"Peter and I are flying back to New York tomorrow." She reached for the phone.

"Don't bother calling Centurion; I'll fly you back myself."

"All right." She turned her back to him and pulled her knees up into the fetal position.

"I'm sorry about this," Stone said.

"It's not your fault, Stone."

They didn't speak again until morning.

31

BY MID-MORNING THEY were off the Islesboro landing field and headed southwest.
An hour and a half later they touched down
at Teterboro, New Jersey, and taxied up to
Atlantic Aviation, next to a chartered jet
waiting for Arrington and Peter.

"I wish you'd stay longer," Stone said to
Arrington as her luggage was being transferred.

"Peter wants to get back to his pony," she
said, "and I'm redesigning the gardens at
the main house, so there's lots of work for
me to do." She kissed him. "Take care of
yourself."

Stone knelt and gave Peter a hug and
watched them board the jet, then walked

with Dino through the terminal building to the parking lot, where Joan, his secretary, was waiting with his car. Half an hour later, they were back at Stone's house.

He went to his office and wrote a check to the Samuel Bernard Foundation and gave it to Joan, along with the file on Dick's estate and a letter to his old mentor. "Please have this hand-delivered to Sam Bernard," he said. "I want it to pass through his hands on the way to the foundation. Then book a table at Elaine's and call Lance Cabot and tell him I'd like to have dinner with him and Holly Barker."

ELAINE'S AND ELAINE were as ever. Stone and Dino shook some hands, then sat down at their usual table, waiting for Lance and Holly.

Elaine came over and sat down. "So, you couldn't stand it up there any longer, huh?"

"It was very nice up there, but I had to fly Arrington back."

"So, you couldn't stand it up there with Arrington, huh?"

"You're not gonna win this one," Dino said.

"I give up," Stone said, raising his hands in surrender. "I just couldn't stand it up there any longer."

"That's what I thought," Elaine said, then moved on to another table.

Lance and Holly arrived, they ordered drinks, then Stone got down to business. "It looks as though our theory of a work-related death for Dick and his family may have been wrong."

"I'm not convinced of that," Lance said.

"There's more news. After Don Brown's death, his niece, a seventeen-year-old named Janey Harris, was kidnapped, raped and murdered on the island. Ed Rawls thinks the two deaths are connected, that Janey told Don something that got both of them killed. Ed thinks it's local, and I have to agree with him."

"And how about the Stone family's deaths. Does he think those are connected, too?"

"Dick's daughter was eighteen, and the two girls had to have known each other. Maybe whatever Janey told Don she had told Esme Stone, too."

"And the killer wiped out the whole family to protect himself?"

"It makes more sense than the Russian mob theory," Stone said.

Lance seemed unconvinced. "For somebody who used to be a cop, it's odd that you would form a theory on so little evidence," he said. "This is an air theory, like air guitar is making music."

Dino spoke up. "I've seen solutions of a lot of murder cases that were based on less, in the beginning. An investigator needs a theory, if only to have it proved wrong. You have to work with the evidence you've got, even if it's thin."

"Lance," Stone said, "have you heard anything from your friend at Langley about who Don Brown wanted the background check on?"

"Not yet," Lance said. "It could be days or weeks before I hear from him."

The waiter brought menus, and they ordered.

When they were halfway through dinner, Lance spoke up again. "My people are not going to buy your local theory."

"It's Ed Rawls's theory," Stone said.

"That won't matter to them. They're not going to be distracted by the deaths of Don Brown and his niece. They won't be inclined to believe that a high-ranking officer like Dick was killed by some information shared between two teenaged girls."

"Lance, the facts surrounding what happened to Dick and his family are not going to be shaped by what Langley believes. They are what they are, and you need to explain that to them."

"You obviously haven't had much experience with large bureaucratic organizations," Lance replied.

Stone laughed. "I worked for the NYPD for fourteen years."

Lance laughed. "Touché."

"Too many murder investigations are shaped by what the hierarchy wants to believe," Dino said, "especially in high-profile cases. When you're working a case, you have to ignore that, or you'll come up with the wrong result."

Holly spoke for the first time. "Who has motive?" she asked.

"Nobody," Stone replied.

"How about Dick's brother?"

"Caleb didn't have a motive."

"Our background check showed he was perpetually short of cash. That'll do it in most murders."

"Yes, but Caleb didn't inherit from Dick, who changed his will."

"Did the brother *know* Dick had changed his will? I mean, you only got the new will a couple of days before Dick's murder."

"You have a point," Stone said. "It came as a surprise to Caleb when I told him. I'll grant you he had motive, and he had a key to the house, so I'll give you means, too, but he didn't have opportunity. The state police put him in Boston at the time of the murders; he and his family didn't arrive on Islesboro until the day after."

"And how good are the state police? They didn't do such a hot job on the first investigation of Dick's murder, did they?"

"Again, you have a point," Stone said.

Holly turned to Lance. "You know, we have an ex-Boston cop, Bob O'Neal, in our group. Why don't I ask him to use his contacts at the Boston PD to reinvestigate the brother's alibi? Maybe Caleb is smarter than we're giving him credit for."

"Good idea," Stone said.

"All right," Lance said, "but tell Bob not to make a career of it."

"Are you going back up to Maine, Stone?" Holly asked.

"Not until I get more to go on," Stone replied. "I've got to make a living, after all."

"If you go back, maybe Lance will give me some time to go with you. I'd really like to get my teeth into this one."

"Maybe," Lance said. "You want to use vacation time?"

"Remember, the Agency has a stake in this."

"Oh, all right. Get your desk cleared."

"I'm happy to have all the help I can get," Stone said, thinking he'd be happy to have Holly up there, in any case.

32

STONE WAS AWAKENED by the telephone too early. He glanced at the bedside clock: 6:30 A.M. He picked up the phone. "Hello?" he croaked.

"It's Ed Rawls."

"And good morning to you, Ed."

"Did I wake you?"

"Yes."

"Sorry. You better get back up here, Stone."

"What's going on?"

"All hell has broken loose, that's what."

Stone pressed the button that raised the head of his bed and rearranged himself. "What do you mean?"

"The people on the island, both locals and

summer folks, are up in arms. They had a meeting at the yacht club yesterday."

"And what happened at the meeting?"

"Mostly they just aired their complaints."

"About what?"

"Lack of police protection, mostly. They've sent the state police a request to have officers stationed on the island round the clock until this situation is resolved."

"Sounds like a good idea."

"What's not a good idea is they're arming themselves. Sergeant Young told me they've had something like a couple of dozen applications for carry licenses, the most ever in one day from one town, and this is a village. Several carloads of people went over to Ellsworth yesterday afternoon."

"Is there something ominous about Ellsworth?"

"No, it's just that the only gun shop in this part of the state is in Ellsworth, a place called Phil's. There are more guns than people in Maine, but for some reason, not very many gun shops."

"I'm trying to find this alarming, Ed. Are you afraid they're going to start shooting each other?"

"Something like that. Everybody's really on edge. They were all shocked by the killings of Dick and his family and Don, but Janey's murder has really got them spooked. A bunch of people have just packed up and left."

"I can understand that, Ed, but why does that make it important for me to get back up there right away?"

Rawls cleared his throat. "Well, your name came up at the meeting."

"In what regard?"

"Somebody, I forget who, asked a question that implied that you might have had something to do with Dick's murder, since you inherited his house. The guy was shouted down, but the thing is, the idea is in the air now."

"Oh, swell. Did somebody mention that I was in New York at the time of the murders and that I didn't even know about Dick's murder until the day after?"

"I said you weren't on the island that night, but that just started a discussion about how anybody could get onto the island in a boat. I think you need to be seen up here dealing with this. There's another meeting at five o'clock this afternoon, and I think you ought to be here for it."

Stone clicked on the TV and went to the weather channel just in time to see the national radar displayed. "All right. I'll be there," he said. "But I don't know what I can do to placate them at this point."

"Just being there will let them know that you're not afraid to show your face. That'll mean something."

"All right, Ed. I'll see you this afternoon." Stone hung up and called Holly.

"Hello?" She didn't sound sleepy.

"Good morning. It's Stone."

"Good morning."

"I just got a call from Ed Rawls. He thinks I'd better get back up there today, before the merry villagers torch my house and slay my cattle."

"What?"

Stone explained the best he could what he didn't understand himself. "Can you be ready to go at, say, one o'clock?"

"I'm sure I can. I'll talk to Lance."

"Pick you up at one?"

"I'll come to your house."

"Okay, bye." Stone hung up and called Dino.

"I've got to go back to Maine this afternoon." He explained the situation. "You want to go?"

"Can't do it; a couple of big cases landed on my desk while I was gone, and I have to deal with them. Maybe later."

"Go back to sleep." Stone hung up and struggled out of bed.

THE MIRAGE TOUCHED down on the Islesboro airfield at 3:30 that afternoon, and he was surprised to find not a single airplane parked on the ramp. When he had departed the day before, there had been at least half a dozen there.

Seth Hotchkiss met them in the station wagon. "Glad you're back," he said, and that was all he said.

The drive through Dark Harbor was a little spooky; no cars were on the street or parked in front of the shop. He and Holly parked, went inside and found Jimmy Hotchkiss at his desk in the back office. He was wearing a gun on his belt.

"Hi, Jimmy," Stone said.

"Hello, Stone. I thought you'd left the island."

"I just flew Dino down to the city and

brought back another friend." He introduced Holly.

Jimmy stood up and shook her hand. "I'm glad you're back, Stone," he said. "You know about the meeting this afternoon?"

"Yes. Ed Rawls called me."

"I think you should be there."

"I will be. Where is everybody? The village is deserted, and there are no airplanes at the airport."

"A lot of folks ended their summer yesterday," Jimmy said. "We've got a couple of state cops due in this afternoon. I found them a rental, so they're going to stay on the island for the rest of the summer. They'll be at the meeting."

"See you there," Stone said, and left.

SETH PUT STONE'S BAGS in the master bedroom and Holly's in Esme's room; Stone didn't correct him. The phone rang.

Stone picked it up. "Hello?"

"It's Lance. Put Holly on an extension."

Stone paged Holly, and she picked up. "Okay, we're both here."

"I finally got an answer from Langley

about the inquiry Don Brown made right before his death."

"And?"

"He wanted to know if Caleb Stone's twin sons, Eben and Enos, had criminal records."

"Did he say why he wanted to know?"

"No. He just asked that they be checked. He stayed on the phone while they ran the search."

"What did they come up with?"

"Zip. They checked in both Boston and in New Haven, since the twins are at Yale. They're clean. Even the campus police didn't have a bad word to say about them. They're apparently upright lads."

"One more dead end, then?"

"Looks that way."

"Thanks, Lance."

"Have you heard anything else since you got back?"

"A bunch of people have packed up and left for the summer; a bunch of others have bought guns."

"Swell."

"There's a town meeting at five o'clock, and the state cops are supposed to be there. Maybe they'll have something new."

"Good luck," Lance said, then hung up.

33

STONE WALKED OVER to the yacht club, passing a group of children playing in the parking lot watched over by two women. Nobody was taking any chances.

Inside, people were gathered in little groups, talking quietly but earnestly. Stone shook the hands of a few people he'd met before. He waved at Caleb Stone, sitting at a table with his twin sons. A moment later, Sergeant Young of the state police and another uniformed officer walked into the club, and the commodore rapped on a table with a beer bottle for quiet.

"Good afternoon," he said. "Sergeant Young from the state police is here and would like to speak to us." The commodore stepped aside, and Young replaced him.

"Hey, everybody," he said. "I've met a lot of you, but I'd like to introduce my colleague, Corporal Tom Best. Tom and I are going to be living on the island for the rest of the summer, or until there's an arrest for the crimes that have occurred here. We've had a telephone line installed." He gave them the number, and many people wrote it down. "You can call us anytime, night or day, if you have anything important to report. Make that anything at all, whether it seems important or not; we need all the information we can get.

"Now, I want to bring you up to date on our investigation, tell you what we're doing. We're running criminal record checks on everybody on the island, full-time and part-time residents, and yes, this means you, no exceptions. We're particularly interested to know if anybody on the island has ever been arrested or convicted of a crime of a sexual nature, so if there's something like that in your background or the background of a person you know, I urge you to come to me directly about it, rather than wait for the record to turn up.

"We're also rechecking the ferry records to see who was and wasn't on the island at the time of the first murders, those of Richard Stone and his wife and daughter. There are no records of which private airplanes were parked at the airstrip at that time, but a resident who lives within sight of the airport has told us what he remembers about who was here, so we have a pretty good list of owners. Tom and I are going to be visiting every single residence on the island, so you will be seeing us at your house pretty soon. We'll be talking by telephone with those residents who have recently left the island to return to their homes.

"We are going to determine from these interviews the name of every single person who was on the island the day the Stone family died, the day Don Brown died and the day Janey Harris died, so we'll be asking each of you about that, and believe me, we're going to verify every statement you make, so I want the truth from everybody first time out. Anybody who lies to us will immediately be treated as a suspect.

"Now, anybody have any questions? I'd rather you ask them now, because I don't want to have to go over this again with every person I meet." He looked around the room.

A man raised his hand. "We heard that you had determined that Janey had been raped."

"That's true," Young said.

"Did you recover any DNA evidence during the postmortem examination?"

"I can see you've been watching *CSI* on television," Young said. "The answer is no, we didn't. The body had been in the water for several hours, and that would have helped remove any superficial DNA evidence or hairs or fibers that could have been of use. We found no DNA internally, either, which could mean either that being in the water removed it or that the perpetrator used a condom."

Another man raised his hand. "Was there any connection between the firearm used to kill the Stones and the one used to kill Don Brown?"

"No," Young replied. "They were each killed with their own weapons: the Stones with a .380 and Brown with a .45."

Another hand went up. "How did the killer achieve entry into the Stone and Brown homes?"

"We believe that both homeowners failed to secure their properties and that the killers just walked in. Mr. Brown didn't have a security system in his house; Mr. Stone had a very good system, but he did not activate it that night. This should be a lesson to all of you who have security systems or who plan to have them installed. If you don't arm them, they're not security systems; they're just a bunch of useless wires and keypads. I want every home on this island to have its doors and windows closed and locked at night, and every security system armed."

"Do you have any motive for any of these murders?" somebody asked.

"All we have now is supposition. If any of you has any reason to believe that any person had a motive in any of these killings, please see me after the meeting. That could be crucial information. There's something else I want to talk to all of you about." He looked around the room. "I'm aware that a number of you have applied for a license to carry firearms and that others of you have purchased weapons. Corporal Best is going to pass out a brochure to all of you that summarizes Maine law on the possession and use of firearms, and I want each of you who owns a weapon to take steps to see that you are entirely within the law. I will not tolerate the illegal possession or use of firearms on this island. I refer particularly to the securing of weapons to keep them out of the hands of children.

"Further, I want each of you to give serious thought about the circumstances under which you might use a firearm. It would be best if you had a plan of behavior if someone should enter your home, or if you should otherwise feel the need to use a weapon. Tomorrow afternoon at three, Corporal Best and I are going to hold a seminar here at the yacht club on the storage and use of firearms, and you should bring your weapons with you. Do not, however, bring any ammunition. Before you leave your home, check to see that your weapon is unloaded. We will only do dry firing during the seminar. Any other questions?"

From a rear corner of the room came Ed Rawls's distinctive voice. Stone had not seen him there. "At yesterday's meeting somebody expressed some curiosity about Stone Barrington's role or interest in all of this. Maybe Stone would like to address that now."

Sergeant Young turned toward Stone. "Mr. Barrington?"

"Thank you, Sergeant," Stone said. "Dick was my first cousin, my mother and his father being brother and sister. On the day that Dick and his family were murdered, I was in New York City. I didn't learn of their deaths until the following evening, when a colleague of Dick's told me the news."

"I should say that we've verified Mr. Barrington's whereabouts at the time of the murders," Young said.

"I want to tell you all I know," Stone said. "Shortly before Dick's death I received a package from him containing a letter hiring me as his attorney and naming me as his executor, as well as an envelope to be opened in the event of his death. When I opened the envelope, after being informed that he had died, I found a properly executed will, and since I am under no obligation to keep its contents confidential, I will tell you what his bequests were. Dick left the use of his house to me and my heirs in perpetuity; if I choose to sell the house, the proceeds would revert to his estate." He thought it better not to mention the exclusion of Caleb and his family from ownership of the house. "There were a number of personal bequests to friends and relatives on Barbara's side of the family, and the residue of the estate was left to a charitable foundation. Additionally, there were two large insurance policies in the estate: Three-quarters of their combined value went to Caleb Stone, and the other quarter to the foundation."

"Why did Dick leave his house to you?" somebody asked.

"Quite frankly, I don't know, and Dick offered no explanation in his letter to me. I had seen him only once, for dinner, about eight years ago, since the summer I spent on this island when we were both eighteen. Dick said he planned to see me on his next trip to New York, when he might have explained things more fully, but, of course, that trip never took place." Stone looked around. "Does anyone have any other questions?" Apparently, there were none.

Sergeant Young spoke up again. "I should tell you, if you don't already know, that Mr. Barrington spent fourteen years with the New York City Police Department, many of them as a homicide detective, and he has been very helpful to me in my investigation.

Any other questions?" No one spoke. "Then, unless the commodore has something else, that concludes this meeting. I'll be seeing you soon."

The crowd broke up, and people moved into the parking lot to collect their children and their cars. Stone shook a few hands, then started back toward his house.

Ed Rawls caught up with him. "That was good," he said. "You've nipped a lot of rumors in the bud."

"I hope so. By the way, Lance Cabot found out who Don Brown wanted checked for criminal records."

"Who?"

"The Stone boys, Eben and Enos."

"And?"

"They were squeaky clean, both in Boston and New Haven, where they're in college. The boys got an especially good report from the Yale campus police. So it's a dead end."

"Yeah, maybe," Rawls said, "but how come Don ran the check on them? He must have had a reason."

"I suppose he did," Stone said, "but there's no way to know what it was." He looked at Rawls closely. "Ed, you seem depressed."

"I'm not depressed," Rawls said. "I'm angry, angry at what was done to these murdered people, all of whom were friends of mine. If I met the man who did this face to face, I'm not sure I could account for my actions."

"I understand your feelings," Stone said, "but what Sergeant Young had to say about firearms was important. If you take a shot at someone the consequences could be worse for you than for your victim. I've seen this happen before: Some citizen fires a weapon at a supposed criminal, kills or wounds him, then he has to deal with criminal charges, followed by a lawsuit. Believe me, it's not a position you'd want to put yourself in."

"I hear you," Rawls said. "See you later." He turned and walked back toward the yacht club parking lot.

Stone hoped to God Rawls had truly heard him.

34

STONE TOOK HOLLY TO the Dark Harbor Inn that night for dinner. He wanted to wipe away all the tension surrounding the murders on the island, if only for the evening.

"So, how is the new job working out?" he asked.

She took a sip of her wine. "Without getting too specific, very well."

"Do you like working with Lance?"

"I do. He can be autocratic at times, but that's to be expected, given the position he's in."

"Which is?"

"Let's just say that he has a lot of responsibility. But most of the time, he's open to the ideas of others, and he's inclined to delegate responsibility among those he trusts, and that seems to include me. I'm lucky, in that being pretty new on this job, I'm getting a lot more responsibility than I would if I had come out of training and started work at Langley."

"From what I hear Lance is held in high regard at the Agency, and that should rub off on you."

"That would be nice."

They ate silently for a moment, then Holly spoke up again. "Arrington was up here for a visit, wasn't she?"

"Well, yes."

"Not a very long one, though. What happened?

"She was upset about the murders: Janey Harris's body was found while she was here."

"Is that all?"

"Well, she and I pretty much agreed that there's no permanent relationship in store for us."

Holly smiled. "That's awfully nice to hear. I'd hate to think that I'm up here only as an investigator."

"Don't worry, you're not." He poured her some more wine.

"I got a little worried when you let Seth put our luggage in different rooms."

"I was just catering to Seth's sensibilities; I didn't want to shock him."

"Can Seth hear what goes on in the house?"

"No, his place is well out of earshot."

"That's good," Holly said. "I wouldn't want him to hear your pitiful cries tonight."

Stone laughed. "If it makes you feel any better, Seth and his wife are on the mainland tonight. They went to dinner at her sister's house in Rockland, and the last ferry is at seven P.M., so they're staying the night. We can lock down the house and not worry about being disturbed."

"The best of all possible worlds," Holly said.

THEY WERE DRIVING HOME when Stone's cell phone vibrated. "Hello?"

"It's Ed Rawls."

"What's up, Ed?"

"I thought you ought to know that Janey's mother just told me her daughter's diary disappeared."

"When?"

"She can't be sure, but since her death. She saw her in her room writing in it the afternoon before the evening she disappeared."

"Could she have had it in a pocket or purse?"

"I asked about that: It was big, about eight by ten, so probably not. Her mother thinks someone came into the house, searched her room and stole it."

"So whatever Janey might have told Don Brown might have been in her diary?"

"Right. Do you know if Esme had a diary?"

"As a matter of fact, I do, and I've got it in a safe place."

"Have you read it?"

"No, but in light of the theft of Janey's diary I'm going to read it tonight."

"Let me know if there's anything relevant in it, will you?"

"I'll call you in the morning." Stone hung up.

"What's happened?" Holly asked.

"Janey Harris's diary has disappeared, but I've got Esme's at home in the safe."

"And Rawls thinks there was something in the diary that might have led to her murder?"

• • •

THEY WERE HOME in ten minutes. Stone unlocked the door and stepped into the entrance hall, ready to tap the alarm code into the keypad there. He stopped. "Didn't I set the security system before we left?"

"Yes, I saw you put in the code."

Stone looked at the small screen on the keypad. "Well, it's not armed now."

"Who could have disarmed it?"

"Only Seth and his wife would have the code, and they left before we did."

"Could you have entered the code incorrectly?"

"Possibly. Maybe I got a digit wrong."

"Or maybe not," Holly said. She reached into her purse and came out with a Walther PPKS.

Stone unholstered the little .45 on his belt. "Let's have a look around," he said quietly. "We'll go together, room by room, starting upstairs."

The two crept up the stairs, listening. They did a standard police search, entering each room, checking each closet, any place that could hide a man. Stone paid particular attention to Esme's room and the little bedroom across the hall that she had used as a study. This was where Peter had found her diary. There was no sign that anything had been disturbed.

They went back downstairs and searched the kitchen and dining room and the garage, then went into the study.

"Uh, oh," Stone said.

"What?"

Stone nodded toward the back door. The vacuum cleaner sat just inside the door to the terrace. He went over and opened the canister. "Bag's gone," he said.

"Just like before."

"Exactly like before."

"But nothing seems disturbed."

"Let's look more closely," Stone said. They worked the whole room, looking for some small sign that someone had been there.

"As far as I can tell," Holly said, "everything is exactly as it was before."

Stone tried the door to the terrace. "Locked."

"Didn't you say that Dick had some sort of special locks?"

"Yes. They use a key that you can only get from the manufacturer."

Holly put her gun back into her handbag and came out with a small leather case. "You said the door to the terrace was locked?"

"Yes."

She walked over to the door and tried it, then got down on her knees and opened the little case, which held a selection of lock picks. "Standard issue," she said. "I'm supposed to be able to open just about anything."

"You did a pretty good job on Dick's safe, as I remember."

"This is going to be harder," she said, then went to work.

Stone walked around the study again and opened Dick's secret office. It seemed undisturbed. The weapons were still in their cabinet. He went back and watched Holly work.

She stood up and put her lock picks away. "I can't do it," she said. "I mean, I'm not a genius at this, but the training I got at the Farm made me a lot better than all but the best burglars. These locks are made by a company called Assa, and we were told about them in our training. The U.S. Government uses them in special security situations."

"I want to read Esme's diary," Stone said. He went to the cabinet that held the safe and opened it. "Holy shit," he said.

"What?"

"It's gone."

"What's gone?"

"The safe. Come and look at this."

There were four crudely cut holes in the base of the cabinet, where the safe had been bolted down.

"He used a hammer and a chisel," she said. "Took the whole thing right out. I guess he couldn't open it."

"Right," Stone said.

"And if he couldn't open that little safe, he certainly couldn't have opened the terrace door," Holly said.

"Then he must have used a key," Stone replied.

"Does anybody else have a key?" She asked.

"Not as far as I know. Caleb Stone had one, but he returned it to me."

"And he couldn't have had it duplicated," Holly said, "since only the manufacturer has the special key blanks required."

"Right," Stone said.

35

STONE WOKE SLOWLY the following morning. Holly was lying naked next to him on her belly, and his hand rested on her ass. He found it companionable to wake up with her next to him, warm and bare.

He ran a finger up her ass, between the cheeks.

"Hmmmmm," she muttered. "More."

"More what?"

"Just more."

He rolled over and lay on top of her.

"You're nicely heavy," she said.

He was growing in size, and in response she opened her legs wider. "More," she said.

"Where?"

"Anywhere you like."

She was wet, and he slipped inside her.

"Good choice," she said.

Stone moved slowly in and out.

"That's so good," she breathed, pushing back against his belly.

"It's better than that," Stone said, close to her ear. "You're in wonderful shape."

Holly continued pushing rhythmically against him. "They toned us up at the Farm."

"Thank you, Farm."

Holly rolled over. "I want to be able to get my hands on you," she said, taking him in her hand and reinserting him. She pulled her knees up and rested her ankles on his shoulders. "There," she said. "Now."

Within a minute they had come noisily and lay sweating and panting in each other's arms.

"What a wonderful way to start the day," Holly said.

"It makes me want to go right back to sleep," Stone said.

"Sex renders men unconscious," she laughed. "I'm quoting you."

● ● ●

THEY WERE AT BREAKFAST, eating without much conversation. Holly spoke up. "I want to meet this burglar of yours," she said.

"What, you want a date?"

"Thanks, but I'm all booked up," she said, kicking him under the table. "No, I'm just surprised you aren't paying more attention to him."

"Dino and I eliminated him as a suspect."

"On what grounds?"

"Since his father's death and his own release from prison, he's become a valued member of the community; he's married with a child; he earns a very good living making very expensive cabinets; and he's too smart to foul his own nest, especially such a small nest. He also has nothing in his record to indicate that he's interested in committing crimes of a sexual nature, raping and murdering teenaged girls."

"Still, he has a lot of skills that make him a suspect."

"I actually had him go over this house and give me his opinion on the security features. He was impressed."

"Let me get this straight," Holly said. "You gave a high-class burglar a tour of your home, pointing out all the security features?"

"Yes, and actually he pointed them out to me, not the other way around."

"God, you're naive, Stone."

"I am not."

"Don't you know anything about burglars?"

"Of course I do; I worked burglary for a year on the NYPD."

"How many did you catch?"

Stone hesitated. "Not as many as I would have liked."

"There you go," Holly said. "A smart burglar is notoriously hard to nail. If he doesn't get caught or seen on the property or leave fingerprints or DNA, and if he has a fence unknown to the police, he's damn near bulletproof. These guys know this. Even the ones who get caught learn from their mistakes and go right back to work as soon as they're out of the joint. Very high recidivism rate among burglars. There's also a significant sexual component to these crimes; burglars are often rapists. They get caught for that rather than for the burglaries."

"All right," Stone said. "I'll introduce you to the guy."

Mabel Hotchkiss bustled into the kitchen. "Oh, you're already eating," she said. "I wanted to make breakfast for you."

"We fixed our own," Stone said. "How was your evening on the mainland?"

"We enjoyed it very much," Mabel said, starting to clean up the pots and pans they'd used.

"You should have stayed longer."

"No, one night there is enough. I like to get home."

"Mabel," Stone said, "can you ever remember anyone getting into this house who shouldn't have been here? Anyone outside the family?"

Mabel shook her head. "Mr. Stone said that could never happen, because of steps he'd taken."

"Has either you or Seth ever lost a key?"

"No, we each have one; mine's in my purse, and Seth's is in his pocket. Why do you ask?"

"I'm still trying to figure out everything."

They finished their breakfast, then Stone got out the MG and they drove north on the island.

"I don't know what our excuse is going to be for this visit," Stone said.

"Why do we need an excuse?"

"I don't want to appear to be harassing the man," he said.

"Leave it to me."

They turned into Hal Rhinehart's drive and stopped next to the shop. Rhinehart was at his drawing table in his office, working on a set of plans. "Good morning," he said.

"Morning, Hal. I want you to meet Holly Barker, a friend of mine."

Rhinehart shook Holly's hand. "To what do I owe the pleasure?" he asked.

"I wanted to ask you about something," Holly said.

"Go ahead."

"You know the Stone house has Assa locks."

"Yes, and they're the best."

"If you wanted to get past one of them, how would you do it?"

"I'd find another way in," he replied. "I wouldn't waste my time working on an Assa."

"I'm talking about the Stone house, specifically," she said.

"That's a very tight house," he replied. "If I really wanted to get in, I'd try and steal a key from somebody. Otherwise, I'd pass it up for something easier."

"Could you get a duplicate key made?" Holly asked.

Rhinehart shrugged. "I'd try and bribe the locksmith who installed it. He'd have to order a key or a blank from Assa, in Sweden. The trouble is, there's no locksmith on the island; Dick Stone would have to have found one in a larger city to come and do the work, and there's no way to know which one."

"Suppose the bribery didn't work. How would you get a key?"

"If I were in New York, I'd follow the maid to the subway and steal her handbag. As you can see, getting past an Assa would be a major pain in the ass."

"Could you pick it?"

"I tried that once for two bloody hours and got nowhere. When you put the key into an Assa and turn it, something like ninety-two things have to happen inside the lock before it will open."

"Could you make a copy of a key?"

"Sure, if I could get a wax impression. Then it could be cut from a solid piece of metal. That's also a major pain. There are simpler ways to make a living as a burglar."

A young woman carrying an infant came into the office. "Oh, I'm sorry. I didn't know you were busy," she said.

"This is my wife, Helene," Rhinehart said, "and our baby, Dede. She's nine months old."

Holly made the appropriate noises with the baby. "Thanks for your help," she said. "We'd better be going." They said their goodbyes and went back to the car.

"Well?" Stone said.

"All right," she said, "Rhinehart sold me. He's a reformed character."

"Good questions about the locks," Stone said.

"Yeah, but no good answers. I'm stumped."

"So am I."

"I guess we'll have to pursue other leads."

"What other leads?" Stone asked.

"Well, there is that," she said.

36

BACK AT THE HOUSE, Holly came into the study where Stone was reading the *New York Times.*

"Have you got the key to Dick's secure office?"

"Sure." Stone took the key off his ring and handed it to her. "I guess Lance wouldn't mind."

"It's Lance I want to contact," she said, unlocking the door. She went into the little office, inserted a data card into the computer and switched it on. When prompted, she entered her user name and password.

"That's a lot of digits for a password," Stone said.

"Big-time encryption," she said. She

tapped in more keystrokes. "Ah," she said. "I caught Lance at his desk."

"What do you want to tell him?"

"I just want to bring him up to date, and I want to get more information about the Assa locks." She continued typing, stopping now and then to read the replies.

"You're using regular instant messaging?"

"It's highly irregular instant messaging," she said, "but the result is the same." She typed a few more keystrokes, then ended the session. "He'll get back to me."

"I'm going back to the *Times*," Stone said. "There's the crossword yet to do." He went back to his chair, grabbed the paper and put his feet up on the ottoman.

"I'm going for a run," Holly said. "Want to join me?"

"I'm too comfortable," Stone replied. "Go armed."

"You think that's necessary?"

"How many more murders do you need on an island this size to make you cautious?"

"Oh, all right."

"And stick to the roads; don't run down any trails."

"Oh, stop it."

"I just want to know where to look for your body later."

"All right, all right!"

HOLLY WENT UPSTAIRS AND changed into sweats and sneakers, strapped her 9 mm on, then left by the front door and headed toward the main road past the house. She stopped at the end of the driveway and did some stretching, then headed down the road, running lightly on the left side of the road, facing traffic. The day was bright and cool, perfect Maine weather. She had gone about a mile when a police car began coming toward her. It slowed as it approached, then stopped, and the passenger-side window rolled down.

"Morning," a uniformed officer inside said.

"Good morning," Holly said, stopping and going to the open window.

"I'm Sergeant Young of the Maine State Police," the man said. "Who might you be?"

"I'm Holly Barker. I'm staying with Stone Barrington at the Dick Stone house."

"I'm glad to know that," Young said. "My partner and I are interviewing every living soul on the island in connection with the recent killings."

"I can sympathize with your task," Holly said. "I'm a retired police officer, and I've done my share of canvassing, though I've never interviewed a whole population."

"Only about six hundred, locals and summer folk," Young said. "Where did you serve?"

"First I was an army MP, then I retired from that and became chief of police of a small town in Florida, Orchid Beach."

"How long have you been on the island?"

"Arrived yesterday, with Stone," she said. "My second visit with him, though the last one was only a couple of days."

"How long you staying?"

"I don't know, really. Until Stone kicks me out, I guess."

"What do you do now, Ms. Barker?"

"Oh, I live the soft life."

"I see you keep in shape."

"Sporadically."

"Well, enjoy your run, but please keep to the roads. We don't know exactly what we're dealing with here, so be careful."

"I will, Sergeant."

"Is Stone at home now?"

"Yep. Doing the crossword."

"I'll drop in on him."

Holly said goodbye and continued her run.

STONE ANSWERED THE door to find Sergeant Young there. "Come on in, Sergeant," he said.

"Thank you. I just met your lady friend, Ms. Barker, on the road."

"Yes, she's staying here. You want some coffee?"

"No thanks. Already had some this morning."

Stone led him into the study. "I'm glad you dropped by; I want to show you something." He went to the cabinet that once concealed the safe and opened it.

"What happened here?" Young asked.

"We came home last night to find that somebody had been in the house and ripped out the safe that was here."

"What was in the safe?"

"Nothing particularly valuable: papers and such. And Esme Stone's diary."

Young looked at him sharply. "That's the

second diary to go missing," he said. "Janey Harris's was taken, too."

"I don't know if that's what our visitor was looking for," Stone said. "I can't imagine how he'd know the diary was in the safe."

"Who knew where it was?"

"Only three other people: Holly Barker, another woman of my acquaintance who was visiting, and her young son. The boy found the diary in an upstairs bedroom that Esme used for a study, and he was copying her handwriting, which was quite beautiful."

"Did you read any of the diary?"

"No. I felt I would have been intruding."

Sergeant Young made some notes in his notebook. "What time did this happen?"

"I guess between eight and ten; that's about when Holly and I were having dinner at the inn."

"Anybody know you were going?"

"No. Seth and Mabel Hotchkiss were on the mainland last night. But we were in Dick's old MG, which is a pretty recognizable car. Just about anyone who might have seen us would have known it."

"Why do you think he took the whole safe?"

"I suppose because he tried to open it

and failed. Probably wanted to work on it at his leisure."

"Was it an expensive safe? Hard to open, I mean?"

"A friend of mine opened it in a few minutes, without the combination."

"Would that have been Ms. Barker?"

"Yes."

"You have any idea how the thief got into the house? I understand this place is supposed to be very secure."

"We're baffled. Our best guess is he had a key."

"Who else has keys?"

"Seth and Mabel Hotchkiss. Caleb Stone had a key, but he gave it back to me. The locks are by a Swedish company called Assa. They're just about impossible to pick, and you can only get a key or even a blank from the manufacturer through a dealer."

"I've heard about those locks," Young said. "Are you sure the Hotchkisses are the only people with keys?"

"I'll find out," Stone said. He picked up the phone, pressed the intercom button and tapped in Seth's extension. "Seth, can you come to the study for a minute?" He listened, then hung up.

Seth was there in less than a minute. "What can I do for you, Stone?"

"You know Sergeant Young, don't you?"

"Know of him." Seth shook his hand.

"Seth, who else outside the family might have a key to the house?"

Seth shrugged. "Nobody that I can think of. Dick was very strict about not giving a key to anybody but family. Caleb has one."

"He returned it to me awhile back," Stone said.

"Then just me and Mabel."

"No repairmen, workmen, maybe the contractor who built the house?"

"Nope. After the locks were installed, I always had to be here to open the door for anybody who came to fix anything. I fix most things myself."

"Any questions, Sergeant?"

"What have you had to have fixed by somebody else?"

"That Viking stove in the kitchen needed some adjustment once. Mabel let the fellow in and stayed with him while he did it. The installer of the TV and audio stuff made several trips, but I was always with him."

"Nobody else?"

"Not that I can think of."

"What about regular maintenance? Furnace, air conditioning?"

"I clean or replace the filters myself; I know how to light the pilot light."

"Plumber? Electrician?"

"I do that stuff."

"That's all I've got," Young said.

"Thanks, Seth. Oh, you should know that somebody got into the house last night and stole Dick's safe out of the cabinet."

Seth looked dumbfounded.

"I'll tell you about it later."

Seth left the room, and Stone heard the back door close.

Holly came back from her run and entered the study. "You two guys don't look too happy," she said.

"Good guess," Stone replied.

37

STONE AND HOLLY had lunch on the rear terrace, enjoying the sun, and as Mabel was taking away the dishes the doorbell rang. Dick Stone had installed an outside bell, apparently for occasions like this.

Stone went to the door and found the remaining three Old Farts standing there.

"Good afternoon," Rawls said. "We disturbing you, Stone?"

"No, gentlemen, come in," Stone replied, waving them inside. "We're sitting out on the terrace."

Stone led them out onto the terrace. "Holly Barker, this is Ed Rawls, Harley Davis and Mack Morris."

"How do you do, gentlemen?" she asked.

They all muttered greetings.

"Stone, forgive me," Rawls said, "but we need to speak to you alone."

"Relax, Ed," Stone said. "Holly is one of you; she works for Lance Cabot."

Ed's eyebrows went up. "Oh?"

"Yes, and she's helping me with our, ah, situation. Anything you can say to me, you can say to her."

The three men sat down around the table.

"Can I get anybody anything? A sandwich? A beer?"

"Maybe later," Rawls said.

"What's up, Ed?"

"We've been over and over this thing, and we've come to some conclusions."

"I'm all ears," Stone said, leaning forward and putting his elbows on the table."

"First of all, we think we're dealing with two different people," Harley said.

"How so?"

"We think one person killed Dick Stone and his family and another, unconnected person killed Janey Harris."

"I suppose that's possible," Stone said. "Do you have any ideas about who either of them is?"

Rawls spoke up. "Stone, I hope you'll take this as reluctantly offered."

"All right."

"We think Dick and his family were killed by Caleb Stone."

Stone looked at the three men: They all looked dead serious.

"Tell me your reasons."

"Money," Mack said. "Dick's wife's money."

"Money is always a good motive," Stone agreed.

"Until Dick changed his will, we suspect that Caleb was his heir. Caleb's never had a lot of money, and he has a reputation for living close to the line. He's got two sons who've been educated expensively, a house in Boston and one here to run. He's into his middle years with no hope of making much more than he is now."

"All that seems to be true," Stone said.

"And we guess he has a key to this house."

"He doesn't anymore; he gave it back to me."

"After Dick and his family were dead?"

"That's true."

"He probably knows the security system

code, too, unless Dick changed it," Mack said.

Holly spoke up. "These are all good points, Stone."

"Yes, they are. I'll find out whether the security system code has been changed."

"Why don't you see if you can find out what was in Dick's old will?" Harley asked.

"I suppose I can ask Caleb for it, but he's under no obligation to give it to me."

"Maybe you could ask him what caused Dick to change his will," Rawls said. "Obviously, there was some sort of incident, some family breach for Dick to do such a precipitous thing. We've done some asking around on our own, but we haven't been able to find out a thing. We suppose that it was something private, personal between the two brothers."

"Again, I can ask, but I have no reason to believe Caleb would tell me."

"It's worth a try," Rawls said.

"What about Janey?" Stone asked. "Why do you think her killer is a different person?"

"The crimes are very different," Rawls said. "There was no sexual crime in the deaths of Barbara and Esme, and they were all simply executed, two of them in their bed. We think Janey's murder was one of opportunity, and the murderer was your garden-variety rapist-killer. You can find those anywhere, and our guess is that, eventually, Sergeant Young is going to figure out who this one is."

Harley spoke up. "We think Janey knew her killer and that she wrote something about him in her diary; that's why it was stolen."

"What about Don Brown? Who do you think killed him?"

Rawls looked uncomfortable. "We think it could be either the Stones' killer or Janey's. I'll admit, we're on shakier ground here, but we think the Stones' killer is the more likely suspect, and that's Caleb."

"Frankly, Ed, I think your original idea of Don's being killed because Janey had told him something is the better theory, and the theft of her diary supports that."

"Yeah, that's good," Rawls replied, "but we have the similarities of the Stones and Don being killed under similar circumstances: I'm talking about being shot with their own guns and the vacuum cleaner being left by the door. There's nothing to connect Janey's killer with Don's."

"Something else has come up," Stone said. He told them about the entry into Dick's house the night before and the theft of the safe. "So another girl's diary has been stolen, and the vacuum cleaner was left by the door, as when the family was murdered. That's a connection."

"But how did your burglar know the diary was in the safe?" Rawls asked. "For that matter, how did he know that Esme even kept a diary?"

"As to the diary, I think the killer could have supposed that most or all teenaged girls keep diaries, and he had to find both of them, if they existed, in order to protect himself."

"But how did he know it was in the safe?" Harley asked.

Stone shrugged. "Because he'd looked everywhere else in the house, and the safe was the only place left?"

"Maybe," Rawls said. "But I think we should concentrate on Caleb for the time being."

Holly spoke up. "The state police have verified that Caleb was in Boston when the Stone family was murdered. How do we get around a solid alibi?"

"Maybe it isn't as solid as they think," Rawls said.

"These killings are like a crossword puzzle," Stone said. "You think you know the answer to both the across clue and the down clue. They both seem solid, but when you write them both down, they don't match in the middle. When that happens, it means that one of the words is wrong. Maybe both of them."

"Are you still thinking about Kirov and the Agency connection?" Rawls asked.

"Well, it's still on the table, though I think it's not as strong a possibility as it once was. It looked pretty good when it was all we had."

"Look," Rawls said, "let's pull out all the stops with Caleb: Look again at his alibi, check his finances, look at the old will, the works. If he doesn't pan out, then we can turn our attentions elsewhere."

"All right," Stone said. "You work your end, and I'll work mine, and Holly can work whichever end appeals to her."

"Okay," Rawls said. The Old Farts got up and shuffled out.

Stone went to the phone and called Caleb Stone.

"Good afternoon, Stone," Caleb said amiably.

"Caleb, can I buy you lunch at the yacht club tomorrow?"

"Sure, but we should be there by twelve o'clock; it gets crowded."

"Fine, twelve o'clock. And Caleb, if you have a copy of Dick's previous will handy, will you bring it?"

"I don't have one here, but I'll call my office and have them FedEx it to me. It should be here by lunchtime."

"Thanks, Caleb. See you at noon tomorrow."

38

STONE ARRIVED AT the yacht club promptly at noon to find Caleb already there. A FedEx envelope was on the table. Caleb shook his hand.

"I've already placed an order for two burgers and fries. I hope that's okay," Caleb said. "The kids gang up on the kitchen around this time, and we could wait half an hour if we don't get our order in early."

"Great."

"You want a beer?"

"Sure." Caleb retrieved two beers from the counter and set them on the table. He tore open the FedEx package and removed a blue-bound document, scanned it quickly and handed it to Stone. "That's the previous will, which was superceded by the one you gave me."

"Thanks, Caleb." Stone tucked it into his pocket.

"The substance of it was that he left all his assets to Barbara and she to him. If she predeceased him, then everything would go to Esme in trust, until she was thirty, with me as the sole trustee. If they died together, say, in a car crash—or as they did die—then everything would come to me."

"I understand," Stone said. Their burgers arrived, and they began to eat. "Caleb, I know you've already been through this with the state police, but I'd like to go through the time line with you. Until all this is substantiated, they'll still consider you a suspect, but I'd like to do what I can to eliminate you as such."

"I'm a suspect?"

"Everybody on this island is a suspect until eliminated by an alibi, and the police are trained to always start with family. This whole thing is baffling to the police and to me, and the only way they can clear the case is to start with everybody and narrow it down."

"I understand. Do I need a lawyer?"

"No, I'm not a policeman; I'm just doing what I can to help."

"All right, ask me anything you like."

"Let's talk about the day before the night of the murders. Can you give me an account of your day and evening?" Stone took out a notebook and opened it. This was a common cop technique with suspects: If they knew everything was being written down, it concentrated their minds on getting it right.

"It was a normal day. I was at the office by eight-thirty A.M., as usual. I worked through the morning, ordered in a sandwich, ate lunch at my desk, then worked until six-thirty. I had a lot of dictation, letters involving several estates. My wife came to the office at six-thirty, and we had a drink. Then, at seven, we went to a retirement dinner at the Ritz-Carlton for Alden Hayes, head of our litigation department. It was Alden's last day; he was retiring to Florida. We got home around ten, watched a program on television, then the eleven o'clock news. We were asleep by eleven-forty-five."

"Who else was in the house?"

"Only the twins; we don't have any live-in

help. The boys had gone out to dinner and come home late."

Stone noted all the times. "Tell me about the following day."

"I had breakfast with my wife; the boys were still asleep. I was at my desk by eight-thirty. Shortly after that I got a call from Seth Hotchkiss, telling me what had happened. We had planned to leave at noon that day for Islesboro; I called home, gave the family the news and told them to get ready for an immediate departure. We were on the road by ten-thirty, in two cars. My wife and I drove the Suburban, and the boys followed us in their car."

"What kind of car do the boys drive?"

"A BMW convertible. One of the nice things about having twins is that they don't mind sharing."

"What time did you arrive on the island?"

"We came over on the three o'clock ferry, so we would have landed at three-twenty, and fifteen minutes later we were at home. I went over to Dick's house and talked with the state police, who were still there."

"Were the bodies still in the house then?"

"No. Thank God, I didn't have to see that."

"You still had the key to Dick's house at that moment?"

"Yes, the one I gave to you later."

"Where was the key?"

"It was in a little key cupboard in the butler's pantry. There are so many keys in our lives these days, I keep the spares there, all labeled."

"Did you have the security alarm code?"

"Yes. The key wouldn't have been much use without it."

"Do you know if Dick set the alarm at bedtime, as a matter of habit?"

"No, I don't. I think Dick probably had the alarm installed to use when he wasn't on the island, but I don't think he would have used it every day. He mentioned to me when he was building the house that, with Seth and Mabel living on the property, he wouldn't have bothered with the security system, except that the State Department insisted."

"Did you know much about Dick's work?"

"Not really. When it came up in conversation I got the impression that it was pretty unremarkable diplomatic work."

"Did you know that he didn't work for the State Department?"

"But he did," Caleb said. "His degree was in international relations, and he took the foreign service exam before graduation, then went to work at State shortly after that."

Stone shook his head. "That was a cover. Dick was a career CIA officer."

Caleb appeared dumbfounded. "Are you certain about that?"

"Perfectly. Operations people at the Agency commonly have diplomatic cover."

"But when he was still in this country and I called him at work, it was through the State Department switchboard."

"It may have sounded that way, or State could have rerouted the call to Langley."

"You're saying that my brother was a spy?"

"He was a high-ranking officer in the Operations Division of the CIA. I don't know how much actual spying he did. At the time of his death he had been promoted to Deputy Director, Operations, but he hadn't started the job yet."

"I knew he was coming back to Washington, but I thought it was as an Assistant Secretary of State."

Stone shook his head. "That job is a key

position at the Agency, one of the top three."

"Well, I'm glad Dick did well at his work," Caleb said.

"From what I know, he was highly regarded." They had finished their burgers now, and Stone had most of what was needed. "Just one more thing, Caleb."

"What's that?"

"When did you last see Dick?"

"He came to the house for drinks after his return from London. He was on the way to Washington. That was a week or so before his death."

"Did you spend any time alone with him?"

"A few minutes." Caleb looked over Stone's shoulder toward the water; he seemed to be remembering the occasion.

"What did you talk about?"

Caleb looked down at the table. "Family business."

"Tell me about it, please."

Caleb shook his head.

"This is important, Caleb. If you don't tell me about it, then you're going to have to tell the police."

"It had nothing to do with his death, if that's what you mean."

"Caleb, immediately after you saw him, Dick changed his will, excluding you. I have to infer that his action was a result of your conversation with him on that occasion."

"It was deeply personal and not relevant to the investigation," Caleb said. "I won't discuss it with you, and if you're in touch with the state police, you can tell them that I won't discuss it with them, either. Ever." Caleb stood up. "Now, if you'll excuse me, Stone. Lunch is paid for." He left the table and walked out the door.

As Caleb left, the commodore of the yacht club entered the club, deep in conversation with another man. They spoke to other people, and whatever they were talking about seemed to spread around the room.

Stone got up, walked over to the commodore, shook his hand and asked what was going on.

"There's been another murder," the man replied.

39

HOLLY LET HERSELF INTO Dick Stone's hidden office, inserted her data card into the computer and logged on. There was an encrypted e-mail waiting for her, asking her to contact Lance Cabot soonest. She called the Barn, the code name her unit used for their offices, and was told that Lance was out until 3:00 P.M. and was not available on his cell phone. She asked that he call or e-mail her when he returned.

With Stone gone for lunch, she had nothing pressing to do, so she changed clothes, strapped on her 9 mm and went for her daily run. Since Lance was not reachable by cell phone, she left her own in the study.

She did her stretching exercises, then

turned left out of the Stone driveway and began running at a steady clip, keeping to the left, so that she faced oncoming traffic.

As she warmed up, she increased her pace, taking longer strides and breathing deeply. Holly was not a big fan of running, but it seemed to be the only thing that would keep both her ass tight and her weight down.

She came around a curve into a straight stretch and saw a car coming toward her. She had allowed herself to stray in to the middle of the road, and she moved left to give the car plenty of room to pass.

Oddly, the car seemed to follow her movement. She moved off the pavement to continue running on the firm dirt of the shoulder until the car passed. It appeared that it was going to come uncomfortably close to her, and it was slowing. The sun was reflecting off the windshield, and she could not see the driver.

Holly put her hand on her gun holster for reassurance and continued to run. The car came within a couple of feet of her as it passed, and she was conscious of someone beginning to lean out the window.

Then, as she began to turn to look over

her shoulder, she heard the squeal of brakes, and something hard struck her in the head.

STONE RETURNED FROM the yacht club to the house to find Holly gone and reckoned she was out running. After the news he had been given, he hoped she had remembered to go armed. The doorbell rang.

"Afternoon," Sergeant Young said when Stone opened the door. "Have you heard the news?"

"Yes, but no details. Come on in."

The two men went into the study and sat down.

"Tell me," Stone said.

"Two young housewives, Joan Peceimer and Terry Brown, played golf together late yesterday afternoon and left in the same car, telling someone they were having dinner together at Brown's house. This morning, Brown's car was found abandoned in a dirt lane, and we started a search. Joan Peceimer's body was found in the water, in Dark Harbor, much like Janey Harris's."

"And the other woman?"

"Still missing."

"Good God. Two of them?"

"Just between you and me, I don't think there's much chance of seeing Terry Brown alive again."

"Then what we've got here is a full-blown serial killer," Stone said.

"No doubt about it," the sergeant replied. "And he's accelerating the pace of killings."

"They had to know him," Stone said.

"You think so?"

"Otherwise it would have been very difficult for him to kidnap two women. They must have recognized him when he approached them."

"Well, that's not a startling conclusion, given that everybody on this island knows just about everybody else."

"What steps are you taking?"

"Peceimer's body is on its way to the M.E. in Augusta. My partner has organized a search party of volunteers, and they're covering every inch of the island. I've got half a dozen more sergeants on the way here. There's not much more I can do."

"I had a conversation with Ed Rawls and his buddies yesterday," Stone said. "They think that Dick's family and Don Brown were killed by one man, and Janey Harris by another. They have a point."

"That had occurred to me," Young said. "If you accept that premise, then it seems to me that the idea of the Stone family's murder is probably related to Dick's work."

"I don't know, Sergeant. It's hard for me to accept that we've got some European assassin and a serial killer on this small island so close together in the time line."

"I've seen weirder, and I expect you have, too," Young replied. "Frankly, I don't know what to think, and my superiors in Augusta are all over me. The papers are going to have a field day, too; there's already a reporter from Boston here, and we can expect TV crews when word gets out about these two women."

"The Old Farts' principal suspect is Caleb Stone," Stone said. "I've just had lunch with him, and we went through his alibi thoroughly." Stone read Young his notes, then tore out the page and handed it to him. "If you can substantiate all this, then Caleb is in the clear."

Young read through the notes again. "We already have substantiated it," he said, "point by point. Caleb's in the clear, as far as I'm concerned."

"If the alibi checks out, then I'm with you," Stone said. "Nothing about Caleb strikes me as guilty. The only thing he wouldn't talk about was his last meeting with Dick, when Dick was passing through Boston on his way back to Washington. He says it was family business and deeply personal, and he wouldn't talk about it. He told me to tell you he wouldn't talk about it to you, either."

"Do you think what they talked about might be relevant to all these killings?"

"I can't think of anything they might have said that would precipitate the situation we have now. Certainly not the murders of Janey Harris and Joan Peceimer and possibly Terry Brown."

"Doesn't seem likely," Young said. He got up. "Well, I'd better get back to work. Thanks for having a go at Caleb; you've saved us some time. Where's Holly?"

"Out for her run, I expect."

Young's eyebrows went up.

"Don't worry, she's armed, and she's very, very capable of taking care of herself."

"She gives that impression," Young said.

They shook hands, and the sergeant left.

40

STONE SAT DOWN in the study with a book to await Holly's return. Over the years he had found that if he distracted himself from a problem for a while, his subconscious seemed to work on it in the background, and it would become clearer.

He read on for half an hour, then became drowsy. He rested his head on the back of the chair for a moment, and shortly he was sound asleep.

When he awoke, the shadows were long outside, and he looked at his watch: nearly seven o'clock. Mabel Hotchkiss came into the room.

"Excuse me, Stone, but will you and Holly be dining in tonight?"

"Yes, I think we will," Stone said, standing up and stretching. "I was asleep for a while. Did Holly come back from her run?"

"I've been in the kitchen, so I haven't seen her," Mabel replied.

Stone sat down, picked up the phone and pressed the page button. "Holly? Are you in the house?" He could hear the echo of his voice around the place. "Holly?"

He hung up, then picked up the phone again and called her cell phone. He was shunted immediately to her voice mail.

"It's Stone," he said. "I'm worried about you. Please call me the minute you get this message. If I'm not in, try my cell phone." He hung up.

Holly had been gone way too long, he reckoned. He grabbed his cell phone from the desk, then went and backed the MG out of the garage. At the end of the driveway, he stopped and wondered which way she had gone. A right turn would take her toward the village; he turned left, assuming she would want empty roads.

He drove along the road at a steady twenty miles an hour, checking every driveway as he passed. As he came around a curve he saw Holly down the road, running toward him, apparently just returning home. Where the hell had she been?

He slowed to a stop and pulled over, letting her run on toward him, vaguely angry with her for having worried him. As she ran, she pushed her sweatshirt hood off her head, and she wasn't Holly. She was a teenaged boy. He flagged the boy down.

"Evening," he said. "My name is Stone Barrington."

"Oh, yes," the boy said, "from the Stone house. I'm Tyler Morrow." They shook hands. He appeared to be sixteen or seventeen.

"Have you seen another runner along your route?" Stone asked.

"A couple of them," Tyler replied. "A man and a woman; I didn't know either of them, which is unusual around here."

"Were they together?"

"No. I saw them separately."

"Can you describe the woman?"

"Oh, let's see: mid-twenties, dark hair, five-three or -four, slim."

Not Holly. "Are you sure you didn't see another woman? I'm looking for a friend of mine who runs out this way."

"Nope. Just the two."

"Thanks very much, Tyler. If you should encounter a woman in her late thirties or early forties, five-nine, a hundred and thirty pounds, medium brown hair, will you please ask her if her name is Holly, and if it is, ask her to call Stone on his cell phone right away?"

"Sure. Be glad to." With a wave, Tyler Morrow continued on his way.

Stone put the car in gear and began his search anew. He drove all the way to the southern tip of the island, checking every side road and driveway, seeing no sign of Holly. He turned the car around and got out his cell phone. No signal, low battery.

On his way back he turned down every side road and checked it, and by the time he got back to the house it was dark and lights were on inside. He garaged the car and let himself in. "Holly?" he yelled. "Are you home?"

Mabel came out of the kitchen. "I was just upstairs putting away some linens, and she wasn't anywhere up there," she said.

"Thank you, Mabel."

"What time will you want dinner?"

"I'm sorry. I don't want to eat until Holly is

back. Can you put dinner in the fridge for us, and we'll heat it up later?"

"It's beef stew," she said. "You can heat it in the microwave."

Stone went to the phone and called Sergeant Young.

"This is Sergeant Tom Young," a recorded voice said. "Please leave a message, and I'll call you back as soon as I get in."

"Sergeant, this is Stone Barrington. Holly Barker has not returned from her run, and I'm very concerned. I'm not sure exactly how long she's been gone, but it's several hours, and she's never stayed out this long when running. I think you should let your search parties know about her. Please call me at your first opportunity." He hung up, and his eyes came to rest on the coffee table. Holly's cell phone was there. He picked it up and saw that it was switched off. She had no way to communicate.

He put the phone down and called Ed Rawls.

"Rawls," the big man drawled.

"Ed, it's Stone. You've heard about the two missing women?"

"They're not missing any more," Rawls said. "They found the first body this morning. I've just come back from working with one of the search parties. Somebody in a boat who was patrolling the beach found the second body in the water a hundred yards out early this evening."

"Oh, Jesus," Stone said.

"Why did you call?"

"Holly is missing. She went out for a run hours ago and never came back. At least, I assume she went running; she didn't take a car."

"Oh, Jesus," Rawls said.

41

STONE SAT IN THE darkening study, waiting for Sergeant Young to call him back. Lance. He should call Lance. He dialed his cell phone number and immediately got Lance.

"I'm out of the office," Lance's voice said, "and it's unlikely I'll be able to return calls for a day or two. You can leave a message, if you like."

"Lance, it's Stone. Holly is missing, has been gone for several hours. This is very alarming because two women were murdered on the island yesterday. I've notified the state police, who are conducting a search of the whole island anyway. If you get a chance, call me and tell me if you have any ideas." He hung up.

Stone heated up some of the beef stew Mabel had prepared, but he couldn't eat much. He wanted a drink or some wine with dinner, but he felt he had to keep a clear head. But for what? Young hadn't called him back, he couldn't reach Lance, and Holly might be out there somewhere, dying. He couldn't imagine how someone could take her, armed and prepared as she was. He called Ed Rawls.

"Ed, Holly still isn't back, but something occurred to me."

"Tell me."

"Sergeant Young believes that whoever took the two women yesterday was known to them. It occurs to me that, since Holly was armed, she may have know her kil . . . her abductor. She's not the sort of person to be taken easily."

"Makes sense to me," Rawls said. "Who've you got in mind?"

"I don't know; that's the problem. She hardly knows anybody on the island."

"Who, exactly, does she know?"

"She knows Seth and Mabel Hotchkiss, but they're not candidates for this. She knows Sergeant Young, and he's not a candidate, either. And she knows . . ." Stone stopped.

"Who, Stone?"

"Hal Rhinehart."

"Who?"

"The cabinetmaker north of the village."

"Oh, yeah. I knew his old man. You think he's a candidate?"

"He has a criminal background," Stone said. "Dino and I busted him for a string of burglaries years ago, and he did four years or so."

"Have you told this to Young?"

"No, he hasn't returned my call. I can't get hold of Lance, either."

"Why don't you and I pay Rhinehart a visit? I'll pick you up in ten minutes."

"Okay, and bring your shotgun." He hung up.

Stone armed himself, put on a jacket and waited at the end of the driveway for Rawls, who turned up quickly in his Range Rover. He got into the car.

"Tell me about this guy," Rawls said.

"Master burglar, very sharp mind."

"How'd he meet Holly?"

"I took her to his workshop; she wanted to

meet him for herself. We both eliminated him as a suspect after that visit. The guy has a successful business, which he inherited from his father, and he has a wife and a baby. He seemed stable and happy with his circumstances."

"Is he strong enough to overpower Holly?"

"Yes, if he could neutralize her before she could get hold of her weapon."

"That's good enough for me," Rawls said.

They had passed through the village and were headed north. "There's the sign up ahead," Stone said. "Drive on past, and we'll work our way back."

Rawls drove past the house without slowing and, when he saw a narrow road to the right, cut his lights and turned in, using his gears to slow the big vehicle so as not to use his brakes, thus turning on the brake lights. Through the trees on their right they could see both the workshop and the house. The workshop was dark, but lights burned in the house windows.

"How do you want to do this?" Rawls asked, grabbing his shotgun from the rear seat.

"First, let's check the workshop and any

outbuildings," Stone said. "Then we'll see what we can see through the house windows."

"All right. Is this guy likely to have an alarm system?"

"Yes," Stone said. "Come on." He began walking through the trees toward the workshop, and Rawls followed.

HOLLY CAME TO SLOWLY. Her head hurt on the right side. She tried to put a hand to it, but found herself spread-eagled on a bed, her hands and feet tied. Her mouth was taped shut, and so were her eyes. There was something in each ear, too, shutting out sound.

All she could do was smell, and she concentrated on that. Mildew. Maybe saltwater. She tried rolling back and forth on the bed as far as she could, to see if she could feel the weight of her firearm. She thought it was still there. The bed made squeaking noises. Bare springs under a thin mattress. The mildew smell was coming from the mattress. Old. Disused. She thought she picked up the smell of rotting wood, too.

She tried twisting her hands and feet to

shake loose at least one limb. She felt the head of an iron bedstead, rusted. She was tied to that. God, her head hurt.

STONE AND RAWLS worked their way around the workshop to the side away from the house. A breeze brought the scent of the sea, apparently not far away, through the trees. Stone could see some small source of light inside the workshop, and he crept closer for a look through a window.

Suddenly, they were bathed in bright light. "Shit, motion detectors," Stone said. "That'll bring him running. Let's get out of here."

They ran in the direction opposite the one they had come, hiding behind some bushes. They flushed a deer, which ran toward the house as the porch light of the house came on and Hal Rhinehart came out the door, a shotgun in his hand. He raised it to his shoulder for a shot at the animal, but it was gone. "It was just a deer," he shouted to his wife.

He came toward the workshop, the shot-gun at the ready, and circumnavigated it, then went back into the house and turned off the porch light.

"That was a near thing," Rawls said.

"Yes, it was. I'm glad he didn't have a dog with him."

"You think the house has those lights, too?"

"Probably. I expect he has two alarm systems, one for the workshop and one for the house. You noticed that only the porch light went on when he came out?"

"Yeah, he probably hadn't armed the system."

"He may have by now."

"You've been inside the workshop?"

"Yes, a couple of times."

"What's in there?"

"A big workroom with a lot of power tools, an office, a storeroom, or what appeared to be one. Probably a paint shop, too."

"Let's see if there are any other outbuildings," Rawls said.

They walked through the woods, keeping the house on their left. "All I see is what appears to be a shed for tools or wood," Stone said.

"Well, Young and his crowd would have

searched the premises by now, wouldn't they?"

"I don't know where the hell they are," Stone said.

He didn't know where the hell Holly was, either.

42

HOLLY WOKE UP with a start. It had been chilly, but it was warming up. Must be daylight. The tape over her eyes allowed no light to enter. She needed to pee really badly, and she struggled again with her bonds, trying to free herself. If she could just get one hand free . . .

Then she heard a noise, a door closing. Footsteps, lightly, on stairs, then somebody was in the room with her. She tried to speak but could only make noises through her nose. She listened carefully.

Someone approached the bed where she lay. There was a metallic clank next to the bed, then whoever he was grabbed her sweatpants by the thighs and pulled them down. She struggled, but he pulled down the cotton underwear she was wearing, too, then put an arm under her waist, lifted her off the bed and shoved something made of cold metal under her ass. A bedpan. She peed, long and gratefully.

When she had finished, he removed the bedpan, pulled her panties and sweatpants up. Then she heard the sound of paper or cellophane being crinkled. Suddenly, the tape was ripped off her mouth.

"What the hell . . ." she was saying, but something was crammed into her mouth, filling it. Candy bar. She chewed madly, trying to swallow so she could talk, but the second she got it down, he was pouring water into her mouth. She swallowed, washing down the candy bar, but before she could speak, she heard a ripping noise, and her mouth was taped again. Duct tape, she reckoned. He seemed to inspect her bonds, one at a time, to be sure they hadn't loosened.

She heard him walk across the room and open a door, then the sound of the bedpan being emptied and a toilet being flushed, then running water. He walked down the stairs, and she heard a door open and close. He hadn't said a word.

STONE LAY ON HIS BED trying to sleep, telling himself he would be no good to Holly if he was exhausted. Finally, very late he dozed off. He woke to the sound of the ringing telephone. He rolled over in bed and grabbed it. "Hello?"

"It's Sergeant Young. Has Holly returned?"

"No, Sergeant, she hasn't, and I'm beyond being just worried."

"I'm sorry I didn't get your message earlier, but I've been to the mainland and back."

"Can you keep an eye out for her in your search?"

"We've completed most of the search," Young said. "I had forty people tramping every foot of the island, and we've done two-thirds of it. Then the second woman's body was found, and I called it off because nobody was missing anymore."

Stone looked at his watch: eight-fifteen. "Well, you've got to get the search going again," he said, "because whoever is doing this has taken Holly, and he's getting more dangerous."

"Why more dangerous?"

"It's a pattern with some serial killers: Their pace accelerates, they enjoy it more and more. Sometimes they become more reckless, as if they want to get caught."

"But some of these people go on for years, almost on a regular schedule."

"Not this guy. He wants more and more, and he's getting it. He may stop for a few days, but he won't be able to resist starting again. Three women in less than forty-eight hours: Doesn't that tell you something?"

"I'll get on the phone and get some people together. What time did you last see Holly yesterday?"

"About noon, when I went to lunch with Caleb Stone."

"So we can ignore the parts of the island we searched after noon and concentrate on the rest."

"Good idea. Have you searched Hal Rhinehart's place?"

"Not yet."

"Please go there first."

"Why?"

"Rhinehart has a criminal background.

Dino and I got him for a series of high-end burglaries in New York years ago. He's done time."

"Did any of the burglaries have sexual overtones? Did he rape any of his victims?"

"Not that we knew of, but still . . ."

"All right, we'll start there."

"I want to come with you."

"I'll pick you up in half an hour." Young hung up.

Stone got dressed and had some cereal in the kitchen while Mabel protested that he should eat some bacon and eggs. He was waiting at the roadside when Young drove up in his patrol car. There were two men in the backseat who looked more like locals than summer people. Young introduced them, then drove on north.

"You don't look so good," he said as he drove.

"I didn't get any real sleep," Stone said. "I'm tired."

"I understand."

They reached the Rhinehart sign and turned into the drive. Hal Rhinehart came out of the house as they drove up, apparently on the way to work.

"Morning," he said, looking doubtfully at the four men. "What's going on?"

"Mr. Rhinehart," the sergeant said, "we need to search your place."

"Have you got a warrant?"

Stone spoke up. "Come on, Hal," he said, "we're looking for a woman who disappeared yesterday. You know we can get a warrant, but if you don't let us search, then you'll automatically be a suspect. Just let us get this done."

"All right," Rhinehart said, "look wherever you want. I was just about to open the shop." He handed Stone a key. "Let yourself in while I tell my wife what's going on."

"Stone," the sergeant said. "You take one man and go through the workshop. We'll take a look in the house."

Stone headed for the shop followed by his fellow searcher. He unlocked the door and walked in. "Here's how we do this," he said to the man. "You take that side of the shop. Look in every room, every closet, every cupboard, every box—anyplace that's big enough to hide a human being. Look particularly for trapdoors that might hide a stairway to a basement. Don't miss anything."

The man nodded and started his work.

Stone went into Rhinehart's office and, trying not to make a mess, searched every corner of it, pulling back a rug to expose the floorboards. Satisfied there was nothing there, he opened another door and found a storeroom full of tools and paint cans. He moved everything that might conceal another door or a trapdoor. Nothing. He moved on to the paint shop and was joined by the other man.

"I didn't find nothing, and I looked hard," the man said.

Stone nodded, and the two of them continued their work. Finally, satisfied that no one was hidden in the workshop, they walked to the house. The front door stood open.

"Hello," Stone called. He opened the screen door and walked in. Nobody was in sight. He walked through the nicely furnished living room to the kitchen, where he found Mrs. Rhinehart feeding her baby. "Good morning," he said. "I hope we're not causing you too much trouble."

"It's all right," she replied. "I know you've got to find that lady who's missing."

"Where is Sergeant Young?"

"I think they're all in the cellar," she said, pointing toward a hallway.

Stone walked into the hall and found an open door, with stairs leading down. He walked downstairs and found Sergeant Young and his other searcher standing, talking to Rhinehart.

"Anything in the workshop?" Young asked.

"Nothing."

Rhinehart turned to Stone. "This is because of my record, isn't it?"

"Hal, they're searching every house and outbuilding on the island," Stone replied. "Every structure has to be cleared, and the woods and beaches, too. It was just your turn."

Rhinehart nodded.

"I think we're about done here," Young said.

They all trooped up the stairs. Young thanked Rhinehart and apologized for the intrusion, and the four men got into Young's cruiser.

"I guess that clears Rhinehart," Young said.

"I guess so," Stone replied.

"I'm taking you home so you can get some rest."

"All right."

Young dropped Stone at the top of the driveway. "I'll call you the minute we find anything."

Stone noted that he didn't say "Holly" or "her." She had already become an object.

43

STONE WENT BACK TO THE HOUSE, and Mabel brought a sandwich on a tray to the study.

"You look terrible," she said. "Eat; you need your strength."

"Mabel, when was the last time you saw Holly?"

"Well, after you left for your lunch appointment, she had a sandwich, then she did some work in that little room of Dick's while I was vacuuming, then she changed into her running clothes and went out. I saw her stretching when I took out the garbage."

"What time was that?"

"Pretty close to one o'clock," she replied.

Stone looked at his watch. Holly had been

missing for twenty-four hours. After that long, the chance of recovering her alive fell off sharply as the hours passed. And after forty-eight hours, she was very likely dead. There were exceptions, he knew, and that was what kept the hopes of friends and relatives of missing people alive. There was that girl out in Utah who was kidnapped and held for more than a year. But that rarely happened.

Thinking of friends and family, he suddenly had an awful thought: He had not called Hamilton Barker, Holly's retired master-sergeant father. He opened his address book and picked up the phone.

"Hello?"

"Ham?"

"Yep."

"It's Stone Barrington."

Ham's voice brightened. "Hey, Stone, how are you?"

"Not so good."

He became wary. "What's happened?"

"It's Holly; she's disappeared."

"What do you mean, 'disappeared'?"

"First of all, Holly and I are on an island in Maine called Islesboro. There have been some kidnappings and murders here; some of them were women."

"Anybody who tried to kidnap Holly would have his hands full," Ham said.

"I know that," Stone agreed. "Nevertheless, she went out jogging yesterday at this time, and she hasn't been seen since. A search of the whole island is under way, but she hasn't been found yet."

"What's the name of the island again?"

"Islesboro; it's in Penobscot Bay."

"Hang on a minute." Ham left the phone, and Stone could hear him talking to a woman, probably Ginny, his girlfriend. "Stone, I've got an atlas here. I see Penobscot Bay."

"It's a long, narrow island off Camden."

"Got it. Does it have an airport?"

"Yes."

"Here's Ginny, tell her about it."

Ginny picked up an extension. "Hello, Stone?"

"Yes, Ginny. Nice to hear your voice."

"Tell me about the airport."

"It's a paved strip, twenty-four hundred feet long; the runways are one and one niner. The identifier is five seven bravo, and the unicom frequency is 122.9."

Ham spoke up. "We're on our way, Stone. We'll call you from our fuel stop and give you an ETA. Can you meet us?"

"Wait a minute, Ham," Stone said. "The strip is unlighted, and there's no way you can get here before dark in . . . what are you flying?"

"A Bonanza B-36TC," Ginny replied. "We just bought it."

"It's a good twelve hundred nautical miles, so you're at least six or seven hours away; even with a tailwind by the time you're airborne it will be mid-afternoon."

"We're coming," Ham said.

"I want you to come, Ham, but please, at least spend the night at your fuel stop. There are trees at the southern end of the runway and a house at the other end. It's a short strip, and you do not want to land there at night."

"He's right, Ham," Ginny said. "We'll take off this afternoon, spend the night along the way and take off again early tomorrow morning. We'll be there around mid-morning."

"All right," Ham said, resignedly.

"Call me when you take off tomorrow

morning, give me your ETA and I'll meet you at the strip."

"Okay," Ginny said. She gave him her cell phone number. "Call us if there's any news. I'll get the message at the fuel stop."

"All right," Stone said, "and I'll have a bed for you here."

Ham spoke up again. "Stone, where's Daisy?"

"Holly left her in a kennel in New York."

"Goodbye," Ham said, and hung up.

Stone hung up. Now he was going to have a distraught father on his hands, not that Ham was the sort to show his distress.

The phone rang. "Hello?"

"Stone, it's Lance. I'm sorry to take so long to get back to you, but I've had something of an emergency here. I tried to call Holly on her cell phone, but I was sent straight to voice mail. What's happened?"

Stone told him, as briefly as possible.

"What's being done?"

"The state cops have organized a search party, and they're walking every inch of land and searching every house on the island."

"Good. I may be able to help with that."

"I think they've got it covered, Lance."

"I have other ways of covering it. I can't

get there before tomorrow morning, though. Will you meet me at the airport?"

"Of course. What time?"

"Let's aim for eleven o'clock. I'll call you if there's any change in my ETA."

"Lance, a favor. Will you bring Dino with you?"

"Of course."

"And bring sidearms."

"Of course. Is there anything else I can do for you?"

"One other thing: Bring Daisy."

"She's not with Holly?"

"No, she's in a kennel. I don't know which one."

"I'll find her. See you tomorrow."

Stone hung up feeling a little better. Help was on the way.

44

STONE STOOD AT THE Islesboro airstrip and scanned the skies. Seth Hotchkiss stood beside him.

"There," Seth said, pointing.

Stone followed Seth's finger to a black dot low in the sky. "You have an eagle eye, Seth."

"So did my daddy. Runs in the family. Which lot is in this airplane?" Seth had brought his pickup truck to help.

Stone squinted. "This is the Bonanza, I think. Holly's father, Ham, and his girlfriend, Ginny, who's the pilot, will be in that. I'd like you to take them back to the house and get them settled in a guest room, while I wait for the other bunch. I'll put Lance and Dino in the guest house."

"Ayup," Seth replied.

The Bonanza was straight in for runway one now, and he saw the landing gear come down and heard Ginny reducing power. She cleared the trees and dropped the airplane on the numbers, braking hard. Stone stood on the tarmac, his hands raised, to show her where to park.

Ham was out of the airplane immediately, even though Ginny had to let the engine idle for five minutes to allow the turbocharger to cool before shutting down.

"How are you, Ham?" Stone asked, shaking his hand.

"Not good. Any news?"

Stone shook his head. "Let's hope no news is good news. Shall we get your gear into the truck?"

The two men opened the rear doors and transferred Ham's and Ginny's luggage to the pickup, then Ginny shut down the engine, stepped out onto the wing and locked the door behind her. She jumped down and gave Stone a hug.

"I'm going to send you back to the house with Seth Hotchkiss, here," Stone said, introducing them. "I have to wait for Lance Cabot and Dino Bacchetti; they'll be here any minute. Seth and his wife, Mabel, will get you settled. We should be there in time for lunch. I've asked the state policeman in charge, Sergeant Young, to come over early in the afternoon."

Ham nodded and ushered Ginny into the pickup. They had been gone perhaps ten minutes when Stone heard, before he saw, another airplane. Five minutes later a Pilatus PC12, a big, Swiss, single-engine turbo-prop, had taxied to parking and cut its engine. Daisy was the first out, running to Stone and making a fuss over him. Lance and Dino followed, while the pilot put their luggage into the station wagon. Stone got it started and headed for the house.

"Any developments?" Lance asked.

"None at all. Dead silence. At least no-body has found a body, as in the other cases."

Dino spoke up. "I don't see how anybody could take Holly."

"It's not that hard," Lance said. "Even a well-trained, aware person can be lulled into thinking he's safe long enough to be cap-tured or killed."

"Thanks for bringing Daisy," Stone said.

"It was harder getting her out of that kennel than getting an agent out of a foreign jail. Dino's badge did the trick, finally. I had to sign a form, releasing them from all liability."

"You said you had some other means of searching for Holly," Stone said to Lance.

Lance glanced at his watch. "I do, but it will be another couple of hours before the materials will be in my hands."

AT THE HOUSE, Lance went directly to Dick's secret office and got on the computer. Stone watched as he loaded a stack of acetate sheets into the printer.

"Now we wait," Lance said. "Is lunch ready?"

They sat down around the kitchen table, while Mabel served the food and Stone took everybody through every step of the past two days.

"Any questions?" Stone asked, finally.

Ham spoke up. "Is it true that after forty-eight hours the chances of getting a missing person back are about nil?"

"No, it's not true," Stone said. "Not in this situation, at least."

"Why not this situation?"

"First, because it's Holly, and she is much more capable of dealing with these circumstances than your average abductee. If she has even the slightest opportunity, she'll kill her abductor and get out of wherever she is. It's unlikely that he has any notion of how much danger he's in."

Ham nodded, seeming to take some comfort in that idea.

They were on coffee when Lance looked at his watch. "Excuse me, I want to see if I've had anything from Langley yet." He got up and left the table.

Seth came in from outdoors. "Stone, can you come down to the dock for a minute? There's something I want to show you."

"We're expecting Sergeant Young shortly, Seth. Can it wait?"

"I don't think so," Seth said.

Stone got up and followed, and everybody else followed Stone. Seth led them down to the dock where Dick's yacht and the Hinckley picnic boat were docked.

"This is what caught my attention," Seth said, pointing at a corner of the picnic boat's stern. "Did you do that by any chance?"

The corner was damaged, as if it had been hit from above by something heavy.

"No, I didn't," Stone said. "This boat was pristine the last time I was aboard."

"I didn't think so," Seth said. He produced a bucket with a Plexiglas bottom. "Come over here and take a look." He put the bottom of the bucket in the water astern of the boat and held it while Stone looked into it. The six-foot-deep water, which was clear but dark, became even clearer. A cubical object about eighteen inches on each side came dimly into view, half sunk into the muddy bottom.

"It's got to be the safe," Stone said.

"What safe?" Dino asked.

"Dick's safe from the study. Somebody got into the house and sawed it out of where it was bolted to a shelf in a cupboard."

Seth said, "I reckon the feller muscled it down here to the dock to load it on a boat, and he slipped up and dropped it, hitting the boat's transom. The safe went into the water, and nobody could get it out of there alone without some equipment."

"Seth," Stone said, "is there a wet suit among Dick's stuff?"

"Yes, in the garage," Seth said, "but it's Dick's size, and he was smaller than you or me."

"Would it fit Dino?"

"Hey, wait a minute," Dino said.

"I reckon it would," Seth replied.

"Will you take Dino inside and get him into the wet suit? Hit him over the head, if you have to. Then find some rope and a shovel."

DINO STOOD ON THE dock wearing the wet suit, a mask and a snorkel. "Now what?" he asked.

"It's going to be just like that time you told me about in the Bahamas," Stone said. "Remember how much you enjoyed the snorkeling?"

"This is Maine, not the Bahamas," Dino said. "That water is fucking cold."

"That's why you're wearing the wet suit," Stone said. "See? We've thought of your every need."

"But . . ."

Stone pushed him into the water.

Dino sputtered to the surface. "You're going to pay for that, goddammit!"

"Now, here's what you do," Stone said,
handing him a shovel and a length of rope.

45

STONE LET THE water drain off the safe, then dried it carefully, before he and Seth carried it into the house.

"What do you think it weighs?" Stone asked Seth.

"Fifty, sixty pounds," Seth replied.

"Could one man handle it?"

"You want to try?"

"Nope."

"I reckon a pretty strong fella could handle it. 'Course, he might drop it trying to get it into a boat."

They got the safe into the study, laid some newspapers on the desk and rested the steel box on top of it, lying on its back.

Lance was working away at the computer in Dick's office.

"The dial is gone," Stone said.

Lance spoke up. "That means they tried to open it, failed, then sawed it out of the cabinet."

Stone peered at the safe closely. He could see the bolt that locked it through the crack between the door and the jamb. "I don't have a clue how to handle this," he said.

"Send Dino back in the water to look for the dial," Lance said. "It'll simplify things."

Dino was out on the deck, half out of the wet suit. Stone went out and broke the news to him.

"Your turn," Dino said.

"Put it back on, Dino; you're the only one the suit fits."

Dino sighed and began struggling back into the wet suit. "What am I looking for again?"

"The dial from the front of the safe. It's got to be . . ." Stone stopped. "Wait a minute." He went back into the study and opened the cabinet where the safe had been. He rummaged through some papers on the shelf below, and his hand found something of solid metal. He held up the dial. "Never mind, Dino; I found it."

"Great!" Dino yelled from the deck and started getting out of the wet suit again.

"Got it, Lance," Stone called.

"In a minute," Lance replied. He made more key-tapping noises in the little office.

Dino came into the study in a towel. "I'm going to get a shower," he said. "Anything else that has to be retrieved from the bottom is gonna be retrieved by somebody else."

"All right, all right," Stone said.

"And remember, I have a gun." Dino went through the kitchen out to the guest house, where he and Lance each had a room.

Lance came out of the little office. "Okay, let me have the dial," he said.

Stone handed it to him.

Lance inspected the safe closely, then fitted the dial back onto the stem protruding from the front of the safe. "Now we find out whether it's on right, or whether I have to take it off again and rotate it a hundred and eighty degrees. I don't suppose any of you has a stethoscope on you?"

They all looked at him blankly.

"That's what I thought." He pressed an

ear to the safe and began slowly rotating the dial.

"I didn't know you were a safecracker, Lance," Stone said.

"Jack of all trades, definitely master of none."

"Holly opened it, now that I recall."

"We attended the same safecracking academy. Now be quiet; I can't listen to you and the safe at the same time."

Stone walked over to an easy chair and took a seat.

Lance stood up straight, turned the handle on the safe door, opened it and peered inside. "It's a mess," he said.

Stone walked back to the desk and looked inside the safe. The estate papers he had stored in it were a sodden mass. He lifted them out in a big lump and deposited them on the newspaper. Then he reached inside and brought out Esme's diary. It was heavier than before, being soaking wet. He opened the cover and found the pages stuck together, the ink running.

"Have you got a hair dryer?" Lance asked.

"In my bathroom upstairs," Ginny replied.

"Ginny," Lance said, "would you like to help?"

"Of course," she replied, running over to the desk.

"Will you take the diary upstairs, put it on a table and start drying it?"

"Sure."

Lance reached into a desk drawer and found a letter opener. "Use this to separate the pages as they dry, but don't force them."

"Okay." Ginny took the diary and went upstairs.

A bell sounded in Dick's little office almost simultaneously with the front doorbell.

Lance disappeared into the office, and Seth went to the front door and came back with Sergeant Young, who looked tired.

Stone introduced him to Ham; he'd already met everybody else.

"Anything new?" Stone asked.

"I'm afraid not. We've pretty much started the search over again, and this time we're concentrating on the beaches and shoreline."

"Why?" Ham asked.

Sergeant Young looked away.

Stone spoke up. "Because the bodies of the missing women were all found in the water."

Ham nodded.

Lance came out of the office. "Afternoon, Sergeant," he said, placing several sheets of acetate on the desk. "I have something that might be of use to you in your search. Do you have a current map of the island?"

"A very good one, showing all the houses," Young replied. "I'll get it out of my car." He was back in a moment and spread the map on the desk. "This is the latest map available that shows all the occupied buildings. You can see, I've highlighted the ones already searched in green."

"I see you're better than half finished," Lance said. He picked up a sheet of acetate and laid it next to the map. "This is a thermal image of the island taken from a satellite last night, or rather an image of the north end of the island. In order to get in close, we divided the island in half. This particular image was taken at nine P.M. last evening."

Everybody crowded around. "As you can see, anything that radiates heat shows up in orange, to a greater or lesser degree." He pointed at a house in the village. "Take this house, for example: There's quite a lot of ambient light, and these concentrations are people," he said, pointing to a group, "apparently gathered around the table, having dinner. Outside, you can see another orange object, which is the family car, its engine still warm."

"That's very sensitive," Young said.

"Too sensitive, in fact," Lance replied. "I've ordered other images for after midnight, on the next satellite pass. In those, we'll find many fewer lights and TVs on in the houses, and the car engines will have cooled. What we'll see then is people in their beds."

"What's this in the middle of the woods?" Young asked, pointing to a dark area with an orange spot near the north end of the island.

"Very likely a deer, maybe two," Lance said. "The satellite can pick up heat sources as small as a dog."

Daisy raised her head and made a noise.

"Good dog," Ham said.

"I'm not sure exactly how this will be useful," Young said. "I mean, we can go to every house, search it and count the folks. Maybe we could see if there's somebody extra that we didn't count."

"Right," Lance said. "The after-midnight images should be more useful. Then we can see if there's a person where we don't expect a person to be, in a garage or a woodshed, for instance."

Ham spoke up. "I don't suppose it will pick up a dead body?"

Everybody got quiet. Lance shook his head. "Not unless it's still warm."

46

THE AFTERNOON WORE ON until the shadows were long. Ham, who was asleep on the study sofa, suddenly sat up. "Daisy!" he said.

"What?" Stone asked.

"We're not using Daisy!"

"For what?"

"To track Holly."

Stone slapped his forehead. "Why didn't I think of that?" He ran upstairs to the master bedroom and started going through Holly's clothes, looking for something that had been worn and not laundered, which was tough, because Mabel laundered everything as soon as it hit the hamper. He found a spare pair of sneakers and ran back down-stairs with one.

"Come on, Daisy!" he called to the dog. He grabbed her leash and ran for the door, with Ham and Dino right behind him. When they reached the end of the driveway, Stone rubbed the sneaker on Daisy's face, and she sniffed it eagerly. "Has she been trained to track?" he asked Ham.

"She's been trained to do just about everything," Ham replied. "Daisy! Where's Holly? Go find Holly!"

Daisy reacted at once, pacing around the area, then suddenly, she was moving at a brisk trot up the road, away from the village, on the left side, facing traffic, her nose to the ground. The three men hurried along, trying to keep up with her.

"We should have brought a car," said Dino, who did not enjoy running.

"Why don't you go back to the house and get the station wagon," Stone said, handing him the keys. "Follow along, but don't get close enough to spook Daisy."

The sound of her name caused Daisy to jerk the leash almost out of Stone's hand, and she resumed her tracking.

Stone and Ham jogged along after her,

and a couple of minutes later Stone looked over his shoulder and saw Dino in the station wagon, moving slowly twenty yards behind them.

Daisy rounded a curve and started down half a mile of straight road. Then, after a couple of hundred yards, she stopped, seeming confused. She paced about, sniffing the road and the graveled shoulder, circling back and doing the same area again.

Ham unclipped her leash and pointed at the dense underbrush beside the road. "There, Daisy," he said, pointing, "go find Holly."

Daisy plunged into the brush, and they could hear her crashing around in the thicket, going this way and that, until she came back to Ham and sat down, looking at him.

"It happened here," Stone said. "She was put into a car."

"I don't think a dog can track a car," Ham said.

Dino pulled alongside them in the old Ford wagon. "That's it, huh?"

"That's it," Stone said. "At least we're sure of which way she went." He looked down the road. "South."

They got into the car and drove back to the house.

"Any luck?" Sergeant Young asked as they came into the study.

"Holly ran south, then on a straight stretch. She got put into a car, so we're at a dead end. But at least we know she ran south. Should we concentrate the search there?"

"In a car, she could have been taken anywhere," Young pointed out.

"She could have been taken off the island in a boat, too," Dino said.

"None of the others was taken off the island," Stone reminded him. "I think this guy will stick to his pattern."

"I need a drink," Dino said, heading for the wet bar. "Anybody else?"

Stone looked at the group. "Everybody else."

"I still don't have the after-midnight thermal scan," Lance said.

Dino came back with drinks on a tray. "How's Ginny doing with the diary?"

"She'll let us know when she gets somewhere," Ham said.

They sipped their drinks quietly.

"At least we know the guy's got a boat,"

Stone said. "Otherwise, he wouldn't have dropped the safe in the water trying to get it out of here."

Sergeant Young, who was staring into his drink but not drinking it, spoke up. "Just about everybody on the island has a boat."

"Yeah," Stone said, racking his brain for some other thought that might help.

Ginny came down the stairs with the diary and some sheets of paper. Everybody stood up as she walked toward the desk.

"What have you got, Hon?" Ham asked.

"Are you people drinking?" she asked. "Why am I not drinking?"

"Dino, get the girl some bourbon," Ham said, looking over her shoulder as she spread out her papers.

"What I'm doing here is working backward through the thing, drying pages one at a time, then trying to read the handwriting. It's gorgeous handwriting, but the ink has run from being wet, and that makes it slow going, but I'm copying out everything I can get and numbering the pages to correspond with the diary."

"What is she saying?" Stone asked.

"Well, it's mostly high school girl stuff," she said. "The last entry is the day before the family got to Islesboro. She mentions that they have to make the five o'clock ferry the next day."

"Is there any other mention of Islesboro or Dark Harbor in the days before they arrived?"

"She's looking forward to going, she says, and right here, she mentions that and says "'. . . especially with X and Y neutralized.'"

"Any idea what that can mean?" Stone asked.

"There's a Z mentioned, too."

"Are these people male or female?"

"Z seems to be female, but I can't tell about X and Y. These could be friends of hers at school."

"But what does she mean by 'neutralized'?"

"I don't know. 'Made harmless,' maybe?"

"How do you make somebody harmless?"

"Take away their weapons; take away their freedom of action?"

"How far back have you gotten?"

"January," Ginny said. "It's slow going."

"She's glad to be going back to Islesboro, now that X and Y are neutralized," Stone said. "X and Y must be on Islesboro, too."

"Z, too," Ginny pointed out. "She says that Z will be relieved, too."

"So, both Esme and Z would have been anxious about returning to Islesboro for the summer, if X and Y hadn't been neutralized?"

"That could fit what she's saying."

"Does she give any hint about why they have to be neutralized?"

"Not so far."

"Go back further in the diary, Ginny. Go back to last summer, say the month of August."

"That part of the diary is in very poor condition," Ginny said, "but I'll try." She grabbed her drink from Dino and went back upstairs.

"Dinner will be ready soon," Stone called after her. "We'll let you know." He sank back into a chair.

A bell chimed in the little office, and Lance got to his feet. "Something coming in," he said. "Maybe the new thermal scan." He went into the office. A moment later he came out with some sheets of paper.

"What is it?" Stone asked.

"It's a report from one of our people who used to be a Boston cop. You remember, we checked to see if Caleb Stone had a criminal record? His boys, too."

"Yes, and they were all clean. The report from the New Haven police and the Yale campus cops had the boys clean there."

"Well, this isn't much," Lance said, "but the boys had a juvenile record."

"For what?"

"Don't know; the records are sealed."

"Can your man get at them?"

Lance got up and walked back toward the office. "I'll ask him to try."

Stone got up and followed him. "There's something else I'd like to know from New Haven."

47

HOLLY CAME SLOWLY out of sleep, but being awake wasn't much different. She wondered if he was giving her something to make her sleep; she seemed to be doing an awful lot of it. Not that she had anything else to do.

He was giving her precious little sensory input. He came in four or five times a day, she thought. He emptied her, fed her another candy bar and gave her water. Maybe something in the water? She certainly had not felt wide awake since the first day. How many days was it? Two? Three? Four? She couldn't tell. The tape over her eyes kept her from knowing whether it was day or night, and the ear plugs muffled most sound.

He didn't seem interested in sex; he hadn't touched her in any way, except to pull her clothing down for the bedpan. He hadn't found her gun, either, since the sweatshirt covered it, even when she was using the bedpan. If she could just get a hand free. She tried again, but it only hurt worse. Her wrists felt bruised and chafed from trying to get loose.

Why would he keep her, hour after hour, day after day? What use would he make of her? If he wanted her dead, she'd already be dead; if he wanted sex, she'd have already been raped. It didn't make any sense at all. She yawned and dozed off again.

LANCE CAME OUT OF Dick's little office with a sheet of paper. "The FBI has come to life," he said. "They've given us a profile, done by their experts."

Sergeant Young, who had seemed almost asleep, came to life. "I want to hear this."

"He's between twenty-five and forty," Lance read, "lives with his mother, is employed as a skilled laborer or as a white-collar worker with considerable responsibility. His father is dead or was divorced from his mother when he was a child. He's uncomfortable around women, especially those who dress in an overtly sexual manner. People who know him think of him as quiet and pleasant. He's not married, nor does he have a regular sex life."

"The dress code doesn't sound like any of our victims," Young said, "except Janey Harris, who wore the kind of clothes teenaged girls wear these days: you know, bare bellies almost to the crotch, tight T-shirts, that sort of thing. It certainly doesn't fit the two housewives."

"It doesn't fit Holly, either," Stone said. "Any more of the profile?"

Lance shook his head. "They make the usual disclaimers about the accuracy of the profile, and they say they need more to go on."

"I wish to God we could give it to them," Sergeant Young said.

They all sat quietly for a few minutes.

"Anybody want to go for a boat ride?" Stone asked.

"What?" Dino said.

"I'm going to take the picnic boat and circumnavigate the island, while there's still plenty of daylight."

Sergeant Young stood up. "I'd better get back to the land search; I'm not doing any good here."

"Ham, do you want to come?" Stone asked.

Ham shook his head. "I want to stay here in case Holly turns up, and Ginny is still working on Esme's diary."

"Grab a jacket, Dino," Stone said. "It'll be chillier on the water."

They met on the dock, and Stone started the engine. "Will you cast us off?" he said to Dino.

Dino undid the bow, stern and spring lines, then pushed them away from the dock and jumped on board.

"We've got to get you some Topsiders," Stone said.

"Huh?"

"Wingtips don't cut it on a boat." Stone switched on the GPS plotter and let it warm up. A few seconds later, an image of Islesboro appeared on the screen.

"Hey, that's neat," Dino said.

Stone played with the image. "Yes, and

you can zoom in and out, too." He dug out a paper chart from below and studied it.

"Can we get moving?" Dino asked.

"I just want to take a look at possible hazards," Stone said. "Maine is a rocky place."

"Good idea."

Fifteen minutes later they were under way. They passed the yacht club, which seemed mostly deserted.

"Where is everybody?" Dino asked.

"A lot of people have left the island," Stone said, "and Sergeant Young says a lot of those still here are staying home until this thing is resolved." Stone was staying close to shore, looking intently at the water.

"You looking for rocks?" Dino asked.

"No," Stone replied.

"Oh."

Stone continued to watch the water as they made their way toward the southern tip of the island. He hoped to God he didn't find what he was looking for. He zipped up his jacket against the breeze.

"Besides that, what should we be looking for?" Dino asked.

"Look for places ashore where she might be hidden," Stone replied.

"She could be hidden in any house on the island," Dino said.

"Most of the houses are occupied by families who are spending the summer here. Look for other outbuildings—barns, sheds, that sort of thing. If we find something that looks promising, we can always get Young and his people to go search it."

Dino looked intently toward the shore. "We're grasping at straws," he said.

"I know," Stone replied. "But I don't know what else to do."

48

STONE AND DINO ARRIVED back at the dock, tired and cold, a little after seven o'clock. They put out bumpers and made the picnic boat fast, then went into the house. Everybody was sitting around looking disconsolate.

Lance got up and went into the little office, silently waving Stone to follow him.

"What's up?" Stone asked.

"I've heard from our ex–Boston cop," he said. "He found nothing new in Caleb Stone's background, but something cropped up on his two sons, Eben and Enos. You remember, they had a sealed juvenile record."

"Yes. Was he able to crack it?"

"He was. The twins were arrested when

they were thirteen for torturing and killing small animals, neighborhood pets."

"That's a marker for later criminal behavior," Stone said.

"Yes, but there hasn't been any further criminal behavior. The boys got a year's probation, the family moved to another neighborhood and it was over."

"Anything else?"

"Yes. You asked me to check with the Yale campus police and the New Haven force."

"Right. Anything turn up?"

"Same as before with the Yale cops: They've had no problems with the twins. Neither has New Haven."

"But?"

"But, you were on the money about something else: There are four unsolved cases of kidnapping, rape and murder of women in New Haven over the past two years, none of them students. Three were townies, girls who hung out in local bars, and one was a young housewife."

"Is there anything to connect them to the twins?"

"No, there's nothing to connect them to anybody, so calling the twins suspects is a real stretch. You can't accuse them of four murders because they harmed some animals when they were kids."

Stone picked up the phone and called Sergeant Young's cell phone.

"This is Young."

"It's Stone Barrington. You have a list, don't you, of everybody who's present on the island and those who have left?"

"Yes, I do."

"Will you look up Caleb Stone's family? I'd like to know where they all are."

"Just a minute."

Stone could hear papers being shuffled.

Young came back on the line. "Caleb Stone and his wife are at home on the island; his twin sons left five days ago to participate in a yacht race in Newport, Rhode Island."

"Has the location of the twins been confirmed?"

"We confirmed that they took the ferry, but nothing after that."

"Will you see if you can confirm their location for every day since they left the island?"

"And this is important why?"

"We've learned that the boys have a juvenile record for torturing animals."

"That's not good."

"We've also learned that the City of New Haven has four unsolved murders of local women over the past two years. The boys are students at Yale."

"Yes, I know. Can they connect any of the murdered women to the twins?"

"They have no suspects."

"I've pretty much eliminated the twins as suspects here because of their absence from the island."

"I'd very much like to know if their presence in Newport can be confirmed."

"So would I. I'll call Mr. Stone and find out how to reach them."

"Thank you, Sergeant."

Young hung up.

"What do you think?" Lance asked.

"I think this theory is too thin to mention to Ham; he'd want to hunt down the boys. Still, we don't have anything else to go on, so this lead, however slim, needs to be run down, and Young is on it."

"Oh," Lance said, picking up some acetates, "we've got the thermal images for last night."

"Let's take them into the study; everybody needs to be involved, especially Ham. He's worrying me."

They left the little office.

"We've got last night's satellite thermal images of the island," Lance said.

Everybody gathered around the coffee table, and Lance spread them out and pointed as he talked. "As you can see, at three-twenty-six A.M., when these images were captured, the public parts of town are empty of warm bodies: The yacht club, the Dark Harbor Store, the dining room at the inn are all empty. Everybody is in bed, pretty much."

Ham pointed at a warm spot. "Is that a car?" he asked.

"Yes, probably a police car on patrol," Lance replied.

"What is all this telling us?" Ham asked.

"That people are where they're supposed to be. Nobody's out prowling the island, kidnapping people. They're all at home in bed."

"A lot of empty houses," Stone said.

"That's because so many people have left the island," Lance pointed out.

Mabel Hotchkiss came into the room and announced dinner.

They had finished dinner and were on coffee when the phone rang. Stone took it in the study.

"It's Tom Young," the sergeant said.

"What did you find out?"

"I called Caleb Stone and got a cell phone number for the twins, then I called the number and got voice mail instead of an answer."

"So we know nothing more about their whereabouts?"

"Not exactly. Eben called me back a few minutes later and reported that they were off Martha's Vineyard in a race around the Vineyard, Nantucket and Block Island, then back to Newport. They started this morning."

"Did you believe him?"

"I had no reason not to," Young said.

"If the race didn't start until this morning, then where have they been for the past four days?"

"According to Eben, in Newport, getting the boat ready for the race and partying. I called the Ida Lewis Yacht Club, who are running the race, and the twins are listed as crew on the yacht *Hotshot,* which is owned by a friend of theirs. They have a crew of six aboard."

"Did anybody remember seeing them in Newport before this morning?"

"Nobody at the yacht club. The boat was docked at a marina in town, and I've asked the Newport police to go down there and see if any of the staff remember seeing a pair of large identical twins there the past few days. They'll get back to me."

"Thanks, Sergeant. I'd like to know what you hear."

"I'll call you when I know something." Young hung up.

The others straggled into the study from dinner, Lance first.

"That was Young," Stone said. "He talked to one of the twins; they're aboard a yacht off Martha's Vineyard. He's asked the Newport police for help in placing them in the town over the past four days, and he'll get back to us when he hears something."

Dino played bartender for after-dinner drinks.

Stone didn't know whether to hope his two young cousins were involved in all this, but he wanted *something* to happen.

49

HOLLY FOUGHT TO stay awake. She had a plan now, and she had to have her wits about her when the guy came back to feed and empty her. She tried remembering things; that kind of mental activity might keep her awake. She tried remembering the names of everybody in her high school graduation class. There were only sixty of them at the small military high school in Germany, when Ham was still in the army.

She went through the girls first; they were the most difficult. The boys' names came quicker, starting with Burt Bonner, the athlete on whom she had bestowed her virtue when she was eighteen—bestowed it on him a number of times, in fact. She tried remembering the details of each bestowal; that kept her awake.

Then she heard, or rather felt, the footsteps on the stairs. The house must be fairly rickety, she thought, if she could feel footsteps. He went through his routine, but when he ripped off the tape over her mouth, she was ready for him.

"I have over a million dollars in an offshore bank account," she said quickly.

He crammed the chocolate bar into her mouth anyway.

Holly spat it out. "It's yours. I can wire-transfer it to any bank account in the world in seconds. You can open an account off-shore on the Internet. It's a million two hundred thousand dollars. You can go anywhere in the world on that. This is untraceable money. An offshore bank will give you a credit card that draws on your balance; you can use it anywhere in the world."

He poured water into her mouth, crammed the candy bar in again, and re-taped. Then he went back downstairs.

Did the guy live downstairs and she couldn't hear him because of the plugs in her ears? Or did he live somewhere else and just visit her here?

At least she had given him something to think about. Maybe greed was more powerful than sex or killing or whatever reason he had taken her. She dozed off again. Even the memory of Burt Bonner couldn't keep her awake.

STONE WAS STARTING to get cabin fever hanging around the house, waiting for something to happen. "I'm going to go and get the papers," he said to the group in the study. "Anybody need anything?"

Nobody said a word.

Stone left the house and drove the station wagon into Dark Harbor. He went into the Dark Harbor Shop, bought the *Times* and the Boston papers, then sat down at the counter and ordered some ice cream. He was absorbed in the front page of the *Times* when he heard a deep voice behind him.

"Let me have a box of Snickers bars," the familiar voice said.

Stone turned around to find Caleb Stone standing there.

"A whole box?" the girl behind the counter asked. "That's twenty-four bars."

"My wife likes them," Caleb said. "Good morning, Stone."

Caleb didn't look well. He was pale, and he seemed to have lost some weight.

"Good morning, Caleb. How are you?"

"So-so, I guess. You?"

"All right."

"Bad business about all these murders."

"Yes, it is."

"We're staying home with the doors locked," Caleb said.

"The boys, too?"

"No, they're on a yacht race somewhere off Newport. They left before it got really bad here."

"How are they doing in the race? Have you heard from them?"

"Got a call this morning," Caleb replied. "They were well up in the fleet, they said."

"When will they be back?"

"The race won't finish for another couple of days; they get into Nantucket tonight, where they'll have a lay day, then they'll start the return leg the day after tomorrow." Caleb signed a charge ticket, picked up his box of candy bars and gave a little wave. "See you later, Stone."

"Right, Caleb." Stone finished his ice cream, then headed back to the house.

He found Lance working in Dick's little office. He picked up the phone and dialed Sergeant Young's cell phone.

"This is Young."

"Sergeant, it's Stone Barrington."

"Good morning."

"Good morning. I just saw Caleb Stone in the Dark Harbor Shop, and he tells me the twins' yacht gets into Nantucket tonight, and they have a lay day there tomorrow. Can you get the local police to check quietly if they're actually aboard the boat?"

"I'll make a call," Young said.

"Will you let me know the result?"

"Be glad to." Young said goodbye and hung up.

Lance looked up from the computer. "You're still pursuing the twins angle?"

"What else have I got to pursue?" Stone said.

"Good point. I'm just reading through the notes of the various agents who checked into the Russian mob threat against Dick."

"You're still pursuing that lead?"

"What else have I got to pursue?" Lance

asked. "It's not as implausible as you might think."

"Well, if it's true, it means we have two killers: one of Dick and his family and possibly Don Brown, and one of the women."

"Unlikely, isn't it?"

"But not impossible," Stone said.

50

SERGEANT YOUNG'S CALL was forwarded to the cell phone of Lieutenant Jake Potter in Nantucket, who was sitting in a squad car in the middle of the village, watching tourists turn their ankles on the cobblestones. "Lieutenant Potter," he drawled into the phone.

"Lieutenant, this is Sergeant Tom Young of the Maine State Police."

"Morning, Sergeant, how's the weather in Maine today?"

"A little foggy."

"What can I do for you?"

"I don't know if you've heard about it, but we've had a series of murders on the island of Islesboro."

"I read the Boston papers."

"In connection with that investigation, I'm concerned about the whereabouts of two young men, twin brothers, named Eben and Enos Stone. They may be aboard a yacht in Nantucket. They sailed from Newport yesterday."

"As part of the race?"

"That's right."

"If you want me to arrest them we're going to need a fugitive warrant; you can fax it to us."

"It won't be necessary to arrest them," Young said. "Right now, I just need to determine whether they're actually aboard that boat."

"Description?"

"Identical twins, blond hair, tall—maybe six-three or six-four—over two hundred pounds, muscular."

"Well, I'm glad I don't have to arrest them."

Young chuckled. "It may come to that yet."

"Name of the boat?"

"Hotshot."

"Spell."

"Hotel, oscar, tango, sierra, hotel, oscar, tango."

"Length?"

"I'm afraid I don't have that information."

"Skipper's name?"

"Don't know."

"Home port?"

"Maybe Newport, but I'm not at all sure."

"That was Eldon and Elmer who?"

"No, that's Eben and Enos Stone. And Lieutenant, if you can find out if they're aboard without letting them know you're checking, I'd appreciate it. I don't want them to run."

"What do you want me to do if they try to run?"

"If they do, please try to find out where they're going and call me as soon as possible." Young gave the man his cell phone number.

"I could detain them on some charge or other, maybe dumping their holding tank in the marina."

"I don't think that would help. Anyway, it's not their boat."

"I could think of something else."

"Lieutenant, their father is a big-time Boston lawyer; I don't think that would be helpful. I just need to know if they're actually present on Nantucket."

"Tell me, Sergeant, how is knowing that going to help you?"

"Well, if they're on the boat, then their alibi for my time frame might be good."

"*Might* be good?"

"We're talking about a period of four days. They say they were in Newport until yesterday, partying, and the race started yesterday morning."

"Have you talked to the police in Newport?"

"Yes, and they're investigating as we speak."

"And you just want to know if they're on the boat."

"I want to know if they're on *Nantucket.*"

"And you don't want me to detain them?"

"No, sir, please don't do that."

"I guess you want the collar yourself, huh?"

"I don't have enough evidence for a collar. If they're on Nantucket, I'll have even less. If they're *not* on Nantucket, then I may have some basis on which to proceed."

"Well, I'll drive down to the marina and have a look around," the lieutenant said.

"Thank you, Lieutenant."

"And I'll call you at this number when I find out?"

"Please do that; I'll wait for your call."

"Bye-bye, Sergeant."

The lieutenant closed his cell phone, finished his coffee and started the car. He drove down to the main marina and parked his cruiser on a yellow curb and got out. He strolled down to the marina and walked into the dockmaster's office.

"Hey, Charlie," he said to the man behind the desk.

"Morning, Jake."

"You got a boat named . . ." He consulted his notebook. ". . . *Potshot*?"

Charlie picked up a clipboard and ran his finger down to the *P*s. "That's *Potshot*?"

"Right."

"Nope. Nothing by that name."

"It didn't come in here with the race from Newport?"

"It didn't come in here at all, with anybody."

Jake nodded. He flipped open his cell phone and called Maine.

"Sergeant Young."

"Sergeant, it's Jake Potter, in Nantucket."

"Yes, Lieutenant?"

"I'm down at the marina office; there's no boat by that name in the marina. It's not on the dockmaster's list."

"Well, that's pretty interesting," Young said.

"Anything else I can do for you?"

"Does the dockmaster have a list of people on the yachts?"

"Hang on, I'll ask him. Charlie, do you have a list of the people that come in here on these boats?"

Charlie shook his head. "Nope. I couldn't care less who comes in here on the boats; all I want to know is what I have to find space for."

"No, Sergeant, he doesn't have a list of people."

"Lieutenant, do you think you could just take a walk around the marina and see if there's a yacht named *Hotshot*?"

"Oh, you're looking for *another* boat, now?"

"No."

"I don't understand."

"I'm just looking for the one."

"Potshot?"

"No, not *Potshot, Hotshot*. With an *H* for *hotel*."

"Well, why didn't you say so?"

"Could you ask the dockmaster about *Hotshot,* please?"

"Hang on. Charlie, now he wants a boat named *Hotshot.* You got one of them?" Charlie picked up his clipboard and ran a finger down to the *H*s. "Yep, I've got just one *Hotshot*: dock three, berth fourteen."

"Sergeant?"

"Yes?"

"He's got a *Hotshot* all right: dock three, berth fourteen."

"Great! Could you go down there and have a look at it?"

"Sure."

"Wait a minute. I've got a better idea."

"What's that?"

"Let me speak to the dockmaster, please."

Jake handed his phone to Charlie.

"Charlie here."

"Charlie, this is Sergeant Young of the Maine State Police." He explained his problem and described the twins. "Rather than have a uniformed officer go down to the boat, could you or one of your people go to the boat and tell them there's a phone call for either Eben Stone or Enos Stone in your office?"

"But there isn't a phone call."

"I just want to know if they're on the boat. If they're not, ask if they're in the village or on the island somewhere."

"And if they are on the boat?"

"Ask for a cell phone number and tell them you'll refer the call."

"What call?"

"The imaginary call. If they want to know why the caller never called them, you don't know. All you did was give him the message."

"Okay. I can do that in a few minutes."

Young gave him the cell phone number. "Can I speak to the lieutenant again?"

"This is Jake."

"Lieutenant, thanks so much for your help."

"What help?"

51

JAKE POTTER POURED himself a cup of the dockmaster's coffee and gazed out the window at the yachts in their slips. This state cop, Young, from Maine had something real good going, he reflected. Multiple murders, serial killer, mucho publicity in the Boston papers and TV. Jake didn't like state cops; they always wanted to come in and take over a local investigation. They'd had a real good murder on Nantucket the previous summer, and the Massachusetts state cops were all over it like flies before Jake and his colleagues had really had a chance to break it.

He turned to the dockmaster. "Tell you what, Charlie," he said, setting down his coffee cup and starting to unbutton his shirt. "I'll go down there and check out *Hotshot*."

"Whatever," Charlie said, hardly looking up from his computer.

Jake took off his uniform shirt and his cap and hung them on a coatrack beside the door of the office. Now he was just a guy in a white T-shirt and khaki pants. He pulled the tail of his T-shirt out and pulled it down over his gunbelt, then he left the office and walked down the ramp to the docks, moving slowly, as was his wont. He strolled down to dock 3 and turned right. Long lines of yachts stretched out for many yards on both sides of the walkway.

Jake counted out the berths as he walked, not actually using his fingers, but moving his lips as he read the numbers. He came to berth 14. Two young men were lounging in the cockpit, drinking beer. Neither fit the description of the suspects. Jake walked down the catwalk alongside the yacht and stood next to the cockpit, maybe eight feet from where the two boys sat. They glanced at him, then went back to their conversation, dismissing any importance he might have.

They think I'm just another tourist, Jake thought with satisfaction. "Ahoy, there," he said.

One of the boys looked up at him. "Ahoy?" He chuckled. "What can we do for you, Popeye?"

"I'm looking for two twins," he consulted his notebook, "named Edwin and Elmer Stone?"

"Eben and Enos," the boy corrected.

"Yeah, them. Are they aboard?"

The boy waved a hand. "You see them?"

"Are they downstairs?"

"Downstairs?"

"Down there," Jake said, pointing at the cabin. He hated these Boston pups, the arrogant little sons of bitches.

"There's just us," the boy said.

"Where can I find, uh . . ."

"Eben and Enos?"

"Yeah."

"They went ashore a few minutes ago."

"Where ashore?"

"They had some stuff to buy, beer and stuff."

"When are they coming back?"

"Who knows? We don't sail until tomorrow."

"They got a phone call up at the dock-master's office."

The boy shrugged. "What can I tell you?"

"They got a cell phone number I can send the call to?"

"Yeah." The boy made a little face to show he was trying to remember, then he spat out a number. "Try them on that."

"Got it," Jake said, scribbling the number in his notebook. "Thanks, guys." He turned and walked back up the dock.

THE TWO BOYS WAITED until he was twenty feet away before they burst out laughing. One of them took a cell phone from his pocket and tapped in a number.

"Hello?"

"Which one is this?"

"Enos."

"A cop was just at the boat," he said. "Like you predicted. Funny guy; he actually said, 'Ahoy.'"

"Are you sure he was a cop? Was he in uniform?"

"He was wearing a white undershirt and khakis, and shiny black shoes and a web belt with a shiny brass buckle, and he had a white sidewall haircut, and there was a big bulge on his belt. Who else would he be?"

"What did he say?"

"He wanted you and Eben, and I told him you went ashore for beer. He said you had a call at the dockmaster's office, and I gave him your cell number."

"Okay."

"Everything all right?"

"Yeah, we had a great night with the girls, even if they are underage. Thanks for covering for us; we don't want to deal with their old man."

"Do it once for me."

"You bet."

BACK AT THE DOCKMASTER'S office, Jake got into his shirt and cap before calling Sergeant Young.

"This is Young."

"Hey, Jake Potter, in Nantucket."

"Yes, Jake. What did you find out?"

"I went down to the boat; your boys are here," Potter replied. "I got their cell phone number for you." He read it out.

"Yeah, I've already got that."

"You can reach them on that number,"

Jake said. "Good luck on your case, and don't forget who helped you."

"Thanks, Jake." Young hung up.

Jake strolled back to his car, got in and began driving slowly up the street, looking for a pair of identical giants carrying beer. He was going to keep an eye on these two, and if they did anything funny, he was going to be all over them.

Sergeant Tom Young put his cell phone back into his shirt pocket. "That was the cop from Nantucket," he said to Stone.

"They checked out the yacht?"

"Yes. The twins were aboard."

"So much for that theory," Stone said.

52

STONE WENT INTO Dick's little office, where Lance was working on the computer. "The Nantucket police have verified that the Stone twins are there, on the yacht."

Lance sighed. "I had hopes for that theory," he said. He spun around in his chair. "Stone, I don't want to talk about this in front of Ham, but I think you know that the chances of finding Holly alive are down to slim and none."

"I can't think about that, Lance; I just have to keep trying to figure this thing out."

"I know you feel responsible, but you're not," Lance said. "You told her to go armed."

"She did; her gun is not upstairs, and neither is the holster."

"Then she was incapacitated at the outset, but that's not your fault, either."

"I wish I could feel that way about it."

Dino called out from the study, "Hey, Stone, you and Lance come in here a minute, will you?"

Stone and Lance walked into the study to find Dino and Sergeant Young hunched over the coffee table, looking at Lance's thermal images and the sergeant's map of the island. "What's up?" Stone asked.

Dino tapped the thermal image with his forefinger. "I'm just looking at this house," he said.

"What about it?"

"This is the image from last night. It shows four people, presumably asleep, in the house, at around three-thirty A.M., two people in each of two bedrooms."

"So?"

"So, according to Tom's map, it's Caleb Stone's house."

"And there were four people present last night?"

"Look for yourself. My question is, if the twins are in Nantucket, who are the other two people besides Caleb and his wife?"

"I don't know. Guests maybe?"

"The twins can't be in two places at once, Dino," Lance said, "and we have a sighting of them by a police officer on the yacht less than an hour ago."

"Tom," Dino said, "do you personally know this Nantucket cop?"

"Never met him," Young said. "I just phoned his office this morning, and they put me in touch with him."

"How did he strike you on the phone— sharp?"

"Not really. He kept getting things mixed up: the twins' names, the name of the yacht."

"So, maybe he's mixed up about the twins being on the yacht."

Young produced his cell phone and called Potter's number.

"Yeah?"

"Lieutenant, it's Tom Young from the Maine State Police again."

"Yeah?"

"When you went down to the boat this morning, did you actually see the twins?"

"Ah, no, but the two guys on board said they had just gone for beer. I'm looking for them now."

"So, you didn't sight the twins?"

"Not yet."

"Thanks, Lieutenant."

"You think the two guys lied to me?"

"It's a strong possibility. If you find them, please call me immediately. Goodbye." Young hung up. "He didn't see them."

"I'd like to visit Caleb's house," Stone said.

"Me, too," Young replied.

Ham stood up. "I'm coming, too."

"I'd rather you didn't, Mr. Barker," Young said. "You just stay here, and let me do my job. You, too, Stone."

"As you wish, Sergeant," Stone replied.

"I'll call you after I've talked to Caleb— and his sons, if they're there."

"Be careful," Stone said.

Young left the house.

"You shouldn't get too excited about this, Ham," Stone said.

"No?" Ham replied. "If these twins are here, why are they establishing an alibi for themselves in Nantucket?"

"I don't know, but they may actually be in Nantucket, and we still don't have anything to connect them with Holly."

The doorbell rang, and Stone went to answer it. Ed Rawls stood on the doorstep.

"Come on in, Ed."

"Thanks. Anything new?"

"I'm not sure. We've just learned that Caleb Stone's twin sons have gone to some lengths to make the police believe that they're in Nantucket, but we've learned that they're not."

"We haven't learned that yet, Stone," Lance pointed out. "All we know is that the Nantucket cop looking for them hasn't seen them yet."

"And," Dino pointed out, "we've got these thermal scans that show four people sleeping in Caleb's house last night."

"So, what if they are here?" Rawls asked. "Have you got anything to connect them to any of the murders?"

"Not really," Stone said, "but I find it very suspicious that they seem to be trying to create a false alibi."

"I see your point," Rawls said.

"Sergeant Young has just gone over to Caleb's house to see if they're there," Stone said. "I'll be interested to hear what he finds out."

• • •

SERGEANT TOM YOUNG pulled up to the Stone house, a rambling shingled house sagging with age in places. He walked up onto the front porch and rang the bell.

After a long wait the door opened. "Yes?"

"Mr. Caleb Stone?"

"Yes?"

"I'm Sergeant Young of the Maine State Police. We spoke on the phone yesterday. I'd like to speak to your sons, Eben and Enos, please."

"I gave you their cell phone number yesterday, Sergeant," Caleb replied. "It hasn't changed."

"Yes sir, and I spoke to one of them, but I haven't been able to confirm their whereabouts."

"Well, I'm sorry about that, Sergeant, but I don't see how I can help you. The boys are not here."

"Sir, we have information that four people slept in your house last night. I assume that two of them were your wife and yourself. Who were the other two?"

"We, ah, had houseguests. They left this morning."

"Did they take the ferry?"

"No, they came and left by boat; they're

cruising the coast and just stopped in for the night."

"May I ask their names?"

"Bill and Julie Robertson."

"And the name of their boat?"

"I don't really know the boat's name," Caleb replied. "It's a sailing boat, pretty good size, but I don't know its name."

"How can I contact the Robertsons?"

"Why do you want to contact them?"

"I need to verify their presence here last night."

"Well, I suppose you'll have to wait until they return to Boston in the fall. They're cruising all summer."

"Mr. Stone, would you mind if I had a look around your house?"

"What for?"

"I'd like to see for myself if your sons are here."

"All right. Go ahead," Caleb said, standing aside and holding the door open.

Sergeant Young stepped inside the house, and he heard the door close firmly behind him.

53

STONE FINISHED HIS LUNCH and pushed back from the table.

"I'm going to look for Sergeant Young," he said.

"Take it easy, Stone," Lance said. "He's only been gone for an hour, and we know where he went. Relax and have some dessert."

Stone tried to relax. "Ginny, how are you coming with Esme's diary?"

"Slowly," she replied. "I can go faster, if you don't care if I destroy it."

"Please do it as you see fit, Ginny."

"It's just that it's all these thin sheets, and they've been mashed together by water and the pressure of the cover. If I use the heat from the hair dryer too much, they dry too fast and crumble."

Lance spoke up. "Ginny, if it's too difficult, I can send it back to Langley and let the experts have a go at it."

"We don't have time for that," Stone said.

"You mean Holly doesn't have time for that," Ham said. It was the first time he had spoken during lunch.

"I can do it, Lance," Ginny said, "but it has to be done slowly, and I don't think your people at Langley could do it any faster. I know it would be nice to do this in a lab, to better preserve the diary as evidence, but we have a different priority here, and that's to get Holly back as quickly as possible."

Stone stood up. "I'm going to go call Tom Young and see if he's all right." He left the room.

Ham watched him go. "I think Stone is almost as tightly wound as I am."

Stone came back. "I got his voice mail. I'm going to wait another half an hour, and then I'm going over to Caleb's house." He sat down and tried to eat the apple pie in front of him.

"There are dead spots on this island," Lance said. "Maybe Tom is in one of those."

The doorbell rang, and Stone got up and went to the front door. A moment later he came back into the kitchen with Sergeant Young.

"What happened over there?" Lance asked.

"Let's take a look at those thermal images," Young said.

Stone went to get them and spread them on the kitchen table.

"I searched the whole house," Young said. "Caleb didn't give me a hard time; he seemed to be happy for me to look around." He tapped a finger on two of the sleeping figures. "This is the twins' room," he said, "and it would appear that they're sleeping there. However, there's a guest room one floor up, directly over the twins' room, and Caleb says they had people sleeping there last night."

"Who?" Stone asked.

"A couple named Bill and Julie Robertson from Boston. I checked, and there's a phone listing there, and I got an answering machine. Caleb says they're spending the whole summer cruising the coast in their sailboat and that they came in by sea yesterday and left the same way early this morning. He didn't have the boat's name or description, so I can't ask the coast guard to look for it. I've got somebody checking the Massachusetts yacht registry for the information we need to launch a search."

"So, we're back where we started?" Stone asked.

"I wish to God we could nail down the twins on Nantucket and confirm the past four days of their alibi. I'm beginning to get the feeling we're wasting valuable time on those boys."

"Funny," Stone said, "I'm getting the feeling that they are less and less of a waste of our time."

HOLLY JERKED AWAKE, feeling pain. She felt it again; somebody had slapped her sharply across the face. Then she heard an odd, mechanical-sounding voice.

"Listen to me carefully," it said. "I have decided to accept your offer for your freedom. I'm going to remove the tape over your mouth, and I want you to answer my questions. Say nothing else, just answer. Do you understand me?"

Holly nodded.

"My question is, what do you need to accomplish the transfer of funds?"

The tape was ripped off. Holly panted for a moment.

"Answer me."

"I need a computer and an Internet connection."

"That's it?"

"That and for you to find a way to convince me, beyond any doubt, that the moment I complete the transaction, I will be freed." She heard the rip of duct tape being torn, and a fresh strip was slapped over her mouth.

"I don't know if I can convince you of my intentions," the voice said, "but I will promise you this: If we can't make this happen quickly, you will be dead in less than twenty-four hours." She felt the man leave the room.

Holly felt less drugged than usual, and she forced herself to start planning. First, she had to convince the man that she would cooperate with him, to the extent that he would untie at least one hand. She could still feel the weight of the small 9 mm pistol on her belt under her sweatshirt, and if she could get at that, she would not hesitate to shoot anybody who stood in the way of her freedom.

For the first time, she began to feel something like hope.

She took deep breaths, sucking as much air as possible into her lungs, and her brain began to work.

54

LIEUTENANT JAKE POTTER stood outside the dockmaster's office in the Nantucket marina and trained his binoculars on *Hotshot*. The marina was a hive of activity, as crews readied their yachts for the start of the next leg of the race. Engines started; sails were hauled on deck, shaken out of their bags and bent onto spars and forestays; boats began to leave their berths and motor toward the open harbor.

Hotshot was no different from the others. Jake counted five young men in the cockpit or on deck, each working furiously, and no large blond twins were among them. He had been had. What he would have enjoyed most would have been to remove his Colt

Cobra from its holster, empty it into the yacht's hull just below the waterline and watch it sink.

Instead, he drew his cell phone from its pouch and punched in a number.

"Sergeant Young," a voice said.

"Sergeant, this is Lieutenant Potter of the Nantucket police department."

"Good morning, Lieutenant."

"I wanted to let you know that the yacht *Hotshot* has just left the marina here for the start of the race, and the Stone twins are not aboard. And I haven't been able to find them anywhere in the village. I've had all our people on the lookout for them, and they are not here."

"Thank you, Lieutenant," Young said.

"One more thing: Two young men answering their description left here in a small, private airplane yesterday afternoon. There was no flight plan filed, and I don't have a tail number, but the airplane departed to the northeast, in the direction of Provincetown. That's consistent with a flight to the Maine coast."

"Do you know what kind of airplane?"

"It was a Cessna, nobody could identify

the model, but it was not based on Nan-tucket."

"Do you know if it refueled at your air-port?"

"No, it did not refuel; otherwise, we'd have the tail number."

"Thank you, Lieutenant."

YOUNG CLOSED HIS CELL phone and turned his car in the direction of Dick Stone's house.

STONE WATCHED AS Ginny came down the stairs, clutching the diary and several sheets of paper.

"I've got something," she said. She spread her papers and the diary out on the coffee table and sat down beside it while everyone gathered around her. "I finally realized that I still hadn't gone far enough back in the diary," she said. "Then it occurred to me that Esme had been in London with her parents all win-ter, not here on the island, so what I was read-ing was mostly irrelevant, so I went back even further to last Labor Day."

"And what did you find?" Stone asked.

"The pages were very messy, and the ink had faded or run, but I've written out what I could read. This one entry was a page and a half long, which was unusual for ESE; she ordinarily wrote a couple of paragraphs about her day. Here's what I've got." She picked up a sheet of paper and read:

"'Day started blank.' Where I couldn't read a word, I just wrote down 'blank.' Then there are two or three paragraphs that are completely illegible, then this: 'X and blank said blank blank'—several words unreadable—then 'blank house, blank blank blank drinks. Z wanted blank blank go, so I said okay.' Then more unreadable paragraphs down to the last one: 'Z blank crying, me too. Blank blank Y laughing, drunk. Z threw blank, and I got her out blank blank.' Then the only whole sentence I was able to get: 'Z swore me to secrecy.'"

Lance spoke up. "I want to send the diary to Langley and see if they can recover more of those pages."

"I think you should," Ginny said. "I don't think I can get any more of this particular incident."

"Do you have an interpretation of all this, Ginny?" Stone asked.

"It sounds to me that there are four people involved: X, Y, Z and ESE. It sounds as though Z and ESE were persuaded to go to somebody's house for drinks, then got drunk and Z threw up, and ESE got her out of there."

"Z could be Janey Harris," Stone said, "and X and Y could be Eben and Enos Stone."

"Could be," Ginny said," but there's nothing here that I can read that identifies X and Y. It could be two other boys on the island or two other girls or even two men. Wouldn't be the first time grown men tried to lead teenaged girls astray."

"All right," Stone said. "Here's a theory: Labor Day is everybody's last day on this island. When I spent that summer here, the day after Labor Day, everybody abandoned this place as if it were a sinking ship. By five in the afternoon, the island was practically deserted."

"What's your point?" Dino asked.

"Something happened to the girls while they were drunk—maybe they were raped—but Z, or Janey, swore Esme to secrecy, so she didn't tell anybody, and the next day they left the island with their parents. Dick and Barbara took Esme back to London, and Janey went home to Boston with her parents."

"Okay. Say you're right, then what?" Dino asked.

"X and Y are the twins, and they went back to Yale for the fall semester. Neither of the girls told anyone. Maybe they talked on the phone and reinforced their secret that way. But somehow, Dick Stone learned what had happened. Maybe Esme's mother read her diary."

"Mothers will do that," Ginny said. "Mine did."

"So Dick is furious. On his way from London to Washington, Dick stops in Boston and confronts Caleb with this information. Maybe Caleb doesn't believe it or believes it and refuses to do anything about it, so Dick, in a fit of pique, draws a new will disinheriting Caleb and, by extension, the twins, and sends the will to me."

"Wait a minute," Dino said. "Are you saying that the twins murdered Dick, Barbara, and Esme because they were disinherited?"

"No. What's more important is that *they didn't know they were disinherited*. They wouldn't have known, because Caleb didn't know until I told him."

"So they killed the whole family thinking they would inherit Dick's wife's money? That seems like a stretch, Stone."

"No, no, at least not directly. Esme had talked, or at least her parents had read her diary, so they were at risk for being sent to prison for two rapes."

"So they killed both the girls, and Dick and Barbara were either collateral damage or killed because they knew about what happened. What about Don Brown?"

"Janey must have told him about the rapes, or at least Eben and Enos thought she did."

"Well," Dino said, "your theory covers most of what we know, but what about Caleb?"

"What about him?"

"If his boys raped these girls, then, according to your theory, he knew about it because Dick told him. Do you think he wouldn't do anything about it?"

"I don't think he would send his sons to jail for rape," Stone said.

"How about five murders? Would he take exception to that?"

"It's hard to imagine he would," Stone

said, "but maybe he didn't know the boys were connected to the murders or at least was in denial about them."

"Then there are the other two women on the island who were murdered," Dino said.

"Right," Stone said, "and four more in New Haven."

"Christ," Ham said suddenly. "That just doesn't sound possible. If your theory is right, then these boys from a nice Boston family have murdered, what, eleven people?"

"Ham," Stone said, "when you learn about serial killers on television or in the newspapers, what do people who knew them say after the fact?"

Ham nodded. "That they were nice boys."

The doorbell rang, and Stone let in Sergeant Young.

"I just had a call from Nantucket," he said. "The Stone twins didn't sail on the yacht when it left this morning, but two young men answering their description left Nantucket airport yesterday afternoon in a light airplane, some sort of Cessna."

"You'd better take a seat, Tom," Stone said. "We have some things to tell you."

55

CALEB STONE GOT INTO the big Boston Whaler tied up at his dock, started the engine and motored slowly out to open water, then he increased power and headed for the southern end of the island. Once clear of the island he turned for Camden and increased his speed to thirty. It was a sparkling clear day, and the water was flat.

In Camden he tied up at the local marina and walked a couple of blocks into the business district. He went into a Radio Shack and bought a throwaway cell phone and a kit for hooking the phone to a computer, asking the sales clerk for instructions on how to use it to connect to the Internet.

He then returned to the marina and

headed back to Islesboro. He made it before sunset, having been gone less than two
hours. Then, instead of returning to his own
dock, he motored past it for another half a
mile and, with the engine at idle, turned into
an overgrown creek, dodging low branches
as he went. Within half a minute his boat
was invisible to any passing boat. He continued slowly up the creek until he came to
the boathouse.

The boathouse had originally been an ad-
junct to a large, shingled summer "cottage"
that had been destroyed by fire many years
before. The owners still had the land but
had not rebuilt and had not put the property
up for sale.

He cut the engine and let the boat coast
into the boathouse, tied it up, gathered his
purchases and the other items he had
brought from his house and walked quietly
up the stairs, so as not to wake the woman,
who was tied to the bed, until he was ready.
He checked to be sure she was still asleep,
then he took a small table and chair from
one side of the upstairs room and set it into
a corner, facing the wall.

He opened his computer case and set up
his laptop, which was fully charged, and a

small printer. He connected the cell phone to the laptop and installed the Internet software as the salesclerk had instructed. Everything worked perfectly, and he was soon on the Internet.

He donned the electronic device that changed his voice, something his sons had bought when they were in high school, then he went to the bed, gently untied the woman's feet and duct-taped them firmly together. He bent over her and slapped her sharply across the face. "Time to wake up," he said, his voice sounding mechanical and expressionless.

She came to, and he spoke loudly, to get past her earplugs. "Listen to me carefully," he said. "For the next few minutes, your life is going to be in great danger if you do not do exactly as I say. Do you understand?"

She nodded.

"Your feet are bound together. I am going to untie your hands, and if you make any attempt to fight me or remove any tape, I will hurt you badly. Do you understand?"

She nodded again.

"And don't try to use the gun on your belt; I unloaded it and your two spare magazines a long time ago."

She nodded.

He untied her left hand first, then her right. "Sit up on the edge of the bed," he said. When she did, he took her by the right wrist and elbow, holding her at a distance, and said, "Now hop straight ahead; I'm going to put you in a chair." She did so, and he taped her torso to the chair to restrict her movement but left her hands free.

"Now, close your eyes and keep them closed until I tell you to open them. If you attempt to look at me at any time, I will end your life immediately. Look only straight ahead. Do you understand?"

She nodded.

He pulled off the tape, then took the glasses from his computer case and put them on her. "There is a gun pointed at the back of your neck. Now open your eyes."

Holly opened her eyes and blinked rapidly. Tears streamed down her cheeks. It was the first time since she had been taken that she had been able to see, but she could only see straight ahead and down. She recognized the glasses immediately: They were "foggles," which are used by student pilots in instrument training. They allow the student to see only the instruments in front of him and not out the windshield or to either side.

"The computer in front of you is already connected to the Internet," the mechanical voice said. "I'm going to remove the tape from your mouth, and you will speak only to answer my questions. Clear?"

Holly nodded.

He ripped off the tape, and Holly worked her jaw and her lips for a moment.

"Now, we will open a bank account for me," he said.

"What bank?" she asked.

"How do I choose?"

Holly went to Google and did a search for offshore banks. "Here's a list," she said. "You can open an account with any of them on-line."

"The Malay Bank of Singapore," he said, after a moment.

Holly went to the Malay Bank's Web site and pulled up a form for opening a num-bered account. "Who do you want to have access?" She pointed at a list of options.

"Choose 'anyone with the account num-ber and password.'"

Holly clicked on the correct option. "You

need to specify a password of six to ten letters or numbers."

He was silent for a moment. "PE65000," he said.

She typed in the password, which appeared onscreen as only a series of asterisks, then typed it again for confirmation. The words *Please Wait* appeared on the screen and after half a minute, the message "Your account is provisionally open. A wire-transferred deposit of at least $10,000 must be received within twenty-four hours for the account to be permanently opened. You may change your password at any time by clicking on the 'password change' button and first entering your old password." The new account number followed.

"Print that page," the man said.

She printed the page.

"Now go to your bank account and make the wire transfer," he said.

Holly went to her offshore bank's Web site and began the process. She entered the wire-transfer instructions in the amount of $1,200,000 and the number of the destination account. She had more than five million in the account, the contents of a suitcase full of cash she had taken from an enormous stash of money held by a drug cartel she had broken up during her police days in Florida. She paused when her password was required. A message appeared, saying "After you have entered your password twice, your instructions will be irreversible." She tapped the screen. "You see this?"

"Yes."

"Now, before I type in my password, convince me that you're going to set me free safely." Immediately, she felt cold steel pressing against the nape of her neck.

"You have my word that one of two things is going to happen: Either you will enter your password and I will set you free, or you will refuse to do so, and I will kill you now. Are you convinced?"

Holly typed in the password, then confirmed it. A message appeared, confirming the amount and the destination account.

"Print that page," the man said.

Holly printed it. Immediately, her head seemed to explode. She slumped against the restraining tape as she lost consciousness.

56

HOLLY SLOWLY CAME TO, her face pressed against a cool, rough surface that vibrated. Her feet were still taped together, her hands taped behind her and her eyes taped shut. Only her mouth was untaped. Since her ears were still plugged it took her a moment to realize that she was on a boat, and the vibration she felt was from an engine. There was a slight bumping as the boat skimmed over small waves, and it seemed to be traveling fast. She had no idea whether it was day or night, and she had a terrible headache.

Holly thought about her circumstances and concluded that it was not in her interest to move. She thought it likely that she was being driven into deep water, where she would be weighted and thrown into the water. If this were the case she would have to make a move before the weights were attached. If she could somehow throw herself into the water, then she might be able to swim, even bound as she was. Maybe the water would soak the tape and cause it to expand enough for her to get a hand free. She was going to have to work very hard not to panic when the time came.

The boat began to slow, and Holly tried to prepare herself mentally for what was to come. The boat slowed still further. It was in smooth water now, and, judging from the lessened vibration, the engine was at or near idle. She estimated that the time to make her move was as soon as he began to weight her body.

Then, to her surprise, the boat seemed to bump into something; she felt it through the hull, no more than a nudge. She heard a voice.

"Listen to me. I'm going to move you onto another boat, where you'll be found in the morning."

She felt his hands under her arms from

behind as he lifted her and set her on what felt like the gunwales of the boat.

"Bye, bye," he said, then pushed her backward.

She grabbed a deep breath, but what she struck was something hard. She had tumbled into another boat. She briefly heard the engine of the boat she had just left, then all was silence.

Holly sat up and leaned against something, probably the side of the boat's cockpit. She put her face against it and crabbed her body along its length, until she came to an obstruction. She felt the adjoining surface with her face, and it was a pillow. She backed herself into the corner and began pushing up with her feet, slowly working her way to the cushioned surface. Twice, she fell back to the deck below her, but on her third try she made it to what seemed to be a broad, cushioned seat. She struggled upright and leaned against a corner, then she struggled hard against the tape binding her wrists.

Finally, convinced that she was not going to get free of her bonds, she did the only thing she could do: She whistled. Holly had learned, as a little girl, how to whistle very loudly. She could still bring cabs to a screeching halt in New York City with that whistle, and sound carried well over water. She was probably in a boat moored in the harbor, so somebody ashore might hear her. She whistled, then rested, then whistled some more.

BACK AT THE STONE HOUSE, Dino was looking once again at the satellite thermal images that had been sent to Lance from Langley. "Lance, Stone, come look at this," he said.

Then Daisy, who had been sleeping before the fire, suddenly jerked awake, scrambled to her feet and barked.

Everyone turned and looked at her.

"What is it, Daisy?" Ham asked.

Daisy ran to the door to the terrace and began clawing frantically at it.

Ham got up. "What's the matter, girl?" He opened the door, and Daisy was gone. Ham ran after her and stopped on the terrace.

Everybody else poured out of the study onto the terrace and stood, watching Daisy run.

"She's headed down the dock," Ham said. "Come on!"

The group ran after the dog. Suddenly, Stone could hear a whistle. Daisy had obviously heard it a lot sooner.

"It's Holly!" Ham yelled and jumped into the picnic boat, where Holly lay bound but not gagged.

"Ham," Holly was screaming, "is it you?"

Daisy was dancing around her, yelping, trying to lick her face, while Ham dug into a pocket for his knife.

HOLLY SAT IN FRONT of the fire, trying to eat a bowl of soup. Finally, she gave up, picked up the bowl and drank from it until it was empty. "That's better," she said. "All I've had to eat for days is chocolate bars . . . Snickers, I think".

Stone spoke up. "Jesus, I saw Caleb buying a whole box of Snickers in the Dark Harbor Shop."

"That makes him the guy," Holly said.

Everyone was gathered around her, watching. Even Seth and Mabel had come in from the kitchen. "What else can I get you, Holly?" Stone asked.

Holly stood up and stretched some more. Apart from being sore after being restrained in one position for a long time, she felt remarkably well. "A drink," she said.

Dino went to the bar and got her some Knob Creek on the rocks, her favorite.

"Are you ready to talk now?" Lance asked.

"Ready? All I want to do is talk; I've had my mouth taped shut for . . . how long has it been?"

"You've been gone a little over four days," Stone said. "Was it the twins who took you? Did they put you in the boat?"

"Twins? The Stone twins? No, not them. It was one man, and he was very clever. The only time he spoke to me was through some sort of voice-altering device. I never saw him. I have no idea what he looks like. But the Snickers bars makes me think it's Caleb."

"Why did he let you go?" Stone asked. "Do you know?"

Holly nodded. "Oh, God. I need a computer." She got up and ran toward Dick's little office. The computer was already on. She went onto the Internet and started typing.

"What are you doing?" Lance asked.

"I bought my way out," she said. "I transferred a million two to his Singapore account."

"What are you doing now?" he asked.

"I'm wiring the money back to my account," she said. "I memorized the account number, and he gave me a password of PE65000, like the old Glenn Miller recording, Pennsylvania 6-5000, but I entered EE65000, so he won't be able to access the account until he figures that out. I'm going to send the money back to my account."

Ham stood in the door. "Wait a minute," he said. "Where did you get a million two hundred thousand dollars?"

"Jackson left it to me," she lied. Jackson was her dead fiancé.

"Oh," Ham said.

She typed a few more keystrokes. "There," she said. Then she started typing again. "I think I'll change the password back to PE65000," she said. "That way, when he accesses it, he'll find it empty. I wish I could be there to see his face."

Responding to calls from Stone, Sergeant Young arrived simultaneously with Ed Rawls, and they were brought up to date. "Do you have any idea who this man is, Holly?" Young asked.

"No idea at all," she said.

"Lance, Sergeant," Dino said, "can you come take a look at the thermal images for a minute? I've found something interesting."

Everybody gathered around the coffee table, where the images were spread out, along with Young's map of the island.

"Here's my question," Dino said, pointing to a structure on one of the thermal images. "What is this? I can't find it on your map."

"Well," Young said, "this is the most recent map of the island, completed less than three months ago, but you're right, the structure in the image doesn't appear on the map."

"Look at this," Dino said, pointing from one image to another. "We've got three days of thermal imaging here, and in every one of them we can see one hot spot—one person—in exactly the same position. It doesn't move, day or night."

"Maybe an old person, an invalid?" Young said.

Holly spoke up. "Or me. I've been tied to a bed all that time. Good God, it's me."

57

CALEB STONE MADE his way back to the obscured creek, past the overhanging brush and slowly up the little waterway to the boathouse. As he approached he could see a glow from a window. Someone had lit a candle.

He tied up his Whaler and went upstairs. Eben and Enos sat on an old sofa, looking tired.

"Hey, Dad," the boys said simultaneously. They often spoke at the same time.

"Hello, boys," Caleb replied.

"You got rid of her, huh?" Eben asked. Of the two, Eben was the more assertive.

"In a manner of speaking."

"What do you mean by that?"

Caleb dragged up a seedy, overstuffed chair and sat down. "I let her go."

The twins both sat up. "Are you out of your fucking mind?" Enos asked.

"Certainly not, and watch your mouth."

"Easy," Eben said to his brother. "I'm sure Dad had his reasons."

"I certainly did," Caleb replied. "One more murder on this island and we'd have the National Guard in here. They searched our house, you know."

"Dad, she's going to tell on us," Enos said.

"She doesn't know anything to tell. She's been tied to that bed, drugged, her eyes taped and her ears plugged for the past four days, ever since you left. She hasn't had a moment of consciousness when she could see anything except that computer." He pointed at the laptop, glowing in the dark.

"I don't get it," Eben said. "Where's the percentage in letting her go?"

"For one thing, they'll stop looking for her. For another, she paid her way out."

"Paid?"

"Listen to me, boys. You've got to run; there's no other choice."

"But why? We haven't done anything; nobody has anything on us."

"You've killed some people. They've eliminated all the other suspects and now they're focusing on you. They know you weren't on the boat when it sailed from Nantucket."

"So, we came back. So what?"

Caleb noted that they didn't deny the murders, but he didn't want the details. "How did you come back?"

"We flew the airplane to Rockport, had some dinner and got the last ferry."

"Where's your car?"

"At the house; we walked down here."

"I want you to listen to me very carefully," Caleb said, leaning forward in his chair. "I'm your father, and I love you, but I'm also speaking to you as a lawyer. You've committed several murders, and these days, nobody can get away with that for long."

"Oh, I don't know," Eben said.

"Why did you do it?"

"We had our reasons. Anyway, you taught us everything we know."

"*What?*"

"You taught us how much fun it is beating up on other people. You beat us up, before we got too big to let you do it. You stood on the sidelines and egged us on when we wrestled and boxed. You always wanted us to kill the other guy."

"And you took that to mean that murder is all right?"

"As long as you don't get caught."

"You're going to get caught," Caleb said.

"Why do you think that, Dad?"

"Because murderers always get caught. They're going to check every minute of your last four or five days, and they're going to punch holes in your story."

"We've got it covered," Enos said.

"You think your friends are going to go on covering for you when they find out what the police want?"

"Sure, they will."

"No, they'll be dragged into a police station and told that if they lie for you, they're accessories to multiple murders and that accessories get the same sentences as perpetrators. Haven't you watched enough TV to know that? They'll crack to save themselves, and when they do, you'll find yourselves in jail, then on trial, then . . ."

"You wouldn't let us lose a trial, would you

Dad?" Eben asked. "Not with your legal connections."

"I can't fix a trial," Caleb said. "And if they have the evidence, you'll be convicted, and you'll spend the rest of your lives in prison." Caleb saw that he wasn't getting through to them. "They'll separate you."

"What?" Enos asked, looking alarmed.

"They won't let brothers serve in the same prison; they'll put you in different places."

Enos looked as if he were going to cry.

"You've got to get out of here and tonight," Caleb said.

"How?" Eben asked. "Where would we go? What would we do for money?"

"I told you, the woman bought her way out."

"How?"

"I set up a numbered bank account in Singapore; from there you can transfer funds to any bank in the world just by going online."

"How much did she pay?"

"A million two hundred thousand dollars. It's already in the account." He handed them the sheets that Holly had printed. "Here's all the information."

The boys held a candle over the pages

and read them. "Holy shit," they said together.

"Here's what you do: You take my boat
and leave here at first light for Rockland.
Once there, you take that airplane of yours
and fly west, stopping only at small, out-of-
the-way airports to refuel. It'll take you a
couple of days, but you'll fly to El Paso or
Laredo, on the Mexican border, in Texas.
You'll cross the border, each in a different
city, and you'll travel separately to the Mexico City airport. From there, you can fly to
Brazil, which has no extradition treaty. You
can open a bank account there and transfer
enough funds from the Singapore account
to support you for a year or so."

"Then what?"

"You'll research where else in the world
you can go, then start a small business.
Even a million two won't last forever. Take
the laptop with you and the cell phone,
which is a throwaway. I'll call you from
phone booths every now and then to see
how you're doing and give you advice.

"The cell phone may not work in Mexico,
so buy another one, same in Brazil. Don't
linger in Mexico City. Never use your credit
cards. Leave them with me. I'll dispose of

them. One of you should grow a beard, and you should both dye your hair different colors. Twins your size are too easy to spot. When you travel on trains or airplanes, never sit together; take different hotel rooms. Don't be seen together in public until you're safely in Brazil. Your passports are in the computer case." He took a wad of bills from his pocket. "Here's eight thousand dollars. That will get you to Rio, then you can draw on the Singapore account."

Eben took the money. "Where did you get this?"

"I had a couple of thousand in the safe at the house. I've been cashing checks and using ATMs for a week; I knew you'd need some cash."

"So, Dad," Eben said, "you've created a paper trail. When they start looking for us, they'll look at your bank account and see all these unusual cash withdrawals."

"I'll handle that," Caleb said.

"And how are you going to handle it, Dad? You can't explain those withdrawals; you won't have the cash to show them. You'll be just like our friends. You'll crack, to save yourself, and you'll tell them where to look for us."

"I would never tell them," Caleb said. "You're my sons; I would never give you up."

"Remember that time when we ran away from boarding school? We called you, and you gave us up."

"Come on, boys. You were kids then; you'd done something crazy."

Eben stood up, and Enos stood with him. "We're not kids anymore, and you'd be facing prison. I don't think you'd spend the rest of your life in prison for us, do you, Enos?"

"No, I don't think so," Enos said.

Caleb started to rise, but Eben pushed him back in the chair.

"No," Eben said. "If we're going to burn our bridges, we'd better start now."

58

SETH HOTCHKISS SPOKE UP. "I know what that place is," he said, tapping his finger on the thermal image. "It's an old boathouse. The main house burned down, I don't know, maybe fifteen years ago, and they never rebuilt, so it was taken off your map, Sergeant. But the boathouse is still there. There's a little creek that runs up to it, about right here." He tapped the map again. "But it's overgrown, and I don't know whether it's navigable."

"Would the picnic boat make it up that creek?" Stone asked. "It only draws a foot and a half."

"It wouldn't be the depth that's the problem," Seth replied. "You'd have to make your way through a lot of brush."

"Is there a way to the boathouse by road?" Sergeant Young asked.

"There's an old gate about here on the main road," Seth said, pointing to a place on the map. "There was a dirt track down to the boathouse—I delivered some sails there once—but that would be overgrown, too. You could make it through there in a four-by-four, I expect."

"My Range Rover would do it," Rawls said. "It's got a lot of ground clearance."

Young looked at his watch. "I'm going to have to get search warrants for the two buildings, and I'll have trouble getting people over here before tomorrow morning, when the ferry starts running again."

"Can you get a search warrant this time of night?"

"I can call a judge I know and send somebody over to his house with a warrant, then he can fax it to me here. But there's still the matter of people."

"We've got enough people right here," Stone said.

"You're not law enforcement."

"You've got one cop, two ex-cops, a couple of federal agents, and a retired army NCO," Stone said.

Ham flashed a badge. "It says here I'm a police lieutenant in Florida, even if I am a dollar-a-year man."

"Deputize us," Stone said. "We're all armed, and we know how to handle it. We ought to go in there just before dawn, by land and by sea."

"You want to try the creek with the picnic boat?" Young asked.

"Yes; we can always get out and walk if the going gets too rough."

Young nodded.

"Wait a minute," Holly said. "There's not going to be anybody in the boathouse."

"Why not?" Young asked.

"I don't think anybody lives there. When I was using the computer, the only other light in the room seemed to be candles, and the computer was working on battery power. The place smells disused: no cooking odors, no cleaning fluids or furniture polish recently used."

"She's right," Stone said. "We ought to go into Caleb Stone's house first. The twins have left Nantucket; they might be back home."

"I keep telling you, it's not the twins," Holly said. "It's one man."

"Maybe it's both," Stone said.

Young looked doubtful. "You think it's credible for a father to conspire with his twin sons in a string of murders?"

"Maybe not, but it's credible for a father to protect his sons, even from the law."

"All right, this is what we'll do," Young said. "Stone, you and Dino and Seth take the picnic boat up the creek to the boathouse. Seth, I don't want you going in there. You stay in the boat."

"All right," Seth said.

"Ham, Lance and I will go with Ed in the Range Rover, and the four of us will take the main residence."

"What about me?" Holly said. "I'm going."

"Holly, are you sure you're up to this?"

"Try and stop me."

"All right, you go in the boat with Stone and Dino."

"Good."

"Now, all of you listen to me: Nobody shoots anybody unless he's shot at first or is about to be shot at. Is that perfectly clear? If any shooting happens there'll be a very thorough inquiry, and each of us will be held responsible for any action outside the legal use of firearms."

Everybody nodded.

"We'll keep in touch by cell phone. We'll set them to vibrate, and they'll make less noise than radios. I want everybody to have loaded weapons and two spare magazines. I'll have an assault rifle, in case we need more firepower, and I have a shotgun in my car."

"So do I," Rawls said.

"What I don't have is more than one armored vest. I'm required by regulation to wear that, and the rest of you will be going in bare chested."

"So to speak," Holly said.

"And I don't want anybody to get shot, so you must all use extreme caution. We may be up against three men, and we don't know what kind of weapons, if any, they have. We'll make simultaneous entry to both buildings, entering front and back."

Seth spoke up. "There's no back entrance to the boathouse, just stairs going up from the dock underneath."

"Good. All right, everybody check your weapons and ammo," Young said, looking at his watch. "We have a long day up here, and it gets light early. We should be in position by three-thirty A.M. In the meantime, get some rest, and we'll leave here at three."

59

STONE, DINO, HOLLY AND SETH went out to the dock and got the picnic boat ready for departure. The skies had clouded up, and darkness was complete. Seth got the engine started, and the lights from the dashboard instruments and the GPS plotter offered a little light in the cockpit.

"Look," Seth said, pointing to the plotter screen. "The creek is on the electronic chart; that will make it a piece of cake to find, even in the dark. All we have to worry about is moored boats and rocks, and I pretty much know where those are."

"Let's go," Stone said. "It's going to start to get light soon, and I want to at least be in position off the creek before that happens."

Seth moved the boat away from the dock, and at idle speed they began moving up the inlet, away from the harbor. They could hear nothing, except the rumble of the engine. Seth increased power a little. "We could go faster, if we use the spotlight," he said.

"As long as we can navigate safely in the dark, I'd rather not announce our presence," Stone said.

Then, without warning, they heard the whine of a big outboard engine, and a Boston Whaler flashed past them, rocking their boat with its wake.

"Shit," Seth said. "I didn't hear that coming; he must have been doing twenty knots."

"Was that Caleb's boat?" Stone asked.

"Hard to tell with no light," Seth replied. "Lots of Whalers hereabouts." They continued their way up the inlet, passing moored boats along the way, making seven knots, according to the speedometer. "Creek up ahead," Seth said. "One o'clock and a hundred yards." He throttled back to idle.

HAM BARKER WATCHED from the rear seat as Ed Rawls's Range Rover turned into Caleb Stone's driveway.

"Lights off," said Sergeant Young from the front passenger seat. "I don't want 'em to know we're here until they open the door."

"BMW convertible dead ahead," Rawls said.

"That's the twins' car," Young replied. "They're back from Nantucket."

The car stopped, and Ham and Lance got out of the backseat.

"Lance," Young said, "you and Ham go around to the back door and make sure your cell phone is on. What's the number?"

Lance gave it to him, and he tapped it into his own phone and pressed the send button. Lance opened the phone. "I'm on the line," he said.

"Good," Young replied. "If you hear any kind of commotion or yelling, kick in the back door and come in with your weapons drawn. You've got a flashlight; use it if you have to."

"Right," Lance said, and he and Ham began to walk to the rear of the house.

Ham drew his Colt .45 auto, racked the slide and flipped the safety on with his thumb, then he took a small Surefire flashlight loaded with high-powered batteries from a holster on his gun belt. That light, he knew, was enough to nearly disable a man when it hit his face in the dark. Once, he had seen a soldier throw up after such an experience.

They reached the back of the house, walked quietly up the back steps and waited on the landing by the door. Lance put the phone on speaker, and they could hear the footsteps of Young and Rawls as they came onto the front porch. Then, faintly, they heard a doorbell ring.

STONE, DINO AND HOLLY sat in the picnic boat off the mouth of the creek, while Seth kept it hovering in place, using the joystick to control the boat's movement.

"I see a faint light," Stone said, pointing. "There, through the trees."

"Looks like a lantern or maybe a candle," Dino said.

"We've got some light in the sky," Stone said. "Let's go slowly up the creek, Seth. Dino and I will go onto the foredeck and keep the brush and branches out of the way as much as possible. If you hit anything solid, back off." Stone and Dino crept forward.

The going was easier than Stone had thought it would be. It was as if someone had trimmed the larger branches, leaving only the smaller stuff. For five minutes they moved on up the creek at the rate of a couple of knots, and then there were no more branches, only clear water ahead. The boathouse stood before them, twenty-five yards ahead, a soft glow coming from its windows. Stone looked back at Seth and drew a hand across his throat.

Seth turned off the engine, and they drifted forward, ghosting into the boat bay of the house. Stone and Dino hopped onto the catwalk and stopped the boat's progress. Holly joined them, and they made the boat fast. They had made remarkably little noise.

Stone pressed the speed dial on his cell phone for Sergeant Young's phone and got a busy signal. He closed his phone. "Somebody's upstairs," he whispered to Dino and Holly. "Come on, we're going in." He led the way to the stairs, and in single file they began to creep upward, keeping to the inside of the treads to avoid squeaks. They came to the door, which was ajar an inch. Stone looked inside but could see only a small slice of the room. He looked at Dino and Holly and pumped his fist twice; they were going in.

THE SOUND OF A woman's voice raised in protest coming from the cell phone jerked Ham to attention. "No, you can't come in!" she was saying.

"That's it," Lance said. He turned the doorknob, found it locked, then backed up a step and kicked the door open.

Ham was in the darkened house immediately, his flashlight on, his gun hand cradled on his left wrist. They were in a kitchen, and another door was ahead. He peeped through that and saw a light down a hallway. He could hear the voices clearly now, without the cell phone.

"We have a search warrant, Mrs. Stone," Young was saying. "You sit down over there and don't interfere, or I'll arrest you and handcuff you." The woman's voice stopped. "Ham, you and Lance take the upstairs; Ed and I will take this floor."

Ham went into the main entrance hall and ran lightly up the stairs, gun and flashlight at the ready. All he found were empty rooms, neatly kept. He switched on the ceiling light in what was obviously the twins' room. It was as neat as all the others. He and Lance went through it, checking every closet or cabinet large enough to hold a man, until they were satisfied there was no one on the second floor. They went back downstairs.

Young and Rawls came out of a bedroom. "Nobody but Mrs. Stone in the house. Where are your husband and your sons, Mrs. Stone?" She appeared to be drunk.

"I was sleeping," she said.

"Where are they?"

"I don't know. Aren't they in bed? My boys flew into Rockland tonight."

"Let's get to the boathouse," Young said, and they all headed for the Range Rover.

STONE PUSHED THE door open with his foot, gun before him, and stepped into the room. He saw a double bed, a table, an old sofa, a couple of seedy, overstuffed chairs and not much else. He could see the top of the head of what was apparently a sleeping man sitting in one of the armchairs, his back to them.

Stone switched on his flashlight and approached. "Wake up," he said. "Keep your hands where I can see them." Then he saw the pistol on the floor, near the man's dangling right hand, and he knew what else he was going to see.

THEY WERE GATHERED in the boathouse, looking at the dead body of Caleb Stone, a bullet through his right temple.

"They did a better job on Caleb's suicide than with Dick's," Stone said. "At least, the angle is right."

"The computer was on that table in the corner," Holly said, "along with a little printer and a briefcase."

"The twins think they have a million two in a Singapore bank," Stone said, "and that had to be them in the boat that passed us when we were on the way in. I wonder where they're headed."

Young spoke up. "Their mother said they flew into Rockland."

"We'll never catch them in the boat," Stone said. "Come on, Ed. Drive me to the Islesboro airstrip, and maybe we can beat them to Rockland."

"I'll call for backup," Sergeant Young said,

"but I don't know where our cars are tonight, and I don't know how long it will take them to get to Rockland Airport."

"We don't have time to wait for backup," Stone said. "Once those boys are off the ground, it's going to be hell to find them." He ran for the stairs.

60

THE RANGE ROVER skidded to a halt on the airstrip's parking ramp, and Stone ran for the Malibu. There was no time for the usual preflight inspection. He got the door open and slid into the pilot's seat, and felt the others boarding behind him. Sergeant Young squeezed his long frame into the copilot's seat, and Stone looked behind him to find Lance, Rawls, Holly and Ham filling the other four seats. He flipped on the master switch and checked the fuel: Both tanks were less than a quarter full. Stone had not topped off the tanks at Teterboro, having four on board, and he was grateful for that because, with so much weight aboard, the airplane was going to eat up runway before it would fly. Rockland was no more than a fifteen- or twenty-minute flight, so the fuel on board would get them there.

"Everybody buckle up," Stone said, then began cranking the engine. It coughed to life, and he checked the windsock: light wind, favoring runway one. The other direction, runway one-nine, was slightly downhill, but there were tall trees not far off the end of the runway. He taxied downhill and did a one-eighty turn at the end, watching the engine temperatures come slowly up; he couldn't afford any hesitation or an engine failure today. The temperatures were edging into the green. He jammed his feet onto the brakes and put in twenty degrees of flaps; that would lower his takeoff speed from eighty to seventy knots. He eased up on the power until the throttle was at its stop and let the engine run up to full power. Now or never. With a scared feeling in his stomach he let the airplane go.

The Malibu began its roll all too slowly. Stone flicked his sight back and forth between the runway and the airspeed indicator, watching it inch up. Halfway down the runway, the needle began moving faster, but the end of the runway was rushing at them, where there were scrubby trees and a house. They were running out of pavement, and the ground beyond was rough.

"I want to fly now," Sergeant Young said, his voice sounding strangled.

They were at sixty-nine knots when Stone eased the yoke back a fraction. The airplane left the ground in what seemed like the last yard of pavement, but it didn't want to climb. Stone put the gear lever up and the flaps to zero, hoping for less drag, and held the airplane level, wanting to let it gain airspeed. At eighty knots, with the gear at about ten feet up and the house rushing at them, he tried for more altitude and cleared the roof by what seemed like inches.

"Sweet Jesus," Young said. "Is this thing going to fly?"

Stone leveled off at a hundred feet, watching the treetops flashing past a few feet below them, dodging the taller ones as the airplane struggled to gain airspeed. Then they were over water, inching their way up to five hundred feet. An overcast was, maybe, a couple of hundred feet above them.

"I thought you were going to hit that

boat's mast," Young said as they flew past a moored yacht.

"We're going to do the rest of the flight at this altitude," Stone said. "It'll keep us out of clouds and get us down faster." He leveled off at five hundred feet and eased the throttle back to keep the airspeed in the green. They were using a lot of fuel at this altitude and speed, but the distance was short.

Stone reached down between the seats and handed Young the airport directory. "Look up Rockland and give me the unicom frequency," he said. "There's no tower on the field."

Young took a painfully long time to do so, but finally he said, "One hundred twenty-three point zero five."

Stone dialed in the frequency. "Rockland unicom, November one, two, three, tango, foxtrot. Anybody in the pattern?" No reply.

"Says here their hours are eight A.M. to eight P.M." Young said. Stone looked at his watch: It was a little after five.

"Rockland traffic," Stone said, "anyone in the pattern?" No reply. The sun was up but low in the sky, casting a beautiful glow over the sea. Stone entered the airport identifier,

RKD, into the GPS, and pressed the direct button. The arrow on the horizontal situation indicator swung to his left, pointing the way, and he adjusted his heading.

The sun rose into the overcast, and the light became dull and dusklike. "Twelve miles," Stone said aloud, reading the distance off the GPS.

"I think I see the airport," Young said, "dead ahead."

The airplane's speed was right at redline, and now Stone could see the runway. He switched on his strobe and landing lights, the better to be seen by other aircraft. He grabbed the airport directory from Young and checked the runways: 13-31 was 5,007 feet, the longest. Stone squinted into the distance. He thought he had it in sight.

Then he saw strobe lights on the ground; an airplane was taxiing to runway 31. Stone adjusted his course to put him on a base leg for the opposite runway, 13. He dialed the automatic weather frequency into his second radio. The wind was 310 at ten knots, straight down runway 31. He was about to change direction for that runway when the radio came alive.

"Rockland traffic, Cessna taxiing onto runway 31 for takeoff," a voice said.

"That's got to be the twins," Young said. He began speaking into his handheld radio and putting it to his ear to listen. "Two patrol cars are ten minutes out," he said.

Stone could see the Cessna, its strobes flashing, only a few yards from the runway. At that moment, his engine began to cough. Jesus, he thought, he had forgotten to switch fuel tanks. He flipped the lever to the other tank, switched on the auxiliary fuel pump and prayed. The engine roared back to life. He reduced power and turned from the base leg to the final approach for runway 13.

"You can't land this way," Young said. "They're taking off in the opposite direction!"

The Cessna was starting its roll on 13. Stone put the landing gear down and put in two notches of flaps. "Mayday, mayday, mayday!" he yelled into the radio. "Malibu is declaring a fuel emergency, landing on runway thirteen!"

"Negative, Malibu!" a voice came back. "We're rolling on 13!"

"I don't have a choice!" Stone replied. He

pulled the throttle back to idle. "No power, no fuel! Stop your roll now!" Stone was hot and high, and he put in the last notch of flaps and flipped up the speedbrakes. Still, he was doing ninety knots when he touched down and stood on the brakes.

The Cessna had stopped rolling halfway down the runway. Stone had thought the other airplane would turn off onto the grass, but the pilot seemed frozen. Now the Malibu was rushing toward the Cessna, and Stone could smell his brakes. He braced against the seat back, straightened his legs and pushed on the brake pedals as hard as he could. "Help me with the brakes," he yelled at Young. "Use your toes!" Young started to help. Stone had already decided not to turn off the runway; if he did that, they'd get away, and it was awfully hard to spot a low-flying aircraft from another airplane. Anyway, he didn't have enough fuel to follow them. They'd be gone.

The Malibu came to a final halt less than three feet from the Cessna, with both propellers still turning. If Stone had run head-on into the other airplane, there would have been a real mess, he thought. Normally, he would run the engine for five minutes on the ground before stopping it, to cool the turbochargers, but he yanked back on the mixture control and cut his engine. The prop wound down and came to a halt. The Cessna prop was still turning, but the twins weren't going anywhere; there is no reverse on a piston airplane.

"Cut your engine, Cessna," Stone said into the radio. The twins sat, staring at him, no more than twelve feet away. "Listen to me, boys," he said. "There's still a way out of this."

"Sure," a voice said back. "Just get out of our way."

"The money is gone. It's not in the account."

"What are you talking about?"

"There is no million two in the Singapore bank; we tranferred it back to the original account. The only money you have is what's in your pocket."

There was a long silence.

"Which of you is driving?" Stone asked.

"Eben."

"It's not as bad as you think," Stone said. "If you listen to me, you can still walk."

"What are you talking about?" Eben asked.

"There's a way out of this, if you'll just listen."

"Start talking."

"I'm not your lawyer; I want to emphasize that. But, you can still walk on an insanity plea."

"We're not insane."

"When they question you, tell them you hear voices, and the voices told you to do what you did."

"Nobody's going to buy that."

"They will, if you agree on a story and stick to it. There'll be a psychiatric examination, but if you stick to your story, you'll get through it. You'll do a couple of years in a mental hospital, and then you'll walk." He could see the two boys talking, arguing. Still the Cessna's prop spun.

"Open the rear door, Dino," Stone said. "Do it slowly, and if they run, go after them, but remember, they're probably armed."

"Right," Dino said.

Stone could hear the Cessna engine get louder as Dino opened the door.

"Will you represent us, Stone?" Enos asked.

"I can't do that; any judge would remove me for a conflict of interest. I'm Dick's heir.

But I'll get you the best defense lawyer in the country."

"If you don't get out and move your airplane, we're going to start shooting," Eben said.

Stone could see Enos talking, gesturing, while Eben looked stonily ahead.

"Come on, boys," Stone said. "This will work, believe me."

They argued some more, and then the Cessna's prop wound down and was still. The twins sat, slumped in their seats, looking defeated.

Stone turned and looked over his shoulder. "Before you get out of the airplane, you all heard me tell them I'm not their lawyer, right?"

"Right," everybody said.

Holly spoke up. "We all heard you tell them to act like they're crazy, too."

"Right," Stone said. "And don't forget that when you testify. Now, let's go get them. Me first."

"No," said Sergeant Young. "*Me, first.*"

61

THE FOLLOWING DAY they sat around the living room at the house, their luggage piled at the door, waiting for Sergeant Young to call from Augusta. It was three in the afternoon.

"Lance," Stone said. "It's a good thing they're sending an airplane for you, because we'd never get off the ground with all this stuff." He had refueled at Rockland before returning to the island.

Seth came into the room. "You folks ready to go?"

"Not until we hear from Sergeant Young," Stone said.

As if on cue, the phone rang. Stone pressed the speaker button. "Hello?"

"It's Tom Young."

"Yes, Tom. We're all here. What's going on?"

"First of all, Caleb Stone's wife is dead."

"What? How?"

"Sleeping pills. We're not sure if it was intentional. When my people arrived at her house, they found her. She had apparently been drinking all night, and in her condition, if she had taken even a couple of pills, that might have done it."

"What about the boys? Have they said anything?"

"They did their 'we hear voices' routine, then, gradually, they told us everything," Young said. "They murdered seven women in New Haven before any of the Islesboro killings."

"Good God! Did they confess to all the Islesboro crimes?"

"Yes. It helped that I told them we had Esme's diary. Have you heard anything about that from Lance's people?"

"Lance had a call from Langley. They've recovered a lot of writing that we thought was unrecoverable. It would nail them for the Islesboro murders, even without the confessions."

"Good. Funny, they didn't even ask for a lawyer; they asked for a psychiatrist."

"I don't think the Supreme Court would require you to give them a shrink," Stone said. "And their crazy act won't hold up when you testify that you heard me suggest it to them."

"That was a good move, Stone."

"It was either that or get shot at, and I was in the front seat. Did they say how they got into Dick's house?"

"That was easy; their father had two keys, and he only returned one to Stone. They knew the alarm code, too. Caleb had sent them over there once to pick up something he'd left in the house."

"It sounds like you've wrapped it up then."

"I believe we have."

"Do you need us here for anything else?"

"No, I'll be in touch when I do."

"Then we're off to New York in a few minutes."

"Your airplane engine all right?"

"It did fine on the flight back from Rockland."

"Then have a safe flight. Goodbye and thank you again."

"Thank you, Sergeant. Bye." Stone hung up. "Let's get out of here," he said to his assembled group.

"You had enough of Maine?" Ed Rawls asked.

"For this summer," Stone replied, shaking his hand. "Maybe I'll be back next summer, if nobody is getting dead up here."

Two minutes later, Stone locked the door, got into the station wagon with Dino, Holly and Lance and was driven away.

Author's Note

I am happy to hear from readers, but you should know that if you write to me in care of my publisher, three to six months will pass before I receive your letter, and when it finally arrives it will be one among many, and I will not be able to reply.

However, if you have access to the Internet, you may visit my website at www.stuartwoods.com, where there is a button for sending me e-mail. So far, I have been able to reply to all of my e-mail, and I will continue to try to do so.

If you send me an e-mail and do not receive a reply, it is because you are among an alarming number of people who have entered their e-mail address incorrectly in their mail software. I have many of my replies returned as undeliverable.

Remember: e-mail, reply; snail mail, no reply.

When you e-mail, please do not send attachments, as I *never* open these. They can take twenty minutes to download, and they often contain viruses.

Please do not place me on your mailing lists for funny stories, prayers, political causes, charitable fund-raising, petitions or sentimental claptrap. I get enough of that from people I already know. Generally speaking, when I get e-mail addressed to a large number of people, I immediately delete it without reading it.

Please do not send me your ideas for a book, as I have a policy of writing only what I myself invent. If you send me story ideas, I will immediately delete them without reading them. If you have a good idea for a book, write it yourself, but I will not be able to advise you on how to get it published. Buy a copy of *Writer's Market* at any bookstore; that will tell you how.

Anyone with a request concerning events or appearances may e-mail it to me or send it to: Publicity Department, Penguin Group

(USA) Inc., 375 Hudson Street, New York, NY 10014.

Those ambitious folk who wish to buy film, dramatic or television rights to my books should contact Matthew Snyder, Creative Artists Agency, 9830 Wilshire Boulevard, Beverly Hills, CA 90212-1825.

Those who wish to conduct business of a more literary nature should contact Anne Sibbald, Janklow & Nesbit, 445 Park Avenue, New York, NY 10022.

If you want to know if I will be signing books in your city, please visit my website, www.stuartwoods.com, where the tour schedule will be published a month or so in advance. If you wish me to do a book signing in your locality, ask your favorite bookseller to contact his Penguin representative or the Penguin publicity department with the request.

If you find typographical or editorial errors in my book and feel an irresistible urge to tell someone, please write to Rachel Kahan at Penguin's address above. Do not e-mail your discoveries to me, as I will already have learned about them from others.

A list of my published works appears in the front of this book and on my Web site.

All the novels are still in print in paperback and can be found at or ordered from any bookstore. If you wish to obtain hardcover copies of earlier novels or of the two nonfiction books, a good used-book store or one of the online bookstores can help you find them. Otherwise, you will have to go to a great many garage sales.